Mercy's Mill

Mercy's Mill

by BETTY LEVIN

GREENWILLOW BOOKS

New York

Library of Congress Cataloging-in-Publication Data
Levin, Betty.
      Mercy's mill / by Betty Levin.
         p.   cm.
      Summary: While trying to deal with her new life
with a stepfather and a younger foster sister,
Sarah encounters a strange boy who claims to have traveled
forward in time from the nineteenth century.
      ISBN 0-688-11122-X
      [1. Time travel—Fiction.   2. Stepfathers—Fiction.
3. Foster home care—Fiction.]   I. Title.
PZ7.L5759Me   1992
[Fic]—dc20   91-31483   CIP   AC

FOR PENELOPE AND JACK

Remembrance is more than honoring the dead. Remembrance is joining them—being one with them in memory. Memory is survival.

—Timothy Findley, from *Inside Memory*

Contents

Mercy's Mill

Winter Lightning

S arah could tell that she was being tested. Everything was a test these days.

Trying to detach herself from the kitchen chaos, she edged away from the stuff Mom had collected to get the little ones ready for church. Well, not church exactly. There was day care in the parish house for Linda, the littlest. And Jancy, the foster child, would go to the kindergarten Sunday school class.

Mom filled a baby bottle with apple juice and stuck it in her coat pocket with the ripped seam. Her eye fell on Sarah in the doorway. "I wish you'd reconsider," she urged. "It's a chance for you to meet people."

Meet people with Mom all frazzled and coming apart? Be taken for Roger's daughter just because Sarah was fair like him? Not that he had all that much hair left to show that he was blond. Anyhow, whenever he caught Sarah explaining that he was only her stepfather, he always looked injured. What did he expect? It was the truth, wasn't it?

"Your mother's right," Roger put in. "Jancy had a great time last week. Didn't you, hon?"

Janey nodded, obedient as always.

But Sarah stood her ground. The actual test wasn't whether she would go with her family but whether she would get into a fight with them.

"You'll be alone again," Mom pointed out. "For hours."

Sarah looked her mother in the eye. Was Mom saying she didn't trust Sarah on her own? Sarah's mother turned aside and was busy with Linda's snowsuit.

"You think she needs that?" Roger said. "It's like spring out."

Mom gave a small sigh. Sarah guessed she was giving up. Not about Linda's snowsuit, but about trusting Sarah. Mom and Roger had agreed to act as though they really did trust her. In return Sarah had promised to act as though she were worthy of their trust.

"I'll be fine," Sarah said. "I want to be alone."

"Okay, Garbo," Roger replied. It was some kind of joke he always made when she stayed apart from the family. Sarah refused to smile back at him.

The truth was she didn't want to be alone in this cluttered antique house. She wanted to be where she belonged, back in Brookline, which was the next best thing to living right in the city of Boston. She wanted to be where she could hang out with her friends, where there were always things to do.

Mom kept expecting her to adjust to life way out here in the country. But after nearly six months in what amounted to solitary confinement, nothing had changed.

Sarah watched her family as it hurtled toward the car. Janey, her black braids flying, held out her arms to catch the wind gusts. Roger had to lean against the car door to keep it from being blown shut.

Running. It seems so real that the child can feel the wind's sting. She tilts her face skyward. There is the

*sun, warm on her skin. Warm and cold at once. A
sudden gust snatches her cloth cap. She scrambles
after it as it scuds along the path. Her loose black
hair blows across her eyes. Her apron flies up; her
skirt tangles about her legs.*

As soon as Sarah was alone, she went outside and splashed
in her mother's footsteps. It felt wonderful to be free, especially without Janey, the dark-eyed angel who could do no
wrong. It felt good to be away from Mom's anxious looks, too.

This was the third day of the January thaw, but the warm,
wild wind was new. Sarah gazed up at black and silver clouds
that seemed to beat like great slow wings through a yellowing
haze. She could almost taste the color of it, bitter and hot. It
thickened the air she breathed.

The car suddenly reappeared and pulled up in front of the
house. Mom jumped out, shouted at Sarah to put something
on, and dashed inside. A moment later she emerged with a
diaper bag bouncing at her side. The bottle of apple juice
tumbled from her pocket. Stooping to retrieve it, dripping
from the slush, she called to Sarah, "You sure you won't
change your mind?" The wind raked her black hair so that it
stood up from her face like a bush.

Sarah shook her head. Her own short hair, wind-whipped,
shielded her from her mother's pleading glance. The car
swerved onto the road and turned toward the highway. They
must be late, Sarah thought. And now Roger was annoyed.
Probably he'd sweat and his glasses would slip down his nose.
How glad she was that she wasn't in the car with them.

Sarah crossed the road and headed for the mill. There was
nowhere else to go.

Mill Road was a casualty of the highway, which cut it off
from the rest of the town of Ashbury. There was only the old
house, where Sarah and her family lived at this end of the

road, and the Costa farm at the other end, with its farm stand on the highway and its additional family houses. In between there was nothing but woods, the brook, the power line, and turnoffs where Sunday drivers dumped their rubbish.

The mill, newly built and not quite finished, was supposed to be like the one that had stood across the road from the house a century and a half ago. Sarah's mother planned to sell stone-ground meal and flour in the antiques shop that would be built near the other end of the milldam. An exciting prospect if you were Mom or Roger. If you were Sarah, it was boring and stupid.

From the road the mill looked like an ordinary barn. But if you went around the pond behind it, the building took on a different up-and-down appearance. It seemed to tower over the water, sheathed in ice now, and over the stone dam that merged with the deep wheel pit beside the mill. When no one was looking, Sarah liked to stand on the very edge of the dam or the pit and gaze straight down.

Last August Singing Fish Brook had to be diverted while the dam was rebuilt and the pond dug out. For a while it was possible to see how the old dam sloped down to the stream bed. It felt a little strange to find all those massive stones in perfect formation, as if lying in wait. Although none of the upper part of the dam had survived the years, Sarah could follow its remains all the way to where construction had begun on the mill and the wheel pit. Not so at the opposite end, though, where the antiques and refinishing shop would eventually be built. There the base of the old dam was buried under jumbled blocks of stone too heavy to move.

Until the new dam was completed on the base of the old one, those stones had remained visible, jutting at odd angles and lodged in the rising ground at the foot of Anursnack Hill. Once at twilight Janey had been so spooked by them that she went from her usual placid self into wild hysterics. Roger had to carry her off to the house, leaving Sarah alone with what Janey had insisted were giants. Something had struck Sarah about those stones, too. It had almost seemed as if life did stir among them. It had taken only a moment for Sarah to figure out that it was nothing but shadows shifting and deepening in the last of the light.

Sometimes, though, the feeling still came over her that she was not alone. Someone watching, perhaps. But she never saw anyone.

Now that the water had risen and the pond was full, there was only the top of the dam, like a wall, to see or walk along. Sarah liked to stand right over the tumbling vent where the water gushed through the dam and splashed below to the brook. It felt like daring fate.

Today Sarah detoured around the deep pit with its enormous wooden wheel, which Roger had made and still fussed over. The way up to the dam was slippery with melting snow. Sarah's sneakers were a bit too smooth to get a grip. But how good it felt to be up this high with the wind trying to knock her from her perch. Yesterday, when they had tried to skate on the slushy ice, Mom had made Sarah wear her parka. Now, alone, she was free to wear and do whatever she liked.

Sarah stared at her loopy reflection. There was just enough meltwater on the ice to blur the face she saw there. Everything looked shapeless, her close-cropped hair a yellow smear, her face bloated. She made a grin. The reflection gaped back at her, hideous as a Halloween mask.

Then the darkening sky blotted out her reflection. She cast a look out over the pond. There where Roger had shoveled slush and debris aside to clear a skating area, something black flapped the seeping water. At first Sarah thought it looked like part of a plastic tarp snagged on a branch. But when the wind suddenly dropped, the black thing kept on stirring up twigs and dead oak leaves and empty acorn cups. An eerie darkness covered the pond.

Sarah leaned over the watery ice. For a moment she lost sight of the thing. Then she heard it slapping the water. It looked like a crow trying to lift itself from the debris. Sarah couldn't tell whether it was trapped by the ice or by trash.

Instinctively she turned toward the mill. On any weekday Ken and Frenchy, the builders, would be there. They would come running with a ladder or a long pole to rescue the bird. Now a quick glance backward showed Sarah nothing that would reach the crow. There was only one thing to do. Sarah had to ignore the rim of water that separated the ice from the dam and trust the footing beyond it. Yesterday they had approached the skating area from the shallow end of the pond. Today there wasn't time to go back and all the way around to the wooded side.

She eased herself down onto the ice. The water slid over and into her sneakers. She gasped. It was colder than she expected. A sudden warm gust sent twigs and bits of roots shooting across the surface. In an instant the meltwater was whipped into tiny waves. Trees bent and swung, moaning, creaking. The ice creaked, too.

Hurry, she told herself. Go get that bird and get out of here.

Not that she was afraid. How could she be, with the wind so warm? Still, it forced her down on her hands and knees. Soaked and slightly stunned by her own helplessness, she slid toward the heap. Nothing looked the same anymore. She used a branch to probe the tangle of debris. But there it was, hunched down, maybe cowering from her. And it really was a crow, caught in some kind of plastic netting.

A deep rumble reached her ears. She would have guessed heavy traffic on the highway. Only this was Sunday, when there were scarcely any cars out there. She didn't think thunder. Who would think thunder in January?

Even though the crow didn't struggle in her grasp, she

couldn't pull it free. It took a moment for her to realize that the plastic was frozen to the ice below the meltwater. She would have to break it out.

Using the end of a heavier branch, she pounded and chipped and splashed until a hole finally appeared in the ice. There! She hauled up the crow and freed it from the plastic. Its beak gaped at her in mute appeal or threat. Her hands nearly frozen, she rose unsteadily, only to hear a crack like thunder and to feel the ice beneath her tilt. The water climbed up to her knees and kept on climbing. She still held the crow as she sank in slow motion on the ice that had caved in. With one free hand she tried to grab the edge of the surface ice. It broke off, a jagged slab. She kept grabbing as she slid until she found herself completely immersed. She wasn't actually alarmed. If the ice broke so easily, she could make a path through it and swim to the dam.

Only the water was achingly cold. Kicking to keep moving, she broke off another flake of ice. She was fighting the freezing water, fighting the darkness, the sky all of a piece with the gray-black pond. And then in an instant it was transformed as light flashed everywhere. She didn't need the thunderclap that followed to inform her that there was lightning.

Brad's brotherly instructions came to her. What to do if lightning strikes when you're in the water? If you can't get out, dive down, swim beneath the surface. Head for shore, but keep submerged.

Down she went, the crow still in her grasp. Groping for the dam, she edged her way up and pushed back breaking ice. She gulped the warm air, hauled herself partly up, and set the crow on the dam. She was about to climb up beside it when lightning split the darkness. She could hear it crackle. Plunging back down, she headed for a vent pipe. As soon as she reached it, she propelled herself deeper.

What if lightning struck the crow? All of this for nothing.

Her fingers ached. Her head felt clamped. Her legs could barely shoot her up for air. As she struggled, it came to her that she must be caught in something, maybe a coil of wire attached to the pipe. She tried to reach down to her ankle, but she was too stiff, too frozen. She needed to breathe, but whatever gripped her seemed to want her there.

She had an image of a hand, of fingers closed around her ankle. That was her last clear thought.

And the struggle to break free. Fighting someone.

The next thing she knew she was lying on the bank being horribly sick. She didn't have the strength to move, but she was pulled away from the mess she made and dragged face-down to a cleaner spot. After a while she noticed skatemarks in the softening mud. That meant she was all the way across the pond, far from the dam. How had she managed that? She tried to draw her knees up under her, but as soon as she moved, her stomach heaved. So she just lay there for a while.

When she finally raised herself on one elbow, she was able to turn just enough to look sideways. There was a person be-side her. Her tearing eyes burned when she tried to open them wide. Slitted, they showed her that the person was a boy. Quite long. Not moving.

"Are you all right?" she croaked. Her throat burned, too.

He stirred, lifted his head from his arms, then dropped it down again.

That was some kind of answer. But who was he? Where had he come from? How had he known she was in the pond?

Moving very slowly, she sat up. She had to shield her eyes with her hands. Her face felt puffy to her touch and reminded her of her bloated reflection. It had been a warning then, of what the pond could turn her into. Even now, here on the bank, she felt changed, waterlogged, unrecognizable.

Through her fingers she glimpsed the pond. It had a shriv-eled, angry look as if it wore some ancient skin. Thunder muttered distantly, speaking to itself of new directions. The sky blinked acid yellow. A metallic sheen on the pond's surface forced her eyes shut once more. When she could bear to open them again, the yellow light oppressed her. It was the wrong color for winter, for any time Sarah knew of. *Old* came to mind again. Old light. Worn-out storm.

She began to shiver. Afraid she might throw up again, she followed the boy's example and dropped her head down to her upraised knees. Her nose was running. Since she had nothing to blow it on, she wiped it on the drenched sleeve of her turtleneck. And opened her eyes again.

For a moment she seemed to be underwater. Everything shimmered and wouldn't hold together. She tried to focus on one solid thing, the mill, but it swam from her and wasn't there. Well, yes, part of it was, but not the upper floor. Where was its roof? The mill was ruined, in shambles.

She squeezed her eyes tight and held them shut. When next she opened them, she turned aside, away from the mill, away from the boy, and peered out on open meadowland that she had never seen before. Where there should have been woods the meadow rose in undulations, a split rail fence following its gentle contours. Only there couldn't be a fence. She knew that. She was dreaming through the yellow haze, that old, unnatural light.

She had to fight an urge to cower, to curl into a tight ball and huddle close to the ground like the boy. But when she turned to him, he was sitting up, too, his thin brown fingers shrouding his eyes.

"How did you know I was there?" she whispered.

He faced her, his hands still shielding his eyes. He didn't speak.

She wondered if he could possibly be one of Mrs. Costa's grandsons. But he looked so different, sort of foreign. His skin was the color of oak leaves in winter, a flat brown with a hint of copper. His hair was black. She couldn't see his face very well, but she could tell that he wasn't dressed like any ordinary boy. Of course, his clothes were sopping; they clung to his bony frame.

To gain her bearings, Sarah looked away. She wanted to go home, to get dry and warm. But she couldn't just walk away from him. She glanced across the pond. The mill was all right again. It was whole. She looked sideways; there was no fence, only scrub woods. And, somewhere beyond them, Mill Road crossing Singing Fish Brook, passing between the mill and her house, and curving around toward the highway.

She struggled to her feet. Had this boy been spying on her? He had to have been watching her to have known where she was below the ice and water. He had risked his own life for her.

"Who are you?" she demanded. "What were you doing here?" Was he behind that feeling that came to her sometimes of not being completely alone? "You came after me," she insisted. "Why?"

He mumbled into his fingers.

"What?"

His fingers curled into loose fists that barely supported his chin. "I thought you were someone else," he said to her.

CHAPTER 2

Stranger

S arah peeled off her wet things as she raced through the house. Into her own room to change. Then into her brother's room to borrow clothes. It would have been a whole lot simpler if the boy had come with her. He had started to, but something had come over him when they reached the road. He had stopped short, toed the wet, hard surface, and then pulled up his bare foot as if the road had stung him. After that he had begun to dart anxious glances all around him. When she told him he could wait inside the mill, he had walked directly over to the side of the building where it was perfectly obvious that there wasn't any door. At that point all she could do was leave him there shivering while she went to get him dry clothes.

Rummaging through Brad's things, she picked out sweatpants, because they would fit almost anyone, and a big, heavy sweater with the elbows worn through. She even found the sneakers Mom wouldn't let Brad wear or pack when he went away. There was also an old basketball jacket. She rolled everything into that and ran downstairs.

She stopped in the kitchen for bagels and cheese and apples. Then she poured milk into a glass jar with a tight cover.

In the mudroom she paused. Did she dare take the woolen watch cap from the shelf? She wasn't sure whether it belonged to Brad or Roger. Maybe it was just an extra.

> *The cloth cap scuds along the path until it snags on a root. Just as the child lunges for it, a crow swoops in front of her and plucks the cap free. The crow flaps off, inviting the child to chase it. But there can be no game today. It is the Sabbath. Mamma must already be halfway to the meetinghouse; the child is far behind. Only the crow cares nothing for Sabbath laws. It takes to the air, the cap strings trailing like streamers.*

The boy was back at the far end of the pond. Sarah thrust the bundled clothes at him. When he just stood there, she told him to go and put them on. Slowly he turned, stepping through the slush, heading for the woods.

"Don't go away," she called after him. "I have some food here. It'll warm you up. And I can dry your wet things with mine." She would have them out of the dryer before her family got home.

When he reappeared wearing Brad's clothes and carrying the sneakers, he looked even stranger than before. He had left his own things behind. Probably he didn't trust her with them. Looking down at his bare feet, she noticed two whitish welts encircling his brown ankles.

When she proffered the bag of food, he just eyed it with alarm. What was he afraid of? She showed him the bagel, broke it in half, and began to nibble one piece. Only then did he take the food from her.

The bagel hurt going down. She could barely swallow. But the boy gnawed off huge chunks. When he started to choke, she offered him the milk. He didn't seem to know what to do with the jar, so she unscrewed the lid for him. Maybe she was wrong about his being foreign. Maybe he was retarded. He drank deeply and handed the jar back to her.

"It's all for you," she said. "I can get more at home. All this is for you really." He watched her as she spoke, his eyes glancing from her face to her faded jeans and mucky boots and then to the woods and the mill.

"I will bring back these clothes when mine dry out," he told her. He spoke precisely, as though he had just learned English. So he had to be foreign after all. He had a trace of an accent and a strange manner. His eyes held wariness, maybe even fear. A runaway? Sarah wondered. Was he hiding?

"If you're in some kind of trouble," she told him, "my mother can help you."

"Please," he answered, "tell no one. Not yet."

She shrugged. "Whatever you want."

He gave a slight nod.

"I'll bring some hot food later. Just hang out awhile. I'll be back." She stuffed the empty jar into the bag.

Without a word, he slipped away into the woods.

Back inside her house, Sarah dumped her wet things in the dryer. Probably there would be more stuff to add when the others got home. Mom would never notice how soaked everything was.

Sarah glanced out the window. The yellow light had dulled again. It was pouring now and strangely windless. The rain turned the driveway tracks into pitted rivers streaming down to the road. The day had gone dreary and endless. Away off thunder rumbled. To drown it out, she switched on the radio, but it wasn't working. She tried the stereo, the television, the lights. Nothing. So the lightning had knocked out their power.

Staring out at the miserable rain, she wondered where the boy had gone for shelter. She should have brought him some of Brad's old rain gear. There were always extra foul-weather things hanging in the mudroom.

Sarah picked up a magazine, brought it to the window, and flipped through some of the pages. It was one of her mother's magazines, all about antiques. Probably in the back it carried a small ad for Roger's refinishing shop, which was still where they used to live in Brookline. In civilization, where there were buses and stores—and Sarah's friends.

Sarah wandered into the dining room. As usual, the table was covered with Mom's blueprints and books and papers. Old deeds, for instance. And a copy of the environmental impact study Mom and Roger had to file before they could dam up Singing Fish Brook to make the millpond.

How about a family impact study? These days all they could think about was this house, the mill, and the antiques shop and workshop soon to be built. Brad had escaped just in time. Linda was too young to care, and Janey wouldn't complain even if she did feel lonely and cut off. That left Sarah, who was supposed to be old enough to "understand."

She peered at the copy of an old deed. Maybe she would discover something that would prove that it was illegal to run a mill here and they would have to move back to civilization. But it was hard to make out the old-fashioned, spidery writing. Sarah fetched matches from the mantelpiece and lit the eight candles in the wrought-iron candelabrum. The soft glow warmed the silent room. But she had forgotten to trim the wicks; the candles began to drip all over her mother's papers. Scooping them up, she spread newspaper over the center of the table where the wax fell. After that she tried to restore the papers to their original piles. She came to a book with photographs of gristmills and carding mills and sawmills. It even included pictures of ruins amid weeds and rusted machinery.

Sarah paused. Some of these reminded her of what was lying around the brook last summer. She was turning a page when lightning flashed and something outside, but near, clicked. Thunder ripped through the silence. As Sarah's hands flew to her ears, the pages of the book flew, too. Sarah caught a glimpse of a scene she thought she recognized, a rolling meadow with a rail fence, a mill in shambles.

The thunder fell away. Sarah turned back the pages. She wanted to see if that picture jibed with what she had glimpsed out there by the pond through tear-blurred eyes. She pulled the big book from the table and sat on the floor with it. But she couldn't find what she was looking for. Probably it was something she had noticed ages ago and half remembered, so that it had come into her mind when she was still a bit dazed and was staring into the painful yellow light. That would explain why any picture of a ruined mill would look familiar just now. A lot had happened, that was all. A lot, and not very much.

Just going back over it made her head begin to ache. Suddenly, guiltily, she wondered about the crow. She had set it on the dam and then simply left it there. What had happened to it?

Sarah stood beside the table and listened to the rain drum outside. Nothing muffled its presence, no voices, no footsteps, no whirring refrigerator.

"The way I like it," she said aloud. Too bad there was no one around to hear her.

The car splashed into the driveway. A door slammed, then another. Voices and footsteps mingled, and then the mudroom door burst open, and the house was full of her family. And nonfamily.

Roger put Sarah's half sister down, and Linda just sat on her cushion of diaper and snowsuit.

"What a storm!" Sarah's mother exclaimed. "Did we lose our power here, too?"

Janey held up a drawing for Sarah to see.

"Oh, good," Mom said, "you lit the candles."

"I'll get the lamps," Roger offered, letting Sarah know she might have thought of getting them herself.

As soon as he was out of the kitchen, Sarah flung her arms around her mother's neck and squeezed as tight as she could.

"What's all this about?" Mom asked with a little laugh. "Were you scared of the storm?" She started to hug back, but quick as a wink Sarah pulled away.

"No," she answered. "Of course not."

"Can we have soup for lunch?" asked Janey.

"No," Sarah said again. "The stove won't work. No soup."

"Never mind," Mom told Janey. "We'll make a fire. We'll cook something over it the way they used to in this house long ago. It'll be fun."

"Fun!" Sarah jeered, heading for the stairs. If they were going to play olden times, it would be without her. As she started up, she caught sight of a reddish mark above her ankle. Probably from putting on her boots when she was still wet. Probably from being rubbed there when she had run out with clothes and food for the boy. But there was a sour taste at the back of her throat, a clenching like nausea. That bruise brought back the moment underwater when she could feel something, fingers maybe, clamped around her ankle. Holding her down.

Sarah could feel herself about to turn back to her mother for that rejected hug. She had to hold herself quite still until the impulse passed. And even so, she couldn't quell the feeling that surged up in her, the pure joy, because Mom was home and nothing out of the ordinary had happened—had it?—except that the power was off. Just that.

Running again. The child cannot see her mamma. She
flings her arms out. If they were wings, she would fly
like the crow. She pelts along the beaten ground as
fast as she can go.

Roger assured Janey that there was light upstairs through
the bathroom window. She could go right up without worrying.
But Janey stopped behind Sarah. "Will you come with me?"
she asked.

Sarah swept Janey up and swung her onto the step above
her. "I'll race you," she shouted. "And you have a head start."

"No," Janey begged, "carry me."

Sarah swooped over her. " 'Carry me, carry me!' What will
you give me?"

Janey threw her arms around Sarah's neck and planted a
kiss on her cheek.

Sarah whooped. "That'll get you up and down again," she
declared.

Out of the corner of her eye she caught the look of astonishment that passed between her mother and Roger.

CHAPTER 3

Crow

Monday afternoon Liz Ackerman, the social worker, was just getting into her car as Sarah walked up to the house from the bus stop.

Timed, Sarah supposed. Probably Liz had been ready to leave for a while but had waited for the school bus to make its long loop to deposit Sarah at this end of Mill Road.

Liz greeted Sarah without asking her how school went today. They both surveyed the enormous puddles lying about from yesterday's storm. The unseasonable thaw had not softened the frozen ground, so the rainwater had nowhere to go.

"Anything you feel like talking about?" Liz inquired. "I can spare a few minutes."

Sarah wanted to get out to the woods to see if the boy had come back for the food she left him yesterday. She had waited until it was nearly dark before giving up on him. "I don't know," she answered noncommittally. "Did Roger complain about me again?"

"Should he?" Liz leaned against the fender. She was a large woman, bigger than Mom, but more put together and neat. She didn't loom.

By now Sarah knew that social workers usually took that route, coming back at you with a question, setting you up. But Sarah could field one question with another herself. "How's Janey doing?" Janey was the real reason Liz came by every Monday. Only ever since Sarah had taken off after Christmas, Liz had been spending time with her, too. Liz maintained that she came to see the whole family. Sarah understood that to mean that Liz came to see whichever person was causing trouble.

"Janey?" said Liz. "The same. Treading water. Why? Have you noticed anything?"

Sarah shook her head. "Just the usual." Meaning that this foster child continued to be everything Sarah wasn't.

Liz nodded. "Janey deals with problems by avoiding them."

But what kind of problems could a five-year-old have to deal with? Janey had been with Sarah's family for more than two years. The easiest kid Sarah's mother had ever taken on. Sarah grinned. "I could teach her how to show her feelings."

"She can't show them till she knows them. You're right, though. She does look to you."

"So what do you want me to do?" Sarah retorted. She didn't want Janey's admiration. She wanted as little to do with Janey as possible.

"It isn't what I want," Liz responded.

Sarah was tired of playing hide-and-seek like this. Sometimes Liz seemed almost like a friend, but sooner or later she always turned social worker again.

When Sarah clammed up, Liz went on. "Maybe she looks up to you because she senses you're fighting your own battle. Maybe she would, too, if she knew how."

"I'm not nice to her," Sarah blurted. No sooner were the words out than she recalled catching Janey up in a hug on the stairs. "Well," she added, "except once in a while."

"If you feel like being nice once in a while, see what kind of reaction you get."

What was Liz getting at? She was always suggesting motives and reasons that never occurred to Sarah.

Sarah watched Liz backing her car down to Mill Road. Then she turned toward the house. Inside the mudroom Sarah kicked off her muddy sneakers and pulled off her soaked, stained socks. She padded into the kitchen, where she found Janey on the floor surrounded by crayoned paper. Probably Liz had been getting her to draw pictures again. Sarah didn't believe anyone could learn anything from those scribbles, but it wasn't her business.

"Where's Mom?" Sarah asked.

"Getting Linda up. She had a long nap. We had cookies and cider with Liz."

Sarah rummaged through the cupboard. She was thinking about the boy. If he was actually from around here, then he should be home from the high school by now. If he was from somewhere else, he still might show up. Either way, Sarah didn't want him to think she was looking for him. "Janey, let's go see if the ice is all gone off the pond." If the boy showed up, he would see that Sarah was just looking after her foster sister.

Janey scrambled to her feet. "Can I wear my furry boots?"

"Better be the rubber ones. We'll splash in the puddles."

"Who's splashing in puddles?" Mom asked as she came downstairs with Linda.

"Janey and me. With boots."

"Why don't you wait for it to dry out a little? Or a freeze-up. We're bound to get back to winter weather soon."

"We don't want to wait," Sarah countered. "We want to splash. Liz told me to be nice to Janey. So why can't you just let me?"

Sarah's mother shot her an appraising glance and said dryly, "Nice of you to let Janey know you're trying to be nice."

Sarah flushed. "You made me say it," she mumbled as she stomped into the mudroom.

Janey, unfazed, followed her. All that mattered to her was that she and Sarah were going out together.

Yet once they were on the driveway, Janey could only plod, one solemn foot descending in front of the other.

"Come on," Sarah implored, flapping her arms and making airplane noises. Janey raised her eyes from the narrow stream she trod and cast them worshipfully on Sarah's forced antics.

The mill looked deserted. Ken and Frenchy must have gone home for the day. Water roared through the tumbling vent and crashed to the brook below.

Sarah led Janey around the pond. Two trees had come down in the storm, one of them lying aslant the water. More debris floated on the surface along with gray flakes of ice. For a moment Sarah thought she glimpsed the crow out there. Her stomach lurched. But what she saw turned out to be the partly submerged tip of an oak branch with brown leaves still attached, some of them blackened with slime.

Janey went exploring at the base of the uprooted tree. Sarah slowed. Her boot chafed her raw. It made her ankle recall being caught. Her skin prickled and went hot. She watched Janey pick up a stick and poke at the exposed roots. Leaf mold fell away in frozen clumps.

Janey glanced back at Sarah. "Look," she said.

Sarah tramped over to her and peered down. The root crater was surprisingly shallow. The earth inside it was black and pebbly and shot with white frost. The tree, a pine, seemed to have stepped up out of the ground and then keeled over in a faint.

"Is it dead?" Janey asked.

Thinking she meant the tree, Sarah considered. "Maybe not yet. It will be soon."

"Poor bird," Janey mourned.

Bird! Sarah stared hard. Then she located the object, the crow. It stood hunched and motionless, its eyelids shut, its wings dragged like tattered garments.

"It likes me," Janey declared. "How do you know it will die?"

Sarah shrugged. "It just looks that way. You can try touching it. Gently," she instructed.

Janey squatted at the rim of the crater, then had to stretch out on her stomach to reach the crow. When she stroked the nearest wing, the crow opened its beak, then fell on its side. "I didn't do that," Janey said. "I didn't push it."

"I know," Sarah told her. She was sure the crow was dying. If only they could walk away and leave it.

"Is it a boy or a girl?" Janey asked.

"I don't know."

"Then how can we name it?"

There was no backing out now. Name or no name, Sarah had to try once again to save this bird. Straightening, she pulled off her jacket. And there, on the other side of the crashed tree, stood the boy. Brad's clothes did nothing to mask the strangeness of him. And they were drenched. Sarah expected him to speak first, if only to say, "Hi." But he didn't utter a word. Definitely not normal, she thought. "My sister found this crow," she said to him. "I think it was here yesterday. This same one."

The boy stared. He clambered over and through the pine boughs. When he was able to look down, his eyes grew large.

Janey rose beside Sarah. "You're wet," she told the boy. To Sarah she remarked, "He won't talk to me." Then she tried again with the boy. "I'm going to name it Blackie."

The boy flinched. Sarah guessed it was because he was black. "It's not yours," he declared in his precise, nearly foreign accent.

"Where have you been?" Sarah demanded. "Where do you live?"

"Here," he answered. "Hereabouts."

Hereabouts. Which question did that answer? Shaking her jacket out, she caught the boy eyeing it. Obviously he needed more dry clothes, but this jacket would never fit him. Spreading it on the ground, she addressed no one and everyone. "If I met someone that needed warm things and food, I'd take stuff to them and not tell. I've been helped like that myself." While she spoke, she scooped the limp crow up in her hands. It felt icy, weightless. "That's what I'd do," she went on, "just as soon as I got home. I'd hope the person would wait, because I'd do it right away." By the time she stood up with the bundled crow, the boy was gone.

"I would, too," Janey told Sarah as they started back. She turned to peer into the woods. "He's not waiting," she said. "He's cold, but he won't wait." Then she ran ahead, already beginning to shout for Mom to come and save the sick bird so it wouldn't die.

The child shouts as she runs. The wind throbs in her ears like a pulse. Mamma always waits for her, so she must be near. Probably she is standing there just past the bend.

Sarah had to call Janey back. "Don't," she warned. "Don't mention that boy. Understand?"

Janey blinked and nodded obediently. Clearly she understood nothing. All she could think of was getting Mom. After a moment she tore off again.

By the time Sarah carried the crow into the mudroom, Mom had the laundry basket ready. In the kitchen Linda knocked over a chair and started to shove it around. That would keep her busy for a while.

"I think I saw this crow yesterday," Sarah told her mother. "It was in the ice."

"On the pond?"

The blackness of the sky came back to Sarah, the sudden wind driving that yellow haze before it. The lightning. "I think so," she said.

Mom carried the basket into the kitchen and righted the overturned chair. Linda, distracted, gazed at the disheveled bird. "Kitty," she said.

"Crow," Janey corrected.

Using tweezers, Mom forced milk-soaked bread into the crow. Sarah could see it swallow. It began to shiver. Mom frowned. She said she couldn't tell if it was sick or just cold and hungry. After it had time to warm up, she would take it to the Audubon Society. The people there would know what to do for it.

Sarah went upstairs, where she gathered up another bunch of clothes from Brad's room. Downstairs again, she deposited them outside the front door. Then she went back through the kitchen to the mudroom. On her way she plucked a banana and an apple out of the wooden bowl on the counter and dug into the open bread bag at her mother's elbow. Mom was so engrossed with the crow that she didn't seem to notice. Sarah ran around the outside of the house and made a bundle of the clothes with the food inside.

She splashed down the driveway and across the road and ran all the way to the far end of the pond. She set the bundle on a huge boulder covered with pale green lichen. She shouted into the woods, "There's dry clothes here for you. There's fruit and bread. If you don't come, an animal will eat the food." She held her breath, listening. Not a sound, except for the rushing brook and the throb of traffic on the highway. She waited a moment longer, in case he was just making sure she was alone before he showed himself. Then she headed for home.

CHAPTER 4

Late-Night Show

Tuesday morning Sarah woke up with a sore throat and didn't have to go to school. Bliss. She could stay in bed and drink endless cups of herb tea with honey.

But by late afternoon she began to feel worse. She didn't want to read or even listen to the radio. She dozed in the gathering gloom and listened to the household sounds that welled up from downstairs.

"Just lying there in the dark?" Mom inquired as she passed Sarah's door. "Let's check your temperature again."

Later Mom returned with the small television from her bedroom, which meant she didn't expect Sarah to be bouncing out of bed tomorrow. Sarah handed Mom the thermometer, and Mom handed Sarah the remote. Then she reported that the crow seemed to be holding its own, although the people at Audubon said it was very old and might be getting ready to die. But Janey had made Mom promise to keep the crow. At least for a while.

Sarah registered all of this without much feeling. It was the boy she wanted to know about. Why was he so secretive? If he was in some real danger, shouldn't she say something about him to Mom?

Long after the household had settled down for the night, Sarah woke up, went to the bathroom, and poured herself some flat ginger ale. It burned her throat, but it cleared her head a little. After shutting her door tight, she turned on the TV with the sound down to almost nothing and picked up a movie about invaders from outer space. She was drifting off again when it occurred to her that the invaders were no more weird than the boy. Maybe he was from another planet. That started her giggling. She didn't actually believe in any of that sci-fi stuff. Still, it was convenient to type him one way or another.

Much later, drenched in sweat, she came half-awake. Through sticky eyes she glanced at the television screen, where nothing made any sense. Hours must have gone by, because this was a really old movie in black and white with a muffled sound track. She tried turning it up, but that didn't make the voices more distinct or the music less tinny. She was able to make out the shape of someone being dragged down some stairs into a cellar or dungeon. This looked like the kind of spooky movie she could laugh at with her friends, but not alone in the middle of the night. She switched it off.

> *At last the child catches sight of the meetinghouse.*
> *The goodmen and their wives and children have*
> *started to enter it. But Mamma stands apart, turned*
> *toward the child who would fly to her if she could.*
> *Mamma holds her arms wide. She makes it seem as if*
> *in just the wink of an eye she will clasp the child to*
> *her. That is the way it seems, every time.*

Waiting for sleep to come, Sarah heard a sound that seemed at first an echo of the movie. It went, "Craak," not quite human, but insistent. She lay still. In a moment Mom or Roger would come out of their room and turn on lights and investigate the noise. But they didn't. They slept right through whatever it was.

Sarah switched the TV back on. She stared at the grayish image on the screen. It was a prison of some sort, for there were bars crisscrossing a tiny window through which a shaft of dusty light slanted down to indistinct figures slumped on the floor. The figures barely moved. But someone, it seemed like a child about Janey's size, reached with clasped hands toward the window. Something else blotted the light. A crow? Sarah had crows on her mind. She could hear that eerie voice again: "Craak!" This is a movie, she told herself. I'm supposed to be scared. But she couldn't stand it. This time, when she shut off the TV, she put the remote control under her bed.

She pulled the covers over her head. What she had heard must have been the ailing crow. She listened for it, but everything was quiet. After a while she uncovered her face, turned over, and went back to sleep.

The next day it rained again. So did Sarah's eyes and nose. She dozed in and out of talk shows and game shows and soap operas, one blending into another, continuous yet disconnected. When Mom brought her supper, Sarah mentioned the crow squawking last night. But Mom said the crow was still at Audubon.

"Oh," Sarah answered. "I guess it was the movie. There was a bird in the movie. It might have been a crow."

"I think tonight you shouldn't watch past ten," Mom told her.

"What difference does it make if I'm not going to school?"

"Think school anyway," Mom advised. "You will recover."

Listening to the dreary rain, Sarah thought of the boy out in the woods. "When can I get up and go out?"

"When do you feel like it?"

"Tomorrow," Sarah promptly declared.

Mom looked doubtful. "We'll see." Then she added, "Get some sleep tonight."

Sarah was reminded of all those evenings when Brad was in charge and they had stayed up watching TV until they heard their mother at the front door. Sarah knew she had been allowed to watch with him and with whatever foster kid might be there because then she would have to share the guilt if they were discovered. But Brad never did anything really bad like going out when he was supposed to be baby-sitting. No one in Sarah's family had ever done anything irresponsible until she did.

She tried to stay awake so that she could turn on a late movie. Not that she expected to catch the same one. She just thought she might be able to prove to herself that nothing weird was going on.

One moment she was alert; the next she felt herself groping through sleep to awareness. It was the middle of the night again. What had broken into her sleep? She stayed so still she felt as though she were listening with her whole body, all the way to her fingertips. She heard the drone of trucks on the highway. She heard the hum of some motor inside the house. And now, with a lurch, the burner started up. The floorboards vibrated. But there was no squawk, no crow sound.

She switched on the television with the sound off. There was a talk show. Words flashed on the screen: "This show is taped. No calls please." The next channel had a music video. Then there was a movie with a car chase. Then snow. She moved on. An old sitcom. Another movie. But no prison cell, no dungeon, no crow. Fever could do strange things to the mind. Maybe she had dreamed up that dungeon scene. At least there wasn't any danger of that tonight. She was absolutely clearheaded. And there wasn't anything worth watching on the tube.

The next day the people who had been tending the crow said he was strong enough to go home. Sarah was doing better, too, even though she faced a heap of homework assignments Mom had picked up from school. So Sarah was quick to offer to baby-sit Linda while Mom and Janey went to pick up the crow.

As soon as the car pulled out of the driveway, Sarah bundled Linda into her snowsuit, hiked her down the steps, and carried her around the mill. Everything was frozen again. Her feet didn't sink and slide with every step. Both trucks were here today, the big flatbed and the pickup. Sarah could hear the whine of a power saw. Everything was back to normal.

Except Sarah herself. By the time she made it to the pond she was puffing and gasping.

Linda squirmed. "Down," she demanded, "down."

As soon as they gained the woods, Sarah let her little sister slide down. Linda went charging off and immediately tripped and landed face forward in reindeer moss. Sarah dragged her to her feet, brushed her off, and headed for the boulder where she had left the clothes and food. How many days ago? The boy was probably long gone. Looking for the right boulder, Sarah recalled the lichen stuck all over it. Not this one beside the gray birch, but that one over there. Somehow it all looked different today. The sun showered droplets of bright color everywhere, green and sage and brown.

Linda tugged at Sarah's jacket. "Up," she commanded.

Sarah picked her up and trudged into the open sunshine. There stood the mill, the flatbed just visible to one side, a stack of lumber next to it. And the trees beyond the pond, past the wheel pit. Had she really imagined meadowland and rail fencing? What had made her think the mill was in ruins? She slitted her eyes to see if the illusion could be recovered, but everything was normal. That other day, though, nothing had been what you would expect. The unnatural warmth, the dark clouds, and the yellow cast to the light. The air charged with electricity. So it must have been the storm playing tricks on her when she was already so messed up.

"Home," Linda demanded. "Go home." But now she insisted on walking, which slowed them down. Sarah steered her away from the wheel pit. Linda caught sight of Ken and Frenchy having their lunch break outside the mill door and veered off toward them.

The men made a fuss over Linda before greeting Sarah.

"Back to school tomorrow?" Frenchy teased. "Vacation over?"

Sarah said she supposed so.

"Watch those nails," Ken warned as Linda reached into a keg.

Frenchy handed her a corn chip and then lured her away from the nails with another. "Just tell your mom they're organic," he said, grinning at Sarah.

Trying to sound casual, she asked the men whether they had seen anyone hanging around lately. A boy.

"A boyfriend?"

"Not a boyfriend," Sarah retorted. "I'm talking about someone sort of . . . strange."

The two men exchanged a look. Frenchy went inside the mill. A moment later he returned with a gray coat of some sort. "Speaking of strange," he said, "I found this by the dam." He held it up. Long and full, more like a cape than a coat. "Course, it was all wet. I took it inside to dry." Frenchy shook it out and tossed it into the back of the pickup.

"More cookie," Linda demanded.

"Cookie all gone," Sarah replied, her mind grappling with this cape thing.

Ken said, "We had a feeling you might know something about it. Someone playing dress-up?"

Sarah said, "Could I have it, please? In case whoever left it wants it back."

"If they do, tell them we can't have kids fooling around here. It's too dangerous."

Sarah nodded. "Only I don't know who they are," she explained.

Frenchy retrieved the cloak and draped it over Sarah's arm. It looked filthy. It stank. She couldn't picture the boy with this thing. She remembered a shirt hanging loose over his thin frame. But then everything was soaked, and she hadn't seen all that clearly. And afterward he wore Brad's things, and they were wet, too. If this cloak was his, wouldn't he have looked for it or asked about it?

"Up, up," Linda insisted as they crossed the road.

"You'll have to walk," Sarah told her. "This coat's nearly as heavy as you are."

By the time they were back inside the house both Linda and Sarah were ready to collapse. It was only after Sarah woke to hear Mom and Janey coming through the door that it occurred to her that she had forgotten to give Linda or herself any lunch.

"We have to keep him inside for a while," Janey informed Sarah from the hall.

"Who?" Sarah yawned and stretched.

"The crow. His new name's Barker because he sounds like a dog."

Sarah's mother came tiptoeing out of Linda's room. "What did you do to her?" she asked Sarah. "Linda's dead to the world."

Sarah gave a guilty start. To hide it, she shouted at her mother, "Don't say dead. Not ever. It's bad luck."

"It's what?" Sarah's mother began to laugh.

"I mean it," Sarah railed. "Don't say it, don't say it." And for some strange reason she really meant it.

"All right." Sarah's mother turned away. "We'll go settle the crow," she said. "Barker," she added.

Sarah found that she was lying all clenched up. She didn't feel rested, and she was starving. She would have to find a way of getting some halfway decent food for herself and Linda without letting Mom know that she had put the baby to bed on an empty stomach.

Anyway, she told herself, she didn't have to worry about the boy anymore. She was all done with sneaking things out of the house for him. That was finished.

CHAPTER 5

Name Giving

When Sarah went back to school on Friday, no one seemed to notice. At her old school she would have been pulled into the circle of her friends.

That afternoon, waiting for her bus, she watched the clusters of kids merging and fragmenting. She knew better than to take even one experimental step in their direction. It would be terrible to try to move in and have those clusters rearrange themselves all around her, leaving her out.

The moment the bus left her off she could hear her mother over by the site for the new shop. Sarah headed that way and found everyone there. Mom, on the far side of the cellar hole that had been dug last fall and then covered with plastic and planks, studied a blueprint, her bushy black hair screening her face. Janey and Linda were playing with a tape measure. Sooner or later they would break it, but no one stopped them. Ken and Frenchy were arguing with Mom.

Sarah glanced around and beyond them and glimpsed something moving among the trees. Her first thought was that it was the presence that seemed to lurk near the pond. She tried to focus on it, a dense shadow receding and then emerging again. Could it be the boy? Was he still there?

She dashed to the house, grabbed a shopping bag, and stuffed it full of all the food she could lay her hands on: bread, a bunch of carrots, a wedge of cheese. Something to drink? There was half a gallon of cider.

Running around the far side of the mill and the wheel pit, she skirted the pond and charged into the woods. If he was hungry, he was bound to show up. This time she would make the boy talk.

She planted herself in front of the boulder and spoke into the trees. "I have food. I can't leave it, or they'll see, so you'd better come now."

Nothing happened. Raising her voice, she tried again. How loud could she shout before Mom and the others heard her? Would the water spilling from the tumbling vent drown out her call?

"Here," he said, coming up behind her. "Give it." He tried to snatch the bag from her.

She spun around. "Wait. Talk to me."

He shook his head. "Food first." He thrust his hand into the bag and pulled out the bread. He tore at the plastic wrapping. It stretched and held.

"I'll open it for you," she said. She folded back the plastic. He had already managed to maul the bread inside, but she was able to extract a few bedraggled slices. "It's resealable," she told him. "It sort of zips."

"Zips?" He gulped down some of the bread.

"Like that." She pointed to the zipper on his jacket. Brad's jacket. It hung open, unzipped. To keep him from bolting, she said, "There's cheese to go with the bread. And cider."

The cheese was also wrapped in plastic. "Is it wax?" he asked. "Tallow?"

She shook her head. "Be careful," she warned. "Let me

show you how." To keep his attention, she kept on talking. "My mother doesn't believe in plastic, but she buys things wrapped in it. Figure that if you can." Sarah broke off a chunk of cheese and handed it to him. She pulled out a carrot.

When he had devoured the cheese, he dug out another mangled slice of bread. The food held him riveted, but she kept up the flow of words just the same.

"My mother doesn't believe in disposable diapers or store-bought bread either. Where we lived before, we were upstairs over her shop. When the shop moves here, she'll sell herbs and stuff as well as antiques and flour ground in the mill. And bake our bread again. The store will have a new name: Singing Fish Antiques. She actually thinks her customers will come all the way out here to buy her stuff. She and Roger aren't very real. How come you're still here? What did you do for food this week?"

He shot her a look full of distrust.

"Listen," she said, "if I was going to tell on you, I'd have done it by now."

He gestured with his elbow, both hands clutching the bread and cheese, his mouth full. Swallowing finally, he said, "Little cakes. Down the road. Not cakes. Little pebbles for the chickens."

"Mrs. Costa's chickens? You ate chicken food?"

He nodded. "I did work to pay."

"Mrs. Costa knows about you?"

He shook his head. "But her dog does. I had to make a friend of him at once. I stacked wood by the house."

Sarah watched him fumble with the cider jug until he flipped the cap off. Dropping to his knees, he retrieved the red plastic cap. He sat back on his heels. "Everything is different." He sounded bewildered, drained. "It's the same and not the same."

Different from what? she wanted to ask him as he rose and

drank from the jug. "You need more clothes? I can bring you soap. What is your favorite food? I'm not sure I can get it, but I can try."

"Corn bread," he told her. "I like corn bread fine. And ham and beans."

It would be tricky getting those things. "I'll try to bring you some of that. Not tomorrow," Sarah added hastily. "Sunday."

> *It is against the law to run on the Sabbath. All the children of the settlement are raised in that knowledge. But the child who runs cannot slow her feet any more than she can still her pounding heart. Even as the people turn from the meetinghouse door and stare at her, the child hurls herself toward her mamma. If only this time, this time, she can reach her.*

"Will I know Sunday?" the boy asked.

"Of course. The men won't be working. Roger will probably be fiddling with something at the mill. Sunday is quiet. Less traffic. Fewer trucks and cars," she added as he scowled in bewilderment. She could hear her voice rising. Didn't he get it? What was the matter with him? "On the highway, the big road."

He handed back the shopping bag. To hold him a moment longer, she told him about the crow, which was getting better, although it still looked a mess. This news seemed to make him anxious.

"Let the crow go," he urged.

"We will," she assured him. "He just needs to be taken care of for now." Like you, she nearly added.

"Someone may come looking for him," said the boy.

"Who?" she demanded.

One of the trucks started up with a roar. The boy jumped and then stood stock-still, his eyes on the blue exhaust that plumed up on the far side of the mill.

"It's only a truck," Sarah said to him. "What are you afraid of?"

"Atruck?" he whispered.

"Look." She tried to turn him toward Mill Road, to show him the truck as it clattered away. A trail of blue-black exhaust vapor rose in its wake. "Just a truck," she said. "What did you think it was?"

The boy let out a long, quavering sigh. "I don't know. Every day I have wondered. I thought it might be a kind of railroad train. But there is no tender, no boiler, and I can find no tracks." He brushed one hand across his eyes the way he had done after he rescued her. Something seemed to cloud his vision. "There is much I do not understand. Like that." He pointed at the wheel pit, then strode over to it. Sarah followed. They stood together and stared at the huge wheel.

"It's a waterwheel," she informed him. "It's what they used in olden times. See, it's dry now. But when they open the sluice gate, the water will come through. Where it hits those things, those sort of paddles that Roger calls buckets, it'll turn the wheel, and that will turn other wheels and the millstones that grind the grain. They're all connected."

"I know that. But why a wheel when a turbine is so much more efficient?"

Sarah didn't have a clue. All she could say was that she would try to find out and let him know.

"Sometimes," the boy confided after a pause, "sometimes I fear my eyes are not right. I see things I cannot quite believe. Everything is . . . dull. Not clear."

"Maybe your eyes were affected by being underwater. Maybe they'll get better in a while."

He nodded. He seemed more comfortable with her, almost trusting.

She drew a deep breath and said, "I'm Sarah Grissom. Can you tell me who you are?"

He thought for a moment and then replied, "My name is Jethro. I am called Jethro Philips."

Progress, she thought. She nearly dared to ask him where he came from, but she was afraid of pushing her luck. His name was a start, not an ending.

CHAPTER 6

The Wheel

S arah met her mother on the driveway and asked about turbines.

Mom said, "When we first came here, there were turbine parts in the weeds. Remember?"

"If they belonged to the mill, why didn't you use them?"

"We figured there must have been a waterwheel at some earlier time. We decided it would look more picturesque to have one. By the way, are you in a play in school?"

Where did she get an idea like that? "No," Sarah told her. "I'm not in anything."

"Then what's that filthy cloak doing in your room? I was picking up a little today. All I could think was that it was some kind of costume."

"Frenchy found it," Sarah replied. "He said I could have it."

Mom stopped for Linda, who was tugging a stick embedded in the ice. "Found it where?"

Sarah shrugged. "Around," she said. "Why?"

"I think it's quite old."

So that was why she was interested in it. The cloak might be an antique.

Mom said, "How about if I get it cleaned up and looked at by someone?"

"I don't know. Maybe."

They went inside to find the crow helping himself to left-over granola spilled from a cottage cheese carton.

Janey said, "Barker went to the bathroom on the counter."

Mom said, "You have to be sure to keep the mudroom door shut when he's out of his cage."

She didn't sound very mad. That was because she must think Janey was the culprit. Mom never yelled at Janey. So Sarah didn't feel she had to mention that she had probably left the door open. Mom was so busy cleaning up after the crow that she never noticed that other food was missing as well.

The crow was surprisingly tame. The Audubon people had told Mom that he might have been a pet. Crows were supposed to be very clever, Mom remarked, but this one would have to confine his cleverness to the mudroom until he could be released.

"I thought we could keep him," Janey protested.

"Wild birds need to be free," Mom told her.

"You just said he might be a pet," Sarah pointed out.

"He's my pet," Janey put in.

"And you are my pet," Mom responded with a hug. "Let's wait and see what happens. Remember, this crow is quite old."

Which was just what she had said about the cloak. Sarah went upstairs to have another look at it. Mom had folded it and draped it over the back of Sarah's desk chair. Now that it was completely dry it didn't smell so sour, but it was in terrible shape, the seams ripped and the bottom shredded. Sarah wondered if Mom could sell it for her. Of course, she would have to pay Mom back for the cleaning and mending.

She would also have to share some of the sale money with Frenchy. But that might still leave quite a lot to buy food and other things for Jethro. If he was still here by then.

Janey poked her head into the room. "What's that?" she asked.

"An old coat," Sarah told her. "An antique."

Janey took an experimental step into the room. "What are you doing with it?"

"I might let Mom sell it in her store."

Janey came closer. She never entered the room when Sarah was in a bad mood. "Did it come from that boy?"

"No, not him." So Janey was still thinking about Jethro. "He's still a secret, you know. We can't tell on him."

Janey regarded Sarah with adoring eyes. She wasn't being kicked out of the room. She was actually being spoken to like an equal. "I know it," she replied gravely. But then she couldn't help adding, "How come he's a secret?"

"He just is. No one knows but you and me." To cement that bond, Sarah said, "Let's teach your clever crow a trick."

As Janey started for the door, Mom came through, Linda under her arm. "Well?" Mom asked, seeing Sarah place the cloak back on the chair. "Want me to take care of it?"

"Will it still be mine?"

"If it's as old as I suspect, you may want me to sell it for you."

Sarah nodded and told Mom to go ahead and get the cloak taken care of. Yes, and maybe get a lot of money for it. Then she led the way downstairs to the mudroom.

The crow was fun. Despite broken and straggly tail and wing feathers, there was a purple sheen to his plumage now. He stepped with purpose from one coat peg to the next. When he reached the last one, he dropped rather heavily into the open potato bin.

"I don't think Barker's allowed there," Janey said.

"I'll get some crackers," Sarah said, thinking of all the other food stored in the mudroom. There were onions and carrots and even some butternut squash. Mom wouldn't miss a few if Sarah took them to Jethro. But he would have to eat them raw. "We'll teach Barker to eat out of our hands," Sarah told Janey.

With the cracker box held under her chin, Sarah reached for the crow, which gave one squawk, but didn't bite her, probably because it had a beakful of potato eyes. Sarah placed him on the washing machine and then broke a cracker into Janey's hands. "Now call to him," she instructed.

"Barker," Janey said. "Here, Barker."

The crow pecked at a diaper and then beneath it until it extracted one of Linda's tiny socks.

"Why did the boy say the crow isn't mine? Why did he say that?"

"I don't know. He says a lot of weird things. The reason you shouldn't talk about him is that he's an alien. Mom and Roger don't believe in aliens, so you mustn't ever mention him. Right?"

"Right," Janey agreed without much conviction.

The crow, now unbidden, stepped closer and stretched until he could snatch up the cracker pieces from Janey's hand.

"It worked!" Janey exclaimed. "Barker comes when he's called."

Sarah deposited more cracker bits in Janey's hand. Each time the crow swallowed some, he made a strange, rasping sound like someone with a very sore throat trying to speak.

"You should get Mom to buy a whole lot of cheap bread and keep it out here, and then we could use it to train the crow to do lots of other things."

"That's a good idea," Janey said. "You ask."

"No, you. Mom listens better to you."

Janey nodded solemnly. Her acceptance of Sarah's judgment confirmed Sarah's own conviction that her mother was far more attentive to this foster child than to her own oldest daughter. This small confirmation made Sarah feel triumphant and bereft all at the same time.

As soon as Roger came in, the crow flattened his feathers and went still. Janey wanted to show Roger the trick she had taught the crow, but as long as Roger was there, the crow refused to budge.

Clever crow, thought Sarah. The bird could sense that Roger was no friend.

But Roger was gentle and encouraging with Janey. Maybe the crow would perform later, he suggested, after it had had a rest.

Whispering a reminder about the bread, Sarah followed Janey and Roger into the kitchen, where Mom started in at once about some problem to do with the cellar hole for the new shop. Sarah felt like pointing out that they still had a perfectly good store back in civilized Brookline, but that would only lead to an argument that Roger would win. Sarah needed to find out about the waterwheel for Jethro. She needed to be polite.

That was hard. All her feelings went against treating Roger like a member of the human race. She had to wait for just the right moment, while Janey was swinging from his hand and Mom was retrieving some blueprint or plan from the mess on the dining room table.

"If a turbine is more efficient," Sarah declared, "why have a waterwheel for the mill?"

Roger looked thunderstruck. "You want to know about the mill? You're actually asking me about the wheel?"

To show that she didn't personally care, she told him it was a question for school. But he was still delighted.

"Come on," he said. "I'll show you."

"Can I come, too?" Janey asked.

"Of course."

"Come, too," Linda chimed in.

"No, sweetheart, just the big girls this time. We won't be long."

Janey beamed. Usually she was one of the little girls.

Sarah didn't mind having Janey along. It helped to have someone else with Roger, who talked nonstop all the way to the wheel pit and then slid down inside to point out every detail. "See, it's a replica," he explained. "In the early days the local iron wasn't good enough to be forged into machinery, so everything was made of wood. People used the best of the native trees just like I have. You've got this white oak for the shafting, maple for the cogs. They used elm for the bearings and the teeth on the cogs, but our elm is diseased now. Hornbeam's a decent substitute. And then oak for all the rest—frames, carriages, pitman rods, trundles, and wallowers. Of course, wood on wood causes a lot of friction, so I've had to compromise. Old mills caught fire so easily, from the friction and flour dust. And then there's the balance rynd of the millstones. It does have to be iron."

This torrent of technical information washed over Sarah as she squatted on the wall. Gazing with forced interest at the things Roger showed her, she wondered all over again how Mom could have married this bald wimp of a man. Everything he made or repaired had to fit so precisely and be finished to perfection. Definitely not normal.

Roger didn't seem to notice that he had left Sarah far behind. To show that she was still paying attention, she asked him when the water would be let in to make the wheel turn. He switched right over to a discussion of the hazards of ice.

Fire and ice, thought Sarah. Why would anyone bother to put together something so easily ruined? And then she recalled what she was supposed to be finding out for Jethro. "Why not a turbine?"

"Can I come down there with you?" Janey asked Roger.

He climbed up to get her. "Just this once. Never without me." As he swept her off the wall, Janey twisted around in his arms and clutched his naked head.

"Why not a turbine?" Sarah repeated. "Mom says one was left here."

Roger held Janey at arm's length so that she could lift one of the leather flaps on the wheel buckets.

> *Sometimes when she is running, it is Papa who holds out his arms to her. Nothing prevents her from throwing herself into them. Once on a hot day in June she picked tiny blue flowers beside the brook. Mamma wove them into a garland for the child's head. Mamma gave her a gentle shove toward the mill and sent her to show Papa. The child walked with care lest the garland fall. But when Papa came striding forth, sticky from the heat and wooled with flour dust, she raced to meet him. She could feel the garland bounce and begin to slide. Papa dropped to his heels. Picking her up, he righted the garland. One of the blossoms lay in his floury hand. Blue, she said. Blue from the sky, he told her. And the yellow spot, the eye at its center, that is from the sun. Forget-me-not, he said, as he carried her past the wheel pit. The child leaned toward the splashing buckets.*

Glancing up between Janey's outstretched arms, Roger frowned slightly as he met Sarah's hard gaze and measured the true distance between them. "But I've been telling you," he said. "I just told you. A turbine's authentic for the last century, but it's not as pretty as a wheel. Waterwheels are from an earlier time. Mostly they're what people expect to see. When we're set up here, people will come because all of this looks and sounds so nice. Like a greeting card."

Was there a note of mockery in his tone? Sarah said, "But all that work. The right kinds of wood."

Yes," he agreed, "you have to be a nut to get this involved in the first place. And now we all are, since your mother and I are mortgaged up to the gills. We're all in this together."

"Me, too?" asked Janey in his arms.

"You bet," Roger answered, giving her a kiss. "For always and always."

That hot June day Papa carried the child all the way around to the shallow end of the pond. He walked right into it with her. The child squealed, half in terror, half in delight. Papa told her to become a little fish and give herself to the water the way the crow gave itself to the sky when it fledged and grew its first flight feathers. The child could see the sky on the surface of the millpond blue as the forget-me-nots that drifted from her hair. She sank into the fluid sky. During the swimming lesson the forget-me-nots floated out of reach. But they are here, Papa said, holding her safe in the water, always here.

Sarah could feel herself withdrawing, shutting down, detaching herself from the whole business. Anyway, she had what she needed now. The next time she saw Jethro she had something to tell him, something to give him besides food and clothes. And maybe, in return, he would explain to her how he came to know about turbines being better than waterwheels.

CHAPTER 7

The Alien Game

"What's this about an alien in the woods?" Liz Ackerman let this question drop casually as she stood in the doorway. Sarah, just off the bus, glanced around. Mom was chasing after Linda. Janey was in bed with Sarah's cold. She and Liz were alone.

"It's like a game, sort of," she told Liz.

Liz yanked on one glove. "Part of the new nice Sarah?"

Even though it was obvious Liz was teasing, Sarah stumbled over her reply. "There's nothing to do around here. You have to think things up." She hadn't actually lied.

Liz nodded. "Just bear in mind that your mother and father and I are working hard to keep Janey in touch with reality."

"He's not my father," Sarah retorted. "He's not Janey's father, either."

"That's true. But it doesn't change what I'm saying."

"You don't want me to play space games with Janey?"

Liz shook her head. "Pretend is good and fun as long as you know it's not real."

Sarah could see the problem. Janey had probably insisted that the alien boy was real. "It doesn't matter what I do," Sarah mumbled. "I just mess up."

Liz fished out her car keys. "Is there something else going on?"

Liz was pretty sharp. She wasn't distracted by Sarah's small display of resentment.

But when Sarah shook her head, Liz let it go. It was time for her to leave.

Sarah went around to the mudroom door to gather up food already stashed there for Jethro. The crow sulked inside his cage, his wings like hunched shoulders. Sarah picked over some limp salad greens in a basket and stuck a few lettuce leaves through the wire. The crow didn't stir. Maybe he missed Janey, who was upstairs in bed. Feeling slightly guilty, Sarah hurried back outside.

The pickup was still parked in front of the mill, so she skirted the entrance and climbed the wooded slope to get around the pond. Almost immediately Jethro appeared, casting glances across the pond and all around the mill. Sarah wished she knew what he was on the lookout for.

"Who did you think I was?" she blurted as she handed him a hard-boiled egg and a sandwich with Mom's damson plum jam.

He shot her a baffled look.

"That day you pulled me out of the water. You said you thought I was someone else."

"Yes," he answered. "Mercy."

"What?"

"Mercy."

They could hear a man cough. Whoever was still at the mill must be leaving now. Jethro ducked down.

"Why are you still here?" she asked him. "What are you here for?"

"Mercy," he said again as he stood and faced her.

She met his gaze. Keep talking, she reminded herself. Keep talking or he'll run. "That's homemade jam," she told him. "Watch out for pits."

He nodded. "It's very good. It's good of you to help me."

Fine. Then why wouldn't he explain himself? What was this mercy thing all about?

"You still wear boy clothes," he went on. "Is it to conceal . . . to hide who you are?"

"No. I told you, I live here. Everyone dresses like this."

He shook his head, then tried once again to wipe away an invisible veil from his eyes. "I am trying to understand. It is hard."

"I found out about the waterwheel," Sarah told him. "Roger made it out of the same kinds of wood the old waterwheels were made from. He says even though the last time the mill was working it used a turbine, the waterwheel fits more with what he and my mother want this place to be. He repairs antiques and she sells them. They think their customers will like the old-type wheel."

"When was it?" Jethro asked. "How long ago was the waterwheel?"

Sarah shrugged. "I never remember dates. Anyway, I don't think Roger told me."

Jethro tried again. "Then how long ago was the mill with the turbine?"

"I've no idea," she stated bluntly. This was the weirdest conversation she had ever had.

"Could you find out?"

"I suppose." If only he knew how much she hated going to Roger for anything. "If it's important."

Jethro nodded. "I would like to know."

That sounded only moderately important. It wouldn't be

nearly as high on her list as food and other stuff Jethro might need. "I'll ask," she promised. "And I'll bring more food tomorrow."

He inclined his head. "Where is the crow?"

"In our house. In a cage."

His glance slid away across the pond and rested for a moment on the dam. "She might be looking for him," Jethro murmured.

"Who?" Sarah asked.

"Mercy," he responded with a shade of impatience. "It's Mercy's crow."

"Mercy is a person?" Sarah exclaimed.

"I have been saying so." He sounded almost scornful.

"Oh." Now what? Sarah wondered. "Is she your friend?"

He nodded.

"And you think she might be here? Or might come?"

"We were together," he said. "Then I was here, but she wasn't. You were instead. And her crow."

So that was why he was still hanging out here. He was waiting for someone named Mercy. Suddenly Sarah felt an urge to confide in a grown-up she could count on. Liz maybe. But she couldn't betray Jethro's confidence.

"Don't let him die," he pleaded. "If she can't come for him right away, he'll find her. He always does."

"All right," Sarah said. "I'll go feed him now. Maybe Mom will let me take him upstairs to Janey. That should cheer him up."

Jethro said, "Thank you," and turned as though to leave.

She really wanted to ask him more about Mercy. "If I see her," Sarah added, "how will I know it's her?"

"Mercy," Jethro replied with a trace of a smile, "is not like you."

"Fine. But that could be a whole lot of people."

"Black hair," he said, "as black as her crow, and very long. And she dresses—"

"Yes?"

"Like a girl," he concluded.

So he didn't believe Sarah about her own clothes being ordinary. He didn't exactly mistrust her, but he didn't believe her, either.

Later Sarah studied herself in the bathroom mirror, trying to imagine what Jethro saw about her besides her jeans. How could he have mistaken a girl with short blond hair for one with long hair as black as a crow?

She went to find her mother, to ask if she could bring the crow upstairs to Janey. Mom thought a crow visit might cheer Janey up, but when they got the cage beside Janey's bed, it was the crow that came alive. Janey, flushed and dopey, soon grew sleepy.

"Can he come back soon?" she whispered.

"I'll ask Mom. I can keep him upstairs with me till you want him again." Even as she spoke, Sarah realized that Janey was dropping off. For a moment Sarah stood looking down on her. There was something in that sleeping face that was overwhelmingly sad. Sarah found herself wondering about Janey's life before she came to them. Had she ever been like Linda, who at nearly two was already pushing the world around to suit herself? Janey never pushed anything or anyone. She was more like a small, careful creature that knows itself to be prey.

Sarah touched Janey's forehead and stroked the damp hair away from her closed eyes. Black wisps sprung from the braids. Janey shivered at Sarah's touch, a tiny whimper escaping her. One hand tightened in a fist, raised as if to ward off the shadow Sarah cast across her face.

That night the crow filled Sarah's room with an acrid odor. It made her nostrils burn. There seemed more than bird smell to it, a hint of earth and rot. Sarah covered up her head and breathed in normal bed closeness. But she could still sense that reek of wildness the crow had brought to her room.

When everything was so still that Sarah momentarily forgot he was there, she threw back the covers and sat up. Had she heard a muffled cry? Was Janey calling out from her room?

"Aaowk," muttered the crow.

Sarah peered at a sliver of metallic light. In the instant before her eyes adjusted to the night-dark, the black shapes around her brought back images from the movie scene with its bundled figures in some kind of dungeon, a child writhing, stretching, its face hidden by a fall of tangled hair. But no sooner had she recalled the clasped hands reaching toward the tiny window than the shapes seemed to be reshuffled, restored to their ordinary, recognizable places. Here were her lamp and the chair with her shirt thrown over it, there the desk and the cage. Only the child remained in her mind's eye, the child who seemed familiar and strange all at the same time.

> *She feels her arms swing. They push through the water. Her legs kick with all their might. Are they trapped in her skirt? She cannot free them, cannot move. Yet her limbs tremble as they recall swimming and running. She thinks: The sky in the pond. She thinks: Mamma just out of reach. She thinks: Next time, next time. She will not give herself to the darkness as she gave herself to the sky in the water. Someone coughs. Someone else moans. There is a flapping, and the crow drops down with a crust of bread. It brings the scent of wood smoke and horse leather. The child inhales those good smells. It is first light, a dirty gray revealed beyond the small square of window. But here the darkness holds her captive.*

Sarah burrowed back down beneath her covers, shutting out the crow smell because it had become oppressive, almost sickening, unlike anything she had ever known or imagined.

CHAPTER 8

Snow Day

During the night more than a foot of snow fell. The air was aswirl. Sarah had only to glance out the window to know that school would be canceled. Every snow day was a gift, this one especially.

As soon as she was sure her mother was busy with the little ones, Sarah went into Brad's room to collect some more cold-weather things for Jethro. She had to borrow one of Roger's scarves, but he had plenty more. Downstairs she spooned leftover pot roast and vegetables into a mason jar and helped herself to a handful of dried apricots. She set the clothes and the jar outside the mudroom door and then made herself some toast and sat at the kitchen table for a while. By the time she got up to go out, she just looked bored. No one paid any attention.

It was slow going, floundering through the thick, falling snow. As soon as she passed the mill, she started calling to Jethro. When she finally reached the boulder beyond the pond, she stopped and waited. Except for an occasional snowplow scraping along the highway, there was no sound of any kind.

The stillness was like the snow, baffling and indifferent. The small white pines growing among the hardwoods stood as though clutching themselves against the storm, their branches stooped and burdened.

Then, off to her right where the brook rushed silently beneath its cover of new snow, a branch snapped. Jays screeched, crows flapped up, and snow dropped in successive thuds. For a moment the air exploded with a fine, crystalline dust and, too, with a kind of energy that seemed to Sarah like a living presence. Something told her not to stare, not to seek out whatever hovered just out of sight. She turned and saw a pine tree striding toward her. She let out a gasp. And then she saw that it was only Jethro, with a snow-caked blanket draped around his shoulders and falling to the ground.

"What took you so long?" she blurted. "I'm freezing."

As soon as those words were out, she wished she could unsay them. Jethro's face was blotched with cold; he was shivering.

She thrust mittens and the scarf at him. In her haste she tugged the blanket off one shoulder and saw that the jacket she had given him was wide open. "You should zip that," she told him. But she could tell at once that he didn't understand. "Here, like this." Fumbling with the pull tag, she zipped the jacket closed. After that she picked up the jar and realized that the meat and vegetables had already begun to freeze. What Jethro needed was hot food and a warm place to thaw out.

But as soon as she told him she was taking him inside the mill, he acted as though that were a trap. "You'd better just trust me," she ordered, her own teeth beginning to chatter, "or you'll turn into ice."

"You sound like her," he said, letting Sarah know he had given in.

"Like who?" she shouted through the rising wind.

"Her. Mercy."

Head down, Sarah plodded on. Jethro followed at a cautious distance. At the door she had to wait for him. Inside, he gazed at the cavernous height and the cluttered floor.

Sarah found herself bustling like a nervous hostess. "I was afraid you wouldn't come. I thought you'd get cold feet."

"I did. They are. Feet and hands and everything else."

She didn't bother to explain what she meant. She saw the toolbox Frenchy usually left during the week. He kept most of his tools in the big box on the back of his pickup; he kept extra snacks in this smaller one. Opening, it, she found a started bag of corn chips and some candy bars among assorted wrenches and his good level.

Jethro sat huddled against the wall under the blanket, his eyes scanning the mill. "It's not like it should be," he murmured.

"I'm going back for hot soup," she said. "It may take awhile. You can wait upstairs." If anyone did happen to come, they wouldn't be likely to go up there where the hopper was.

"The stairs are in the wrong place," he said. "So is the door."

She didn't bother to argue with him or to point out that this mill was just built and that there hadn't been one here in about 150 years. "You just go up," she directed. "I'll be back." But he looked so pinched and stiff with cold that she raised the lid of Frenchy's box and extracted one Milky Way.

Turning on the stairs, one hand gathering the blanket around him, the other warily extended, Jethro took the candy and sniffed it.

"Just tear the paper," she instructed. But then she thought of the telltale scraps lying around. "Here, let me." She took the bar and ripped off the wrapping, which she jammed into her pocket. There were the apricots. She had forgotten about them. She handed them over with the candy, which smelled so enticing that it was all she could do not to taste it first.

Back at the house she found the family gathered in the living room in front of a roaring fire. "Can I make soup for lunch?" she shouted from the kitchen.

"Sure," Mom answered, "when it's time."

"Can't I start now?"

Roger said, "Why not? Unless you want to join us."

"No," she called back. "I want to cook. By myself."

She set to work, starting with canned soup, then adding stewed tomatoes, carrots that she cut up, and rice. In the back of the refrigerator she found some old leftover chicken with white fuzz on it. She washed off the fuzz before throwing the chicken into the pot. Then she added celery and an onion. After that she thought she was finished with ingredients until she came across a bag of dried lentils. She tossed a handful of those in the soup as well.

She thought it would be ready in a few minutes, but the lentils she spooned up were hard as pebbles, so she let the soup go on cooking.

"What should I feed the crow?" she called into the living room.

"Janey and I fed him," Mom answered.

So Sarah sat in the kitchen listening to Roger read *The Elephant's Child.* Every now and then Janey's voice joined in or interrupted. Outside, the snow hissed as wind gusts hurled tiny ice pellets against the windowpanes. The soup boiled and began to smell wonderful. When Sarah removed the pot lid, great thick bubbles burst and splattered all over the stove. Quickly she set the lid back and turned the heat down.

A while later she ladled soup into the widemouthed thermos jug. Chunks of things plopped and spilled, but she managed to get the jug full to the top. After that she added a saucepan of water to the remaining soup in the pot, put on her wet outdoor things, grabbed a loaf of bread and a flashlight, and quickly left through the mudroom.

It was hard lugging everything up the mill's steep stairway. On the upper floor there was even less light than downstairs. She paused to set down the jug and switch on the flashlight. There was Jethro beside the hopper. He stared mesmerized as she came toward him. She switched off the flashlight. He reached out a finger and touched the glass. He didn't speak.

The soup was too hot to drink right off. He held the cup in his hands, warming them, then lowered his face to the steamy heat and inhaled. Finally he began to sip and then to slurp up the contents of the cup.

He drank three cupfuls in succession. "Good," he pronounced with a sigh. He proffered the thermos.

"No, keep it. The jug will keep it hot, or at least warm."

He studied the thermos. Then his glance slid to the flashlight. "What kinds of things are these?" he asked.

"Ordinary things," she said. "What kinds of things do they have where you come from?"

He looked puzzled. "Not these. But I come from, well, here. At least it is where I last lived."

"You can't have," she flashed at him. "You don't know anything about this place. You don't know about cars or zippers or thermos jugs. Why don't you tell me the truth?"

He seemed to struggle with her challenge. Finally he asked, "Do you know Mr. and Mrs. Lockwood? Have you heard of them?"

Sarah shook her head.

"They live in your house. I mean, they did live there once. And ran this mill. They took me in."

Sarah pondered all of this. Could Mom and Roger be so far off base about the last time there was a mill here? Or was this boy confusing this place with another? "I've never heard of any Lockwoods," she said, "but we only moved here last fall." He looked so crestfallen that she quickly added, "I bet there are ways to find them, though. Probably other people know where they went." A thought struck her. "Is Mercy their daughter or something?"

Jethro shook his head.

"So who is she?"

"You would not believe me if I said." He broke off.

"Why shouldn't I believe you?" she demanded.

"Because. Because I did not believe Mercy. Not for a long time."

"Come on, Jethro, tell me and let me decide what I think."

He shook his head.

"What's her last name?"

"Bredcake."

Sarah started to laugh and then checked herself. "Okay. Sorry. So tell me."

"She may be lost," he said.

"Lost?"

Jethro frowned. "She is not in your time."

Sarah managed to keep her face straight. No matter what crazy things this boy said, she was determined to keep him talking until he began to make sense.

"She was born here," he went on. "Her father was the miller. Outside the settlement, away from the other homes and the meetinghouse. The Indians come to fish here. They call it Shabokin. In my time it is known as Singing Fish Brook. Mercy believes that for a while it may have been named Sin and Flesh Brook, but I have heard that only from her." Jethro fell silent. He hugged the blanket to him and drew his knees up to his chest.

Guessing that was all she would get out of him right now, Sarah said, "I'll bring you my brother's sleeping bag. It'll keep you warm. You can use the flashlight if you need to go out, but keep it off when you don't need it or the battery will get used up."

He pulled back. She could see that the flashlight spooked him, so she didn't press it on him. She allowed herself one last question.

"How long did it take for you to believe Mercy?"

He frowned again. "I cannot remember. It happened slowly."

Sarah went away quietly, thoughtfully. The town snowplow had come through Mill Road. Crossing easily and then climbing and sinking into the snowbank, she found on the other side that someone, probably Roger, had shoveled part of the driveway. Suddenly she remember the soup left simmering on the stove. She tried to run the rest of the way home.

CHAPTER 9

The Place of the Departed

S arah's mother and Roger had an argument about whether
Sarah should have to clean out the scorched pot. Roger
said it was time for Sarah to take responsibility for her irre-
sponsibility. Mom said Roger was just irritable because he had
to stay home, which was what she had had to do every single
day since they moved to Ashbury. She also said Rome wasn't
built in a day. Sarah wasn't exactly sure what that meant until
Mom pointed out that Sarah had shown signs of being responsible by making the soup in the first place. A positive sign even
if it was burned.

"I like the burned part," Janey volunteered. "I like that
black stuff."

Sarah ducked her head. Whatever Janey was up to, it
seemed to calm everyone down.

"Actually," Roger admitted, turning to the sink and reaching for the scouring pad, "the soup was pretty good if you
didn't scrape up the bottom." Sarah recognized his positive-
attitude tone. "What did you put in it?" he asked her as he
began to scrub.

Sarah listed some of the ingredients that came to mind.

"Did you wash the carrots?" Mom asked.

Sarah nodded. "I even washed the chicken to get the white fuzz off."

Roger whipped around. "Moldy chicken!" he exclaimed, losing his grip on the positive attitude.

"I washed it off," Sarah repeated. "It's no big deal."

Mom said, "Moldy food should always be thrown out."

Roger said, "Then what was it doing in the fridge?"

Mom snapped, "Obviously I didn't know it was there."

"Obviously," he returned.

Sarah said, "It was way in the back. Underneath things."

A look passed between Mom and Roger. It was their fight now; Sarah was out of it. She went away inside her head where a fight swelled to such immense proportions that Mom and Roger split. Mom and Sarah would move back to Brookline. They would live over the store. Even if the moldy chicken ended up making them all sick, it would be worth it.

"I think we need to get out this afternoon," Mom declared. "Before," she added, sending some unspoken message Roger's way, "we all come down with a bad case of cabin fever."

Did moldy chicken give you cabin fever? What would happen if Jethro was sick out there all by himself? "Is cabin fever serious?" Sarah asked.

Mom and Roger laughed. The fight had fizzled. Roger said, "It's what you get from being all cooped up inside when you had other plans. Let's look over that access problem at the shop site. And I'd like to stop in on the mill. I haven't been home before dark all week."

Sarah's breath caught in her throat. She had promised Jethro he would be safe today and tonight.

"Grab that roll of blueprints," Mom said to Sarah as she went for Linda's snowsuit.

"Which roll?"

"On the dining room table."

Underneath the rolled blueprints something else caught Sarah's eye: a photocopy of an old-looking map. There was Anursnack Hill and below it Singing Fish Brook with another name beneath it. Peering closely, Sarah deciphered the faint script: "Shabokin."

Mom came in with Linda under her arm. "Can't you find the blueprints?"

Sarah nodded, still gazing at the map.

"That's us, there." Mom pointed to a tiny square beside the brook.

"The mill?" asked Sarah.

"No. The house. When this map was made, there wasn't any mill, though there had been earlier. And that road curving around Anursnack Hill, that's partly Mill Road and partly the highway. It was probably just a cart road to what they called the turnpike."

"It's the same and not the same," Sarah murmured. Speaking the exact words Jethro had used to describe the mill and the pond made her feel shivery.

Roger, coming in with Janey, said, "Mostly not. That map was made before the highway plowed right through Anursnack Hill. And the Indian name there under Singing Fish Brook indicates that this whole area must have been a sacred place, like a burial site. Shabokin means 'Place of the Departed.'"

Sarah nodded dumbly, trying to reconcile all of this with what Jethro seemed to know. If he was just plain crazy, would he come up with the correct Indian name for Singing Fish Brook?

Puzzling over this, she recalled the other name he had mentioned: Lockwood. Now, as her family surged out into the snowy afternoon, she asked her mother whether the previous owners were named Lockwood.

Mom shook her head. So Jethro didn't always come up with the right names. When Mom asked Sarah why she wanted to know, she just shrugged and said, "Someone told me people named Lockwood lived here once."

Mom thought a moment. "Now that you mention it, the name does sound familiar. Roger, is there a Lockwood somewhere back in the deed?"

But Roger was dragging Janey onto the mound of shoveled snow so that she could slide down it. The question fell away.

The weather helped keep Jethro safe from discovery. Mom and Roger, tramping around the snow-covered shop site, had to take turns lugging Linda because she couldn't manage in the deep drifts. Janey's nose streamed, and Mom was soon out of Kleenex. Sarah volunteered to take Janey to the mill, where the men kept a roll of toilet paper on hand. She grabbed Janey's mittened hand and slogged there through the snow. It was only when she was blowing Janey's nose that it occurred to her to let Jethro know about the toilet paper, too.

"You wait here," she told Janey. "I'm going upstairs for a minute."

"I'm coming, too," Janey declared behind her.

"It's too steep," Sarah objected. "You might fall. I'll be right down." As soon as she reached the upper floor, she whispered Jethro's name. He rose up from the darkest corner.

"I heard the voices," he said. "I should leave."

"You don't have to. Roger thought he'd come over, but they're going back to the house instead."

"Is that the alien?" Janey stood on the top step, her elbows on the floor. "I can't see."

"I told you to wait downstairs," Sarah snapped at her.

"I want to see the alien."

"His name is Jethro," Sarah told her. "Don't worry," she said to him, "it's just my foster sister."

Janey crawled on her hands and knees. "Turn on the lights."

"There aren't any yet. Not up here."

The outside door opened. Mom's voice came up to them. "You girls still here?"

"Ssh," Sarah commanded.

"Why?" whispered Janey.

"Because," Sarah rejoined as soon as she heard the door close.

"Will Mom be mad because the alien is here?"

"He's not staying. Only for now, because it's so cold. He's hiding."

"Oh," said Janey. She looked at Jethro. "Are you afraid of my mother?"

"I don't think so."

"You don't have to be. She's nice to you even if she's not your mom."

"Janey's a foster kid," Sarah explained. "She's living with us for now. She's allowed to call my mother Mom."

"I have watched your mother. Also the men." Jethro spoke slowly. "I don't think they would understand about me."

"I don't understand, either," Sarah pointed out. Before he could reply, she plunged on. "If your friend Mercy is really lost"—and if she's really real, she added silently—"my mother and the police might be able to help you."

Jethro scowled.

"They know how to look for lost people. They might have to take you somewhere because you're still . . . not a grown-up." But he was already shaking his head. Quickly she added, "Our social worker would make sure you were all right."

"No." His head swung from side to side. "After all I've been through. After all Mr. and Mrs. Lockwood went through for us. Do you have any idea what happens to people like me if we're caught?" His voice had dropped again. He seemed more like a shadow than a living person.

Sometimes when the child's legs forget they cannot move, it seems as if they carry her into the sunlight and down to the brook, where tumbling water washes away the filth and bathes the sores. It is usually June again. Forget-me-nots fringe the bank. But when she reaches for them, she finds that her wrists are bound, the iron weighing them down. Even so, she knows they are there. The forget-me-nots are always there.

"How can I know?" Sarah said to Jethro. "Talk to me." She could tell that she was up against resistance stronger than any argument she could muster. "Help me understand," she pleaded.

"And if you can't believe me?"

"No matter what, I won't do anything to hurt you," she promised.

He nodded. "That is good of you. I have met many good people. Are you a part of the underground, too?"

"Do you remember the crow?" Janey spoke up the way she did when Linda needed to be distracted or cheered up. "He's getting better."

"That is good," he said. "I keep thinking that if the crow came through, Mercy may have come also."

"Come through what?" Sarah demanded, trying to pin him down.

"The water," he said. "The way I did."

Sarah peered at Jethro. She could barely make out his features, his expression. But his tone was too straight for him to be fooling around. "Coming through water," she declared, groping for a way to draw him out. "Is that like imagining?"

He shook his head. "Mercy came through that way, too. Before."

Sarah was at a loss. What was he getting at?

"This time I came instead," he went on. "She wasn't sure how it would work. With her, I mean."

"Did you bring the crow?" Janey asked him. "Even though it's someone else's?"

"I didn't want to," he muttered. "I would take him back if I could."

"Back where?" Sarah cut in.

"Here. To my own time."

"Take Barker away?" Janey asked. "Can't we just keep him?"

"What is your time?" Sarah pressed. "What time are you from?"

"From when Mr. Lockwood is the miller. He and Mrs. Lockwood hide fugitives, runaways, and move them on to other stations. To help them to freedom. Do you know about the Railroad?"

"Oh, yes," Sarah replied. There was a wood-stove store in town where the trains used to stop. She had seen the tracks overgrown with weeds.

Jethro let out a long sigh. "I am glad you know of it. So it can't be too long ago. And if Mercy did not come through . . . She thought that if I came away instead of her and led him after me, then she would be safe."

"Led who?" Sarah demanded.

Even in the gloom she could see Jethro shaking his head. "I cannot explain. Not so you will believe me."

He sounded so bleak that she didn't dare push him any further just now. So she said, "Janey and I will go to the house to get the sleeping bag and some other things for you. Janey will help by keeping Mom and Roger out of my way. When I come back, maybe you can explain what you're talking about."

"I'll come back, too," Janey put in.

"Whether or not you do," Sarah informed her, "you have to promise not to mention Jethro. Okay?"

"I promise," Janey mumbled, following Sarah down the steep stairs. "But when can I? Is he still an alien?"

"No. I don't know." Then, recalling that Liz Ackerman already knew about the make-believe with Janey, Sarah added, "Yes, in a way he still is."

Stopping to tear off a length of toilet paper, which she thrust at Janey, Sarah called up to Jethro to let him know the roll was down here on the shelf above the toolbox.

"Toilet paper?" he said.

Sarah told him never mind. Sooner or later they would have to deal with that, and a lot more. But not now. Not until she had a clearer idea of who Jethro really was and where he stood. Or maybe not where. When.

CHAPTER 10

Covering Tracks

Later, as she trudged back to the mill with Janey and the sleeping bag and peanut butter and jam sandwiches and apples, it occurred to Sarah that her life had suddenly been transformed. It was not only more complicated; it was more interesting than ever before. Running away last December had been challenging. For three exhausting days she had managed to keep herself going. But they had been joyless days, and in the end she had been more miserable than triumphant.

This Jethro thing was altogether different. Trying to understand him and help him was like walking into a mystery story and talking with the characters. Probably it would turn out to be just that—a story. After all, he couldn't be from another time any more than he was from outer space. Only a little kid like Janey would fall for all that stuff.

The trouble was that Jethro himself wasn't just someone in a mystery story. He turned purple and shivered when he got cold. He was anxious and confused. She wondered how much more she could get him to tell her. How could she convince him she wouldn't betray him?

But he wasn't inside the mill. Not upstairs, not down. "Go call him," Sarah ordered.

Janey stepped outside. With the wind up, Sarah could scarcely hear her.

"Louder!" Sarah shouted as she scrambled to find the thermos and flashlight. Probably Jethro had taken off with everything he could lay his hands on.

"Sarah," Janey called up to her. "He's out across the pond. He's going away."

"Stop him," Sarah shrieked. Here she had worried about betraying him, and now he was running away from her. Half sliding down the stairway, Sarah banged out the door and around the side of the mill.

"He's by the brook," Janey told her. "He can't hear me."

"Jethro!" Sarah shouted. "Come back."

Jethro hesitated.

"At least come and get the stuff I brought. I lugged them all this way for you."

Jethro began to retrace his steps.

"Why didn't you stay?" she demanded as he approached.

"You didn't say good-bye," Janey put in. "That's rude."

Jethro regarded her. "That is so. I'm sorry. Sometimes I forget to be civil."

Sarah guessed he was ignoring her because she had yelled at him. It grated on her that Janey could get such a straightforward apology out of him.

Back inside the mill Sarah showed him the things she had managed to bring from the house. He bit into a peanut butter sandwich.

"What paste is on this bread?" he asked.

Janey laughed. "Not paste. Peanut butter."

He separated the slices and sniffed the spread. "I have not eaten butter like this before. Butter made from nuts, or do you mean butternut? The nut trees in the woods seem to be gone."

"It's peanuts from the store," Janey informed him.

"Oh," he replied. "You buy the nuts at the store and then grind them to make this food. It is different. It is good."

"And strawberry jam."

"Strawberry jam!" He seized on the words. "We have that, too."

"Listen," Sarah broke in bluntly, "is this some kind of game you're playing?"

The spark of delight dimmed. In an instant his face wore that guarded mask that registered nothing but wariness. "I have not played games of make-believe since I was a child," he told her.

Did he think he was grown up now? "How old are you?" she asked him. Even though she tried to sound neutral, a challenging note crept into her tone.

"I don't know," he replied.

"When is your birthday?" Janey asked. "If you remember your last one, then you can figure out how old you are."

He shook his head. "I cannot tell. I was brought with my mother from an island I do not recall. The sea was bluer than the bluest sky, and there was sugarcane and fish and long, sharp grass. My mother told me so many times. I grew up in the big house with the young master. I was his companion in all things. What he read I read. What he learned I learned. As he spoke, so must I. And we played many games. The games had rules. His rules."

"He sounds mean," Janey said. "Was he your brother?"

"No."

"Do you know Brad? He's my foster brother. He's away now, but he's coming back. Mike was a kind of brother, too, but he was a foster kid like me, and he went away for good."

Something flickered in Jethro's dark eyes. There was a trace of a smile that lasted only an instant. "The one who was not my brother went away, too. It was time for him to go to school.

When his father took him off, the mistress arranged for me to be sent away as well. It was the master who had insisted on having me reared in the house. She never wanted me. As soon as he was gone, I was put in chains. My mother guessed that I would be sold. She had me stolen instead. It took awhile before that could be done. Then I was taken to a big city. Have you heard of Philadelphia? It was a station on the Underground Railroad. I was there for a time before I came here."

Sarah struggled to make sense of this. She knew there was something called an Underground Railroad in history. But what exactly was it?

Jethro gazed all around the mill. "I worked for Mr. and Mrs. Lockwood. I was not their slave. They wanted me to stay with them, but it was not to be. It was not safe. Strangers came. Mercy came. The slave hunter came. At least we thought it was he." Jethro's voice fell away. The afternoon was waning. The great gears and shafts that could still be seen took on an eerie look and seemed to turn the mill into a petrified amusement park. Cold held them all in its aching grip. Janey's nose ran unchecked.

Sarah finally spoke up, urging Jethro to stay the night and leave in the early morning, when it would be light enough to see his way. But he maintained that if he left now, he would still find his way back to the chicken house. Then, by morning, the blowing snow would have covered his footsteps. He would leave no trace.

Sarah loaded him up with the sleeping bag and food. When they shut the mill door behind them and he parted from them, Sarah and Janey started right off for home. It was a bit spooky with the sky gone black and the ground so pale and lumpy. Were they treading on sacred ground? Was this very spot the Place of the Departed?

Papa dug into the base of Anursnack Hill to build an underground storage house for grain and corn. One day he unearthed some bones and a shaped stone and something else that looked like bark with hair on it. He drove his spade into the loose soil and walked into the woods. After a time his Indian friends returned with him. They did not bring their children to play as they usually did. They stayed awhile at the cellar hole, and then they left. Slowly Papa began to spade back the earth he had dug from the hill.

Cars moved along the highway again, but not with their usual whoosh. Snow tires moaned, and chains clanked. The water falling to the brook from the tumbling vent sounded muted, distant, although they knew it to be close.

Turning, Sarah caught a brief glimpse of the flashlight, like a pinprick, wavering among the trees. As she watched, it vanished. Maybe Jethro had switched it off; maybe he held it away from them, lighting his own way to Costa's chicken house. Beside her Janey's raspy breaths and sniffles drove away the ghostly hush that seemed to stalk them.

Sarah grabbed at Janey's sleeve. "Let's run."

They stumbled and raced and then slowed as light streamed out onto the snow-covered ground from the upstairs windows.

"Why did we run?" Janey was gasping and beginning to cough. "Was someone chasing us? Were we scared?"

"Only pretend," Sarah responded. "It was a game."

"Like the alien and his . . ." But Janey couldn't remember the words.

Good, thought Sarah. She didn't supply the phrase: *young master.* "Not exactly," she told Janey. "A different kind of game. We were running away from aliens from outer space. And also," she added as she stamped the snow off her boots, "we were trying to get warm."

CHAPTER 11

Keeping Secrets

O ver the weekend Mom decided that the crow had to stay in the cellar at night to cut down on the smell that seeped through from the mudroom every morning.

Saturday night at supper Sarah asked Mom and Roger if she could have their television in her room and stay up late. They said she could watch something downstairs. Roger even offered to go and rent a movie.

"I just feel like being in my room by myself," she said. She kept her eyes on her plate, but she could tell from the pause that followed that Mom and Roger were exchanging glances. No doubt worried ones.

Finally Mom said, "Is there anyone from school you'd like to have over?"

Sarah shook her head. "I don't know anyone that well."

"Sarah," Mom told her, "you've been here since school started. Don't you think it's time you accepted this move? And made new friends?"

Arguments rose up, nearly choking Sarah. How could she

get to know kids in a place like this, cut off from all humanity? "The only people I get to see around here," she mumbled, "are Frenchy and Ken."

"Don't forget—" Janey started to tell her.

"And other grown-ups," Sarah nearly shouted to shut Janey up. But it occurred to her that if she could get Jethro to show himself, Mom and Roger would look on him as a gift from heaven. Someone Sarah's age, or anyhow not much older than she was. Someone to help put an end to her solitary ways. "You know what the kids in school call me?" she went on. "Gruesome. That's what I am to them." The dismay on her mother's face sent a thrill of triumph through Sarah.

"That's outrageous!" Mom exclaimed. "I'm going to speak to Mrs. Segal."

Sarah scraped back her chair. "You speak to anyone about this, and I'll never go back to school, not ever."

"Sarah's right," Roger said. "She has to deal with this herself. It's not just the kids' attitude; it's hers." He turned to Sarah. "I know how you feel about being legally adopted, but this might be a good time to reconsider taking the family name."

Silence overspread the dinner table. Sarah's face must have registered her absolute rejection of Roger and his suggestion, because as soon as the conversation resumed, she was shut out of it entirely. Mom's voice was low, and words like *obdurate*, which surfaced at times like this, were passed back and forth, the exclusive, nearly foreign language of social workers and parents.

For the moment Sarah couldn't even remember what had started them off on this. It was only after she was upstairs in her room that she recalled her request for the television. She wasn't likely to get it now. There would be a visit from Mom as soon as the little ones were settled for the night. Mom would tell her how hurt Roger was. Mom would also say she was disappointed, which was what she said whenever she was furious and trying to remember the best way to "handle" Sarah.

Sarah stared at the picture of her father that she kept on her bureau. Sometimes when she looked at old photographs, she could almost convince herself that she remembered him the way Brad did. But all she had of him really were a few snapshots of herself in his lap and one that showed him holding her halfway out of the water at some lake. Those and her name—Grissom. She would never give it up.

> *Everything blurs together—the hill, the bones, Papa dragging himself again and then again to the Indian grave he must fill, Papa in the doorway afterward, swaying, toppling. These events form a single outpouring, an emptying of light. Only when the child dreams can she break through the darkness to find him. He holds her, and the sun is there and the cool water with the clouds on its surface and the flowers like sky.*

"Can I come in?" Janey was at Sarah's door.

Sarah nodded at her. "What do you want?"

Janey had no answer. She wandered around the room, reaching but not quite touching anything, looking worried and bewildered. "Are you mad at me, too?" she asked timidly.

"Of course not," Sarah snapped. "Though you've got to be more careful. You were about to mention the alien."

"I wasn't."

"You were. Don't lie."

"It's a lie not to mention him," Janey shot back.

Sarah considered her retort. Considered also her fighting back. She was beginning to act like a real person. If only she were a little older. She might even get to feel like a true sister.

Sarah plumped down on her bed, drew her knees up, and began to talk about trying to get Jethro to change his mind. Janey stood in the middle of the room, her dark eyebrows knitted as she took in what Sarah was saying about how it had to be up to him, not to them.

Janey said, "I feel sorry for him. I bet he's cold tonight."

"At least he has Brad's sleeping bag."

"Where did he go?" Janey asked. "Is he out in the snow?"

Sarah shook her head. Jethro would be safer if Janey didn't know about the Costa chicken house. "He says he found some kind of shelter. He must be all right. Tomorrow we'll get more hot food to him. Or I will. It might be too hard for you to go through the snow in the woods."

Janey sent her a long, level stare, the kind that would unsettle a grown-up. Sarah was reminded that Jethro seemed to like Janey. If *like* was the right word. There was a kind of sympathy between them, an acceptance. Well, that was all right for Janey. But how could you accept what someone said when every statement left you bursting with questions? And how would you convince someone to come out of hiding if you had no idea what he was hiding from?

Get some answers of your own, Sarah told herself. But how?

Sarah returned Janey's look. Janey, a new person in her own right. A new person in Sarah's life. Along with the mysterious Jethro, who might be an alien, a foreigner, or just plain loony.

"You *are* mad at me," Janey said. She reached for one of her braids and began to suck the tip of it.

"No, I'm not. I'm just thinking." Sarah sighed. It wasn't easy handling Janey as well as Jethro. But as this thought struck her, so did the realization that she hated being on the receiving end of being handled. Maybe that was how Janey felt, too; maybe that was why she kept asking Sarah if she was mad at her. "It's hard," Sarah tried to explain. "Secrets are hard to keep, especially when we don't know why we have to keep them."

Janey nodded and let the braid go.

"It's hard for me, too," Sarah admitted. "Not just for you. I can't think what's going to happen the next time we see him. Or even if we will see him again."

"We will," Janey said confidently. "He has Brad's sleeping bag and Dad's flashlight. He won't steal them."

Sarah found herself smiling. There was trust for you. And it was oddly contagious, comforting. Like walking home in the heavy dusk with that smaller hand in hers helping to hold back the presences that seemed to gather all around the mill and the pond.

CHAPTER 12

Picture from the Past

The difference between a TV detective and Sarah trying to figure out the puzzle of Jethro was that TV detectives picked up clues and Sarah didn't. There weren't any. Or else there were too many. Nor were there witnesses, unless she counted Jethro, and he wasn't exactly what was called a reliable witness.

While the family got ready for church, Sarah considered what she ought to pack in a knapsack for Jethro. He had to be bored by now. What about a game or something to read? She scoured her books without finding anything she could be sure he would like. That was another problem about his being so secretive, if that's what it was that made him invent those wild stories as a cover. She really didn't know a thing about him.

Downstairs the usual commotion reigned. Mom came upstairs, asking on her way whether Sarah had seen Brad's navy wool hat. Since Sarah had given it to Jethro, she thought she'd better make a point of looking for it in the mudroom.

Roger had the little ones in the kitchen actually sitting in chairs, Janey in front of Linda pretending to be a choo choo train. That reminded Sarah about the Underground Railroad Jethro had mentioned. Pawing through the hats and mittens in the mudroom, she called out a question about it. To her surprise Roger responded at once. Yes, it existed before the Civil War.

Sarah stopped and turned. "Did it really go underground?"

Roger unstuck the Velcro boot tab from Linda's sleeve and pulled up her sock. "That's just a term. Because it was secret. To rescue runaway slaves."

Sarah stifled a gasp of surprise. "When would that have been?"

Linda started to slide off the chair. Roger hauled her back up. "Not done," he told her. "You're still the caboose." Stuffing her foot into the boot, he said to Sarah, "I just told you. Before the Civil War."

"Well, when was that?" she demanded.

"Don't they teach you anything in school?" he retorted. "I'll get you a book. You can read about it."

"I don't want to be the engine anymore," Janey declared. "Can I go out?"

Roger nodded, set Linda loose, and strode through to the living room bookshelves.

Mom, passing him, said, "Wait, Janey, let me do the top flap. It's really cold today." In an undertone she told Roger she couldn't find Linda's pacifier and she couldn't find his maroon scarf either.

Sarah scuttled after him. Anything to keep him from launching a search for another thing she had loaned to Jethro.

Roger handed her a thick book and told her to look up "slavery" in it. But Sarah found much more than she could possibly read and no answer to her question.

"I just want to know when that Underground Railroad was," she said to him.

By now he had Linda in his arms, bundled against the cold and already beginning to protest. "Look around the mid-1800s," he told her. "Be resourceful. Try 'Fugitive Slave Law.'"

"Why can't you just tell me?" Sarah demanded as the door slammed behind him. She appealed to her mother. "Why won't Roger ever help me?"

"Not now, Sarah." Mom's bushy black hair clouded her face. "We're late."

They always were. They could never seem to organize themselves so that there was time for helping Sarah. Her mind raced. For one tiny second she still had her mother all to herself. "Mom," she begged, "just tell me the name of a famous kids' book from the mid-1800s."

"I can't think," Mom said. "Oh, how about *Alice in Wonderland?* It's from sometime around then." As she opened the front door, a rush of icy air hit Sarah.

"Wait," Sarah cried, thinking it might be famous enough for Jethro to recognize. "Do we have it? Where can I find it?"

"Upstairs," Mom said. "Probably in Janey's room. Also, there's that big edition with all the historical notes." Mom waved toward the bookshelf behind the couch. "Back there somewhere."

Before Sarah could ask her what it looked like, Mom was out the door. The car motor roared. Sarah was left alone.

The book, which she managed to find almost at once, was much bigger than she remembered. But as she skimmed through it, the story began to come back to her about Alice's going down the rabbit hole and then eating and drinking stuff that made her shrink or grow. She flipped back to the beginning and began to look at the small print in the margin that was full of historical information. And there before her eyes was "Alice's adventures underground . . ." The words flew off the page at her. The underground right here in this book, too. She couldn't wait to show it to Jethro.

She had a struggle to fit it into her knapsack, but she was determined, and eventually she was ready to go to the Costa farm, loaded down with hot canned tomato soup in a thermos, bread and cheese and fruit, and an oversize classic children's book that might be some kind of clue to unraveling the truth from Jethro's fiction.

It seemed to take forever to get there. Whatever snow had blown over Jethro's tracks the night before had kept on blowing, leaving behind indistinct depressions in the crusted surface. Following them made every step she took slippery and treacherous. Every time she broke through the crust she had to struggle to free herself.

> *The child's legs keep pumping, but it takes all her strength to raise them, to stretch, to cover any ground at all. She pulls and then lifts first one leaden foot and then the other. She wakes with her muscles twitching, her body drenched and cold. All that striving, and yet she is no closer.*

As Jethro's path emerged into the open, it skirted a vast, snow-covered field. Sarah looked across that broad expanse. She could see low gray buildings that straggled off behind Mrs. Costa's house. She followed Jethro's rounded footprints to a tiny building. Pulling open the door, she saw that it was an outdoor toilet, a board seat with a hole in it. On the wall were pictures from magazines and a toilet paper roll on a string. She heaved a sigh. That was one thing she didn't have to worry about anymore.

Jethro's tracks led her to the end of the farthest building, a long, low shed. Peering through the windows as she walked along it, she saw hens cooped at the end nearest the house and then a lot of empty cots in a double row. Only one cot, not far from the chicken coop, held Jethro curled up in the sleeping bag.

She tried not to startle him as she entered the shed at the far end. But as soon as she opened the creaky door, he tumbled to the floor, bag and all, in a heap. So she had to speak out quickly, to let him know he wasn't discovered. Then she walked up the aisle between the cots, trying to guess what they were there for. All she could think of was some kind of camp, a place where kids might sleep in the summertime. It didn't look very fancy. Who would send their kids to a place like this?

Jethro hauled himself free of the sleeping bag. "You should not be here. Not in the daylight." The chickens clucked as if in agreement.

"What difference does it make?" Sarah retorted. "Mrs. Costa can see your footprints, too."

"But she hasn't. Whenever she does catch me, I will show her all the wood I've carried and stacked. Then she might even let me stay."

Stay here? thought Sarah. "You could come home with me instead and be in a real house. You wouldn't be the first homeless kid my mother's taken in."

He shook his head. "When I know Mercy is safe, then I'll see what I must do to get along."

Sarah shrugged off the knapsack and dumped it on the cot. "Look what I brought," she said to him. She pulled out the thermos and bread and cheese and fruit. While Jethro started to eat, Sarah tugged at the oversize book. "I brought you something to read, too," she told him.

"You have books? Mr. and Mrs. Lockwood kept a very few, and I read them all, but I haven't seen any here. Mrs. Costa has something that makes pictures into stories of some sort. But it isn't to read."

"How do you know what's in Mrs. Costa's house?"

"I go to the window after dark. When she makes the light come all over. Her stove cooks without wood or coal. Have you seen it?"

All Sarah could say was that those things were ordinary, that everyone had them, and that the pictures that made stories were television.

"Television." His lips silently shaped the syllables over and over. Finally he said, "I have seen newspapers now. I know the year we are in. Are there no slaves anymore?"

"Only in stories," she told him. "What kind of stories did you used to read?" She was still trying to extract *Alice in Wonderland* from the knapsack.

"Pilgrim's Progress," Jethro answered. "The best one, though, was full of adventure. It's called *Masterman Ready*. I would read it until the candle burned down."

The titles meant nothing to her. "I suppose *Pilgrim's Progress* is about the Pilgrims landing. I've been to Plimoth Plantation. You walk around while people in costumes do old-fashioned things. They talk with a worse accent than yours."

Looking puzzled, he informed her that Mercy was the one who was hard to understand. "She is more different from me than I believe I am from you," he added.

"And she's real?" Sarah went on. "Not out of a book or a movie?"

"Movie?"

"Oh, never mind." Whatever he was or pretended to be, he wasn't about to be trapped into admitting it was all a fake. At last the *Alice* book came free. "Have you ever read this one?" she asked.

He stared at the long-necked child on the cover and shook his head.

"Heard of it?" she pressed, opening it, showing it to him.

Slowly he shook his head. "Never."

"It's famous," she insisted. "You can't be from the mid-1800s and not know about it." She thrust it into his hands like a challenge.

He sank down on the cot with the book open on his knees.

To give him some time with it, Sarah wandered along the aisle toward the chickens. The closer she came to them, the more her nose burned from the reek of their droppings. A small door led straight into the coop from the front of the shed. She guessed Jethro must know the time of day Mrs. Costa came for eggs and to feed the chickens. She wasn't likely to look beyond them down the desolate rows of bare cots.

Jethro was partway through the second chapter when Sarah came back to him. He looked astonished. "You still don't know this book?" she demanded.

He shook his head.

"Then you can't be from olden times," she asserted.

"I never said I was. I'm from my own time, and it's not old. Mercy is from olden times."

Sarah pried the book from his grasp. She was pretty sure there would be a date at the beginning. She would confront him with a date the way a TV detective confronted a reluctant witness with incontestable evidence. She found the first dates of publication at the back of the book: 1865 and 1866. She showed them to Jethro.

"But that is after my time," he responded. "We just began the new decade. Books have become strange since then if this is what they are like."

Sarah was so letdown that she didn't even bother to point out that Alice was underground like him. The book was nothing but a false lead. Still, he wanted her to leave it with him so that he could read it through to the end. She didn't mind. It would make her load lighter.

To give herself a reason for lingering, she unscrewed the thermos top and poured out a cup of hot soup. Jethro took it and just held it. She was groping for some other real thing from the past to try on him but couldn't think of anything. She found herself moving away from what was provable and solid. "There's this story I sort of know," she began haltingly.

"You might recognize part of it. I mean, there's one part I'm hoping you know." There he sat, slouched on the cot with the soup cup in his hands, remote and bewildered. "There's a kind of prison," she went on, trying to recapture the scene. "Very dark. Do you know what a dungeon is?"

He looked up at her. He was paying close attention now.

"There's someone on the floor. Not alone." As she spoke, she saw it again, the arms outstretched where the single shaft of light slanted down, the hands clasped, reaching. "A child," she said. "A crow comes through a tiny window with criss-crossed bars."

Jethro was so still he didn't seem to breathe. Leaning toward him, she took the cup from his hands. A thin, sweet plume of steam rose and tickled her nose. "You know that story, too, don't you?" she declared. Her hands shook; soup sloshed over the rim of the cup. "I sort of thought you would. Can you tell me what it comes from?"

He shook his head. There was a sudden ruckus among the chickens. Feathers flew, some escaping the coop and wafting down on his black hair. They looked like giant snowflakes. He raised one hand as if to brush them away, but his fingers went to his cheek, which was wet.

Sarah felt terrible. Her good guess had produced something bad. She had no idea what it was about that scene that made him cry. She said, "But, Jethro, it's only a story. A picture. It isn't real."

"It is a picture from the past," he said. "It is true."

"True?" She tried to laugh, but her mouth had gone dry. She could barely make her voice work. "It's a picture out of some story from an old movie, even if it does remind you of something else."

His hands in fists scrubbed at his eyes. The hands remained in fists and came together as though joined at the wrists. "This very thing. Yes, I have seen it. Mercy showed me. She was that small child, much younger then. Bound at the wrists and ankles. The leg irons maimed her. Do you want to hear some of what she told me?"

"Wait a minute," Sarah protested. She wasn't looking for a story about an imaginary person. "I just want facts."

Jethro nodded. "Then listen. This is Mercy. Her father, the miller Goodman Bredcake, befriended the Indians, and they him. But then all the tribes joined King Philip to drive the settlers from this stolen land. So the Indians came to be seen as children of the devil. When Mercy's father sickened and her mother failed to save him with an Indian cure, the settlers blamed her for using a heathen brew. She had always healed their children and their animals. Now they believed her power had turned and that when she crooned to their babies and tamed wild creatures, the devil spoke through her. People began to whisper of witchcraft. And when her husband's sister and her husband came to help run the mill, those whispers were the first things they heard."

"This is a story," Sarah interrupted. She needed to hear Jethro admit this. "A story!" she insisted.

"Mercy's story," Jethro replied. "Mercy's time. Long ago. When she was perhaps five years old. That was when her uncle Zerobabel came with his wife from Connecticut Colony."

"Zero what?" Sarah exclaimed.

"Zerobabel Quelch. An important man, a magistrate."

"Oh, please, Jethro. That isn't anyone's real name."

"That is what I thought, too," Jethro agreed. "He was named for an ancient priest and raised in the belief that he was ordained to seek out the devil and his servants wherever they might be. That is partly why he gathered evidence against Mercy's mother. He claimed that she surrounded herself with familiars to do her bidding."

"What does that mean, familiars?"

"Creatures that serve a witch. The crow, for one. Other wild animals that came to her. And, much later, a great, black cat."

"That's just Halloween stuff. It's stupid."

"It was considered proof. Along with the charm she wore, an Indian gift, and her disregard of the Sabbath law against kissing a child."

"You expect me to believe that kissing was against the law?"

"Not in my time. In Mercy's. But worst of all was Zerobabel's own confession that the widow Bredcake, who was with child, filled his head with unclean thoughts. Only a witch could corrupt so good a man."

In spite of herself, Sarah was fascinated. "Go on," she prompted. Afterward she could let Jethro know that she wasn't really taken in.

"Zerobabel Quelch held Mercy and her mother in their cellar until they could be brought to court in Boston. While they were held there, Indians attacked the settlement and burned most of the houses. But not the millhouse and the mill. Since they spared Margaret Bredcake and Mercy, that became the most damaging evidence of all. Imagine what the settlers thought when they watched from the garrison house as the Indians laid waste the settlement and drove their cattle off. They must all have been ready to condemn Margaret Bredcake then and there. But all they could do was leave and take her with them."

"If that's true," Sarah insisted, "it would be in a history book."

Jethro nodded. "That is exactly what I said. And Mercy replied that she hoped it was written true. She feared that Zerobabel would have reviled her and her mother for all time."

Sarah drew a long breath. "So what happened next?"

"What I started with. Boston. Mercy in leg and hand irons. And feared along with her mother, because the crow came to her with food."

"A little girl like Janey? Come on, Jethro."

"It happened. Margaret Bredcake was condemned to hang, only not until after the birth of her child. So she and Mercy were bound and kept in darkness and filth until the baby was born and died. Until Margaret Bredcake died. Then Zeroba-bel Quelch paid the prison charges, claiming the mill as payment, and Mercy as well. But that is another chapter in her story."

Good, thought Sarah. At least Jethro was acknowledging that it was made up.

"If I am here long enough," he went on, "I will tell you more about how Mercy was used and how she finally struck back. Then you will understand why she so fervently hopes history reveals her uncle's true nature."

"You believe that?" A moment ago Sarah had thought that Jethro had all but admitted that this story was a fiction.

"I believe her, yes." He wiped invisible cobwebs from his eyes. "It takes time, like a house. I have pointed to the framing only. Mercy showed me threads and splinters and crumbs, until I could see all of it, everything that happened."

Sarah handed the cup back to him. The steam was gone. "There's more hot soup in the thermos," she told him. She felt dazed and stupid, because Jethro's story had held her riveted.

"Good-bye," she said, almost as an afterthought, halfway to the door of the shed.

He was still holding the cup, but in that queer way as though his wrists were linked, the cup balanced on the heels of his palms. The soup would be icy before he took his first swallow.

CHAPTER 13

Family Familiar

After Sunday lunch Mom put Linda down for a nap and then went to work in the dining room. Roger spread newspapers on the kitchen floor and started stripping finish from an old chair. So Sarah sat in the living room with the history book Roger had given her. She had to slog through a lot of names and dates before she came to anything like plain information about the Underground Railroad.

It sounded pretty dangerous, not just for the slaves, but for the people who protected them from slave hunters. She couldn't begin to picture this house as one of those way stations on the railroad. But she couldn't help thinking about those presences she kept nearly seeing. No connection, she told herself. She was letting Jethro's imagination get to her.

As she turned a page, her glance fell on a couple of lines written about Massachusetts by a poet named Whittier:

No slave hunt in our borders—no pirate on our strand!
No fetters in the Bay State—no slave upon our land!

Sarah rose and walked into the dining room, where her mother was leaning over the usual mess of plans and papers.

"Mom, what are fetters?" she asked.

Her mother turned, her finger marking the place on a document she had been studying. "You know how to use the dictionary," she said.

"Can't you just tell me?"

"You should learn to be self-reliant," Mom replied.

"Sure," Sarah muttered. "How come you didn't like me being self-reliant when I took off in December?"

"That," her mother exclaimed, exasperation making her lose her place on the document, "is not self-reliance. It's self-destruction." There were tiny pinched lines at the corners of her mouth. Her cloudburst hair darkened her face and shrouded her eyes.

Sarah could hear Roger in the kitchen groan. She retreated to the living room, to the book, but she couldn't read on. Janey came downstairs caught sight of Sarah, and stopped midway. Sarah fetched the dictionary and slung it onto the couch. She took a long time to look up *fetters*. "A chain or shackles binding the ankles," she read. When she finally looked up, Janey was still standing on the stairs.

Sarah forged through the kitchen to visit the crow in the mudroom. "Is there anything I can bring to Barker?" she called to the powers that be.

Roger stopped sandpapering long enough to suggest raw popcorn.

"Can I feed Barker, too?" Janey asked as she slipped into the mudroom.

"Sure," Sarah told her, although she would have preferred to be alone with her thoughts. Jethro had spoken of chains and leg irons. Of course, he might have read about them, too.

As soon as Sarah closed the door to the kitchen, Janey whispered, "Did you see the alien?"

Sarah raised a warning finger to her lips and shook her head.

"You didn't? He was gone?"

"Janey!" Sarah exploded. Then she lowered her voice and explained that Jethro was fine, but they still mustn't talk about him unless they were outside by themselves.

Janey nodded gravely. The crow stepped onto her shoulder and probed her ear. She shrugged and giggled. "He tickles," she whispered.

"You can speak normally," Sarah told her. "I mean," she added hastily, "about Barker."

"Okay," Janey agreed at full voice. "How come the alien doesn't want us to keep him?"

For a split second Sarah heard herself groan like Roger. "We're not playing that game now," she declared brightly, making sure that Roger would hear her.

"Oh," said Janey, not the least bit subdued. "Can we teach Barker that trick again? He only comes when he's called when he feels like it."

"All right." All of a sudden Sarah felt exhausted. She couldn't think with Janey jabbering at her. When she went to the kitchen for the popcorn, she deliberately left the door ajar so that Roger would notice that she was still being nice to Janey.

The two girls stood across from each other. There wasn't much space between them, but maybe that was for the best. The crow didn't have far to go, first to one who called and held out popcorn, then to the other. This was good for him, Sarah informed Janey. He needed exercise to get his strength back.

So when Janey moved over to the door to the kitchen and

the door swung wide, it seemed perfectly natural to give the crow more room. Roger wasn't there anymore. Calling Barker, extending the popcorn, Janey kept backing away.

When the crow took off, Janey gave a little shriek and ducked. Flapping past her, the crow landed on the counter next to the sink. Janey's shriek erupted into laughter. As she reached out to him, the crow dodged her and swooped on into the living room. He hit the mantelpiece and fell to the hearth, where he righted himself, shook out his feathers, and lurched across the rug.

"Everything all right down there?" Mom called from Linda's room.

Sarah hoped Roger was upstairs with her. "Fine," she yelled back. "Sort of," she added in an undertone. "Don't scare him," she warned Janey.

Just then the front door opened. Roger came backing through, hauling a load of logs.

The crow made his sore-throat squawk and lifted off, clumsy in confined flight, but clearly aiming for the outdoors.

"No!" screamed Janey. "Stop him."

Leaping to intercept the crow, Sarah slammed full tilt into Roger's bent back. The logs, with Roger crowning them, tumbled down the steps. The crow swooped to escape Sarah, landed on Roger, flapped his wings, and took to the air.

"Get Barker," wailed Janey.

"What the . . . What were you doing?" Roger spluttered as he picked himself up and confronted Sarah. "You—you pushed me."

Sarah felt herself go hot. She shook her head.

Mom on the stairs with Linda exclaimed, "Not on purpose. It was an accident."

Linda started to cry. Janey clutched herself, sobbing.

Roger stood inside with the door still open behind him. He brushed off snow, but tiny pools formed at his feet and seeped in wavy streams toward crow droppings on the rug. Taking in the mess, he glared at Sarah and said, "If this was a mere accident, heaven help us when you get into serious mischief."

"I didn't," she declared thickly. "It was the crow."

He gave a hollow laugh. "I'm not buying that unless you mean the bird's acting on orders. Is that it? Did he just acquire supernatural powers?"

"Like a familiar?" Mom asked. She was actually laughing now. "You've been reading too much of that seventeenth-century history."

"I'm just saying," he replied a little stiffly, "that I object to Sarah's idea of family entertainment."

What were they talking about? Sarah wondered. The crow as a familiar? That was the sort of remark she expected from Jethro, not Mom and Roger. But *familiar* sounded like *family.* Maybe that's what they meant.

Mom tried to get Janey to blow her nose. "Barker will come back as soon as he gets hungry," she promised. "Or cold."

"We can leave food out for him," Roger said. His voice was back to normal again. But then he was talking to Janey, not to Sarah.

Suddenly Janey pointed and shouted. "There he is. I see him."

"Don't move," Roger ordered. "Don't take one more step."

His sharp command startled Janey and produced a fresh flow of tears. Contrite, he tried to reach across the snow puddles and crow mess to comfort her. "Honey," he said, "just hold still for a second till we get the rug cleaned up."

Janey stood rooted, her face gone white.

"It's all right," Mom said to her. "Dad didn't want you making it worse."

Sarah could see the crow staggering to keep his balance on a snow-covered bough. Janey raised her hands as if to show him that she had popcorn for him. The low afternoon sun poured in through the open door and lit the entry with its scraps of bark and meltwater and the puddles trickling into the crow-spattered rug and Janey beseeching, unmoving, her wrists joined as though fettered.

"Ssh," Sarah said to all of them. Roger came in from the kitchen with paper towels and a rag. "Ssh," she repeated. Even Roger halted. "He'll come now," Sarah told them, calm with certainty. "Just don't move."

And the crow did come. Hesitant, awkward, and listing badly as he flapped down from the tree. But straight enough to make a feeble swipe at Janey's hands before tumbling, with a surprising clatter, to the hearth.

Sarah slammed the door shut. Janey's arms spread wide. "See?" she sang out. "We just taught him again to come, and it saved his life. He knows he's our friend."

"I guess he does," Roger agreed.

"Sarah," Mom put in, "how could you tell he would come just then?"

Sarah couldn't say: I've seen it. The same scene, only different. She couldn't explain: It was Janey like that, and the light. So she just echoed Janey: "He knows he's our friend." But something made her add, "He's our family," as if that could blot out the other word—*familiar*—that sounded so disturbingly like it.

CHAPTER 14

Catamount

Monday afternoon Liz Ackerman met Sarah at the bus stop and invited her into the car. "Want to talk about your blowup with Roger?" she began.

"So he told you," Sarah retorted.

"Your mother did. She said it was pretty upsetting for Janey."

Janey. "Is that what she thought?"

"That's what she said. She didn't have to tell me it was upsetting for you and Roger."

Sarah could feel the heat rising in her. "He won't believe me. He never does."

"Why do you suppose that is?"

Sarah knew she ought to say: Because I ran off. Because I haven't earned back his trust yet.

One of those long silences followed, the kind that vibrates with unspoken arguments. Liz seemed to take a good deal of interest in the controls on her dashboard. Finally she mused, "I think it's kind of interesting, though, that there's a lot going on in your family right now. Don't you?"

Surprised, Sarah found herself asking what was going on.

"I was hoping you might be able to clue me in. Suddenly you and Janey are teaming up. Suddenly Janey the Silent is turning into Janey the Outspoken. Hadn't you noticed?"

Sarah had. But did that mean that Janey had given away any of Jethro's secrets? For the first time since getting in the car, Sarah turned directly toward Liz. "When Janey asks a question, they always answer it. When I do, Roger makes me look it up. He wants me off his back."

"Interesting choice of phrase. Do you think he still thinks you were on his back yesterday?"

Sarah flushed. She had walked right into that. "I didn't mean what happened yesterday. I mean all the time. I just wish he'd stop pretending that he doesn't hate me."

"How about all of us getting together for a talk one evening this week?"

The last time they'd had one of those family sessions with Liz it was to arrange the terms of Sarah's return. "What for?" she mumbled.

"To help get past this. To make life a little easier for everyone. Including you."

"All I need is to be left alone."

"Do you feel like saying that to Janey?"

Sarah shook her head so hard she could feel her neck creak. "I don't mean Janey. You know that."

"How can I know what you mean unless you tell me?"

Sarah mulled this over for a couple of minutes. She longed to blurt out: That's exactly how I feel about Jethro. All at once she could see how hard it was for Janey not to mention him. But the need was overwhelming, and she found herself skirting the subject. "There's a boy I know that's hard to understand. He's much harder than I am. It's like he doesn't know how to say what's on his mind, so it comes out in sort of riddles. Or stories."

"That must be challenging."

Sarah nodded with relief. It felt so good to get even this much said out loud to a grown-up. And Jethro was still safe. "I keep trying . . . trying." Her voice trailed off.

"So it's worth it," Liz concluded with a smile. "Most relationships are, if you can slog through the misunderstandings. We'll work on yours and Roger's and Janey's. We'll try, too."

Sarah couldn't refuse then, even though she didn't really see what it had to do with Janey. She got out of the car and scuffed home through a light, fresh cover of fluffy snow.

It was only after she had her things off that she remembered that she needed to settle up with Frenchy for the candy bar she'd taken for Jethro. She would rather replace the candy than pay him, but there was no way to get to the store on her own. She had some major shopping to do, too. Where would the money come from?

She found her mother coming downstairs with Linda in tow, a slow process, and asked whether the old coat had been sold yet.

"Hi!" Mom said to her with emphatic cheerfulness. "It's customary to greet people before you make demands on them."

"It wasn't a demand. It's a question."

Mom swung Linda over the last step and onto the floor. "You can't expect that cloak to sell quickly. It's not like something pretty for your living room."

"I thought you said it was valuable."

"It is. Someone will come along who wants just that sort of item, but it may take time."

"Well, next time you go shopping, can I come, too?"

"You mean groceries?"

"Yes." Sarah scrambled for some acceptable purpose. "Janey and me are sort of camping out."

"In February?" Mom asked doubtfully.

"We started when it was warmer. Anyway, I want some stuff on hand."

Mom said that as a matter of fact, she was overdue for getting eggs at Costa's and that she wouldn't mind running into town to pick up a few things before the store closed. She seemed to be surprisingly short of things like bread and cheese.

Upstairs in her room, Sarah rummaged through her bottom bureau drawer, looking for money she might have stashed away and forgotten. She came up with almost eight dollars, which looked like more than she ought to spend at one time, but she took it all with her just the same.

She debated with herself about telling Janey about the explanation she had offered Mom. That was the trouble with little kids; you could never really ignore them. If she ever had any of her own, she would make sure that she could afford to hire someone the way her friend Ruthie Boyer's parents did. There was a person from South America or someplace who lived with them and spent the day pulling socks out of Ruthie's little brother's boots and making his crooked zippers work. If you stayed over at the Boyers', Mrs. Boyer just came sailing downstairs in the morning looking perfect and slipping on her coat and gloves and sweeping out the door. Sarah used to dream about moving in with the Boyers, where the grown-ups left you alone and the little kids were taken care of by the South American someone. But since the day during Christmas vacation when Sarah took off from the Boyer house in Brookline and didn't go to meet Roger at the shop, she wasn't even allowed to visit Ruthie anymore.

After what seemed like an hour, Sarah and Mom and the two little ones were on their way. Sarah gazed out on Mill Road with new interest as she tried to gauge the parallel route through the woods. The big field turned out to be farther off than she would have guessed. As soon as Mom turned up Mrs. Costa's driveway, Sarah volunteered to run in for the eggs. Mom gave her money.

When Mrs. Costa came to the door, Sarah remembered to ask for two dozen. Sandy, the dog, waddled over to sniff Sarah's boots.

"I'll have to go back for another box," Mrs. Costa told her.

Sarah took the opportunity to step inside. Mrs. Costa had gone through the door that connected with the garage. Sarah looked to the left. There was the kitchen. Through the window over the sink she could see some of the outbuildings, but not all the way to the long shed.

Mrs. Costa returned hunched with cold. "We store the eggs in the garage," she said. "It's a wonder they don't freeze there. I suppose you people have heard about those big animal tracks around here."

"Tracks?" Sarah's heart skipped a beat. Mrs. Costa must mean Jethro's footprints, maybe Sarah's as well.

"Tracks in the snow. Sonny says it's some kind of big cat. Figures it's come after deer. They're pretty hungry this time of year. They'll come right out in the open, pawing through the snow."

"Sonny saw the tracks?" Sarah asked. He was one of Mrs. Costa's sons. She called them boys even though they had nearly grown kids of their own.

"They all saw them," Mrs. Costa told Sarah. "Took pictures, too. I can tell you I don't go out no more than I have to these days, and never at night. They say those big cats mostly prowl at night."

Sarah was about to ask Mrs. Costa what she meant by big when her mother beeped the horn. Sarah just handed over the money Mom had given her. She had to step over Sandy, who had thumped himself down in front of her.

"Wait now and I'll get your change." Mrs. Costa took a long time picking out coins from an ashtray and spreading them in her hand. While she counted, Sarah took another few steps until she could see into the living room. She glimpsed a glass-fronted cupboard, the back of a fat sofa, and a television console in an ornate cabinet.

"There." Mrs. Costa was wheezing as she dropped the coins into Sarah's hands. "Coyotes, too," she remarked.

Sarah paused at the door. "Coyotes?"

"After the deer. We all see them. In the summer I can't keep the chickens inside when we put up the picking crews in the shed. I expect them coyotes will be getting into the chickens sooner or later." Mrs. Costa sighed. "What can you do? Those animals coming back, it's a bad sign. Makes you think something's gone wrong, if you know what I mean."

When the snow lies deep and the moon writes messages in bold gray strokes on the glistening land, wolves call to each other. Papa says a deer must have fallen or is trapped in a drift. The child stares at the window. All she can see through the greased paper is a faint glow from the moon-drenched snow. With her mind's eye she sees the hungry wolves close in on their doomed quarry. Papa dons his coat and takes his musket. Mamma says they may have deer meat to help them through this frozen season. Poor wolves, she says. Poor, poor deer.

Poor dear, Mamma murmurs to the child at her side, who resists the darkness she wakes to, resists the howling that has put her to dreaming and brought her out of it again. Not wolves after all, but the old woman whose clothes and rotting skin give off a stench that burns the eyes and clogs the throat. The old woman howls and yips and howls some more. The child would cover her ears if the iron cuffs did not prevent her. Poor dear, says Mamma, poor, poor dear.

☐ ☐ ☐

Running out to the car, Sarah decided not to mention the big cat. Mom disapproved of scary gossip.

"What took so long?" Mom wanted to know.

"Mrs. Costa. She talks a lot."

"She must get lonely here all by herself," Mom put in.

"Why doesn't she live with Sonny?" Sarah asked.

"Maybe she doesn't want to. Maybe Sonny and Elaine don't want her to. Of course, she has that smelly old dog."

"Is she very old?" Sarah asked.

"I have no idea." Mom's foot tapped impatiently as they waited at the light to cross the highway. The cars sped by in one continuous whoosh. Sarah found herself wondering whether Jethro would need to have traffic lights explained to him.

They got to the store just before it closed. Sarah split off from her mother, who pushed a cart around with Linda in the seat. Janey wandered between them until she decided that Sarah's purchases were more interesting.

"What in heaven's name is all that?" Mom had sort of sneaked up behind without Sarah's noticing.

Sarah nearly dropped the can opener she had in her hand. "Janey and me are camping out. I told you."

"Well," Mom warned, "don't let those cans freeze. And I don't want you stuffing yourselves on a lot of junky prepared food. I'd rather you helped yourselves from our own supplies."

"Really?" Sarah responded. "It's all right to take stuff from our kitchen?"

"Of course. Within reason," Mom added. "Are you two almost done?"

Sarah nodded. She had one more stop, for cookies and candy bars. She wished she could get over to the Costa chicken house right away, but it was already getting dark. The food for Jethro would have to wait for tomorrow.

On the bus the next morning she wondered how she would

survive what would seem like a zillion hours of social studies and math, but school turned out to be almost interesting. The class had a whole free period to work in the library on special reports. Sarah found out that if you did a report on an author, you could read real books. So she browsed along the fiction shelves sampling some of her favorite writers until Mrs. Segal caught up with her.

"Looking for something special, or just putting off the job?"

Sarah didn't want to make any trouble. "I was sort of wondering." She faltered. "Wondering about doing an old book."

"You mean for older readers?"

"No, I mean from olden times."

Mrs. Segal asked Sarah whether she had some particular book in mind.

"Pilgrim's Progress," Sarah blurted. "Have you heard of it?"

"I certainly have. But I think you'd find it tough going. Are you interested in old books because of your mother's antiques business?"

What a good idea, thought Sarah. She could get Mom on her side if she used old books. "I just heard about *Pilgrim's Progress* and wondered what kind of story it was."

"It's an allegory," Mrs. Segal told her.

Allegory had the ring of something exotic. "I think I'd like to do my report on it," Sarah told Mrs. Segal.

"It's very preachy," Mrs. Segal warned her. "Very religious."

"Oh." Sarah paused. "Well, what else is old?" She tried with all her might to recall the other title Jethro had mentioned.

Mrs. Segal had to go and separate two kids. When she returned to Sarah, she was distracted. She had other kids to help. "Now then," she asked, "have you decided?"

Thinking she already had a head start on the subject, Sarah said, "Yes. The Underground Railroad."

"Excellent!" Mrs. Segal exclaimed. "Go to the subject index of the card catalog and start looking for books about slavery."

But Sarah had already read about it at home. "Aren't there any stories to do with it?" she asked.

"It's history," Mrs. Segal told her. "See if you can find some books before the bell rings."

When Sarah came home from school, she had one history book from the library that didn't look too boring. She dumped it on her bed and filled her knapsack with cans and cookies, the can opener, and a spoon. Janey wanted to carry some of the food in her knapsack. Sarah, about to object, realized she had to bring Janey along to maintain the impression of camping out, so she gave her the cookies.

They had to stop at the mill to pay back Frenchy's candy bar. He didn't seem concerned about Sarah's taking one without asking, but he reminded her that he didn't want any kids fooling around here. Guessing that Jethro must have left something behind, she said quickly, "We were upstairs last Saturday when it was so cold. I didn't think you'd mind."

"I mind you being up there where we just have the hopper set and nothing fastened down. It's a long way to fall."

Heading for the door, she promised to keep her friends out of the mill.

On the way to Costa's chicken house, she had to keep slowing down for Janey, who trailed behind. They were sort of shouting back and forth to each other as they tramped through the snow and didn't hear Jethro coming until he was just in front of them. He looked excited.

"She caught me," he said. "Last evening. I was splitting wood."

"Who caught you?" Janey asked. "How did you get away?"

"Mrs. Costa," Sarah explained to her. "What happened?" she asked Jethro.

"She wanted to know if I was left here on my own. When I said yes, in a way, it seemed to make sense to her. She believes I was here before!"

"What exactly did she say?" Sarah was sure he had it wrong.

"She thinks I came back here because I had nowhere else to go. She wants me to stay in her house. She said I can be in the shed next summer. With the others. I don't know who they are yet, but she gave me breakfast this morning, cooked on that stove. And I saw the moving book, the tele . . . telephone."

"Television," Sarah corrected. "The telephone you talk into."

"Mrs. Costa talks into the television, too," he countered. "She yells at it sometimes."

Sarah shrugged off her knapsack. "I brought you cans of food. I suppose you won't need them now."

"Could I give them to her? She says she'll keep me for work around the place, but she can't pay money until it's picking time. I think she likes me. Anyway, the dog does."

"I like you, too," Janey declared. Her teeth began to chatter.

Jethro grinned at her. "That's good." He unzipped his jacket, took it off, and put it over Janey's shoulders. Kneeling in the snow, he worked the zipper up. Janey was like a small prisoner inside the jacket. He pulled off his hat, Brad's hat, and shoved it on her head.

"Now you'll be cold," Janey said to him.

"It won't matter. I'll be going back to a warm house."

"And will you stay and stay?" she asked him.

"I will stay until I can be certain Mercy does not need me."

Sarah said, "Mrs. Costa thinks you're one of the workers from last summer. What will happen when they come again and don't know you?"

Jethro shrugged. "I'll probably be gone by then."

"Where?"

"I don't know. It feels so good to be somewhere again, I am not ready to think about later. I have hope now, too. Mrs. Costa says that her sons have seen the prints of a big cat. A mountain lion, they call it. I believe," he went on, "that it is like the catamount Mercy's uncle Zerobabel shot into the millpond."

"Wait a minute," Sarah nearly shouted at him. "How can it have anything to do with—with before?"

"The day Margaret Bredcake died there was a violent tempest. Zerobabel believed it was Goody Bredcake's doing, that storm. So when a catamount appeared on the milldam, he was sure it was her spirit."

"You believe that stuff?"

"It wasn't I who saw it. It was Mercy's uncle. He shot it. He saw it fall from the dam into the pond. Because of the raging tempest, he left it there. But the next morning, when he went to haul it out, it was gone. In later years he often told Mercy the water was still tainted by that evil spirit. He began to call it Sin and Flesh Pond. The brook, too. He accused Mercy of drawing her power from that same source, for she was so like her mother."

"Didn't anyone think that maybe the cat was only hurt and swam ashore?"

"Of course," Jethro countered. "Mercy herself thought that. But she used her uncle's fear against him. She did not try to dissuade him from believing the cat to be her mother transformed."

"Then I can't see what some mountain lion that's probably escaped from a zoo has to do with your Mercy. It can't be a sign about her any more than it can be a sign about her mother," Sarah argued. "Anyway, they're just guessing it's a mountain lion. No one's actually seen it."

"But it is an oddity," Jethro insisted. "Mrs. Costa said so. She, too, thinks it is a sign. So why should it not mean that Mercy is near?"

Sarah let out an exasperated sigh. It was impossible to reason with Jethro when he slid back and forth between opposite positions. He needed some hope, but he also needed to keep from talking like this to anyone else. "Let people get used to you being here," she suggested, retreating from the argument. What would happen if he began speaking to Mrs. Costa about catamounts and Mercy and Zerobabel? "Other people," she tried to explain, "might be harder to convince. A lot harder than me even," she finished.

Jethro nodded as he turned from her, but his face was still alight with hope.

She couldn't think of anything more to say. She would have to find some way to warn him to be careful if he didn't want all the people on Mill Road thinking he'd sizzled his brain on drugs or something and was not to be trusted.

CHAPTER 15

Bugged

The family meeting had slipped Sarah's mind. So it came as a surprise when Mom announced Thursday afternoon that they would have an early supper to be ready for Liz coming afterward. Janey insisted on changing into a dress and making a present for Liz, a picture. She had a lot of trouble getting it just right. Since Sarah was busy with homework and Roger was home early, Janey asked him to inspect it.

"Lovely," he assured her. "What exactly is it?"

Janey scratched her head, frowning with concentration. "This is Liz," she declared slowly, "and this is the crow and this is the alien and this is me and Sarah."

Roger nodded. "It is complicated. That's why I needed help getting it explained. I know Liz will like it."

Satisfied at last, Janey set the picture aside.

Liz came in with a light frosting of snow on her hair and shoulders. There was the usual grown-up exchange about driving conditions. Not bad, Liz told them, although she'd heard on the car radio that there was a mess of a traffic tie-up farther west, where a number of drivers had pulled off the highway because they thought they saw a lion.

Roger laughed. "I hoped they're getting an alcohol check."

Liz shrugged. "It's just as likely to be one of those mass hysteria things." She accepted the offer of a cup of herb tea. Janey handed her the picture.

"In case you can't tell," Roger said to Liz, "that's the crow and that's you and—"

"No," Janey corrected. "That's the alien. This one is Liz."

"Oh, sorry," Roger responded. "The alien looks a little like Liz."

Mom came in with three steaming mugs.

"No, he doesn't," Janey maintained. "He has black curly hair and he's brown; he looks like Jethro." Clapping her hand to her mouth, she shot a look at Sarah, who decided that the only thing to do was admit the existence of a boy named Jethro who was staying at the Costa farm. So she nodded and waited to see what would happen next.

Nothing. No one picked up on it. Liz had her mind on the family session.

"Janey and Sarah," she began, "have been discovering each other these past few weeks." She looked at Sarah and at Janey, who was scratching her head again. Then Liz went on to say that it seemed as though the tension between Sarah and Roger was on the rise. Did the one development have anything to do with the other?

Roger cleared his throat and started to speak. It was easy for Sarah to block him out. She had to stay alert to anything more Janey might let drop about Jethro. But something else pushed its way to the forefront of her thoughts: Lion. Big cat. Catamount.

"How do you feel about that, Sarah?" Liz asked her.

Sarah was stumped. She hadn't heard a word.

"That's what I mean," Roger declared. "I can't get any kind of a response but negative. Or silence."

Sarah said mildly, "And I can't do anything right where Roger's concerned." She looked around to see how the others were reacting. Mom was cleaning off Linda's pacifier. These days it was used only as a last resort. Well, then, maybe Janey would speak up for Sarah. But Janey, on the floor in front of Liz, was rubbing the back of her head against the wooden chair arm and didn't seem to be listening. So Sarah said, "He said I made the crow go after him on purpose."

Roger let out a sigh. He explained that in the heat of the moment he might have said something he didn't mean. Could Sarah blame him?

Leaning forward and bending over Janey, Liz parted her hair, and then parted it again. She said quietly, "It sounds as though Sarah does blame you, though. The question is why."

Sarah went very still inside. Liz was speaking on her behalf and not making Roger mad. Liz was forcing him to come out in the open with his feelings about Sarah.

"I suppose," he began after a moment, "I suppose I haven't gotten over what happened last December. It keeps happening over and over for me. The waiting. Calling people. Not knowing."

"It's still painful?"

Roger nodded. Sarah made the mistake of looking at him. To her horror she saw tears in his eyes.

Liz spoke again. "Were you afraid Molly would blame you?"

"I was terrified. But not that Molly would blame me. I was terrified that something awful would happen to Sarah." He fell silent. No one else spoke.

"Who can say what happened last December?" Liz asked finally.

Janey tipped her head back. "I can."

"Okay, Janey. You have a go at it."

"Sarah wasn't home. We didn't know where she was. We couldn't go anywhere. Mom and Dad yelled at each other and cried. I cried, too."

"How did you feel when Sarah came back?"

"Happy. But she was mean. She wouldn't talk to me."

"Were Mom and Dad happy, too?"

"Very, very happy." Janey paused, scratching again, and then added, "Sort of happy. Not exactly."

Liz said quietly, "Before I forget to mention it, Molly, this child's head is crawling with lice."

It was like throwing a live grenade into their midst. Even Liz looked startled at Mom's and Roger's reaction. Lice! Head lice? Where could Janey have picked them up?

"It's really not serious," Liz assured them. "I see lice on kids every day, and not just in poverty areas. Lice are passed around in school."

"But Janey isn't in school," Mom put in. "Oh, Lord," she went on, peering down at Janey's hair, "I wonder how long she's had them. How could I have missed them?"

"Not long," Liz said. "I don't see any nits. It looks like a fresh crop. But just in case, you all should be treated. Wash her things in bleach. You can get a shampoo at the drugstore. Really, it isn't anything to get upset about. Now let's get back to—"

But Mom and Roger weren't finished exploring the source of the lice on Janey's head.

"If we don't know," Mom explained, "we'll just be reinfested."

Roger scratched his head. "It kind of makes you itch just thinking about it," he said with a grin. Then his face went serious. "You don't suppose it's the crow? Maybe we should get rid of him."

"Don't take Barker away," cried Janey. "I promise not to do it again."

"What?" Mom demanded. "Do what?"

Throwing her arms around Janey, Mom drew her into her lap. "Don't worry, darling, we'll get rid of the lice, not the crow. That's what Daddy meant. Isn't it?" she prompted, looking at him over Janey.

He glanced at Liz, then nodded.

"There," Mom crooned, "there's nothing to cry about."

"I don't think human lice are the same as bird lice," Liz remarked. "Human lice get passed on through contact with someone or someone's clothes. Especially hats. Now can we get back to what we were talking about?"

Mom gazed into Janey's eyes. "Have you worn anything that isn't yours, or ours?"

Janey shook her head. Mom told her to get a Kleenex from the kitchen and blow her nose. During this interval Sarah drew a deep breath and plunged in.

"There's this boy over at Costa farm," she informed them. "When we were in the woods and Janey was cold, he put his hat on her head." At least this way Sarah was in control of the information she fed them.

"Is he one of Mrs. Costa's grandchildren? I'll have to speak to her."

"I don't think he's related," Sarah said. If only they could get past this subject before Janey returned from the kitchen. Janey was perfectly capable of letting slip the fact that the hat and jacket were Brad's and that she had worn them home. In desperation Sarah groped for some diversion. But she was afraid to say anything that would lead to more questioning. All she could do was intercept Janey and get her upstairs to play.

CHAPTER 16

The Deep End

When Roger came home the next day, he balked at the delousing shampoo. Mom pointed out that it hadn't killed her. When he still resisted, she lost her temper.

Janey cowered. Linda ripped apart a magazine. Sarah gloated.

Mom declared that she hadn't spent the entire day washing everything remotely connected to Janey's head to risk reinfestation just because Roger considered himself above it all. *He* should try being the homemaker. She wasn't about to go through this again.

Roger reminded her that she herself had volunteered to turn full-time mom while the mill and antiques shop were under construction.

Sarah dragged Janey into the mudroom. "Come on," she said. "We'll take Jethro's things back to him."

But everything hanging from the pegs and stacked on the shelf had been washed while she was in school. Where were Brad's jacket and hat? Janey, who was listening to Mom's and Roger's fight, had no idea. The fight held her in a trance.

Before, at home, when they were shut in the cellar, it
seemed like the cruelest treatment imaginable. But
they were not bound then, and every day Aunty
brought food and emptied the chamber pot. It was
dark, that was all, and there was nothing to do.
Mamma would hold the child and speak of other
times. To drive away the child's fear, Mamma recited
a psalm: The night shineth as the day: the darkness
and the light are both alike to thee. When Uncle
himself came to see them, the child thought he was
setting them free. But he took only Mamma and
kicked the door shut in the child's face. She pressed
against the wood and heard sounds without words.
After a time the door opened again and Mamma was
shoved inside. For a while she would not speak to the
child, would not touch her. And that was more
terrible than being left alone in the earthen darkness.
The words of the psalm would not come.

"What will happen to Linda?" Janey finally whispered.

"What do you mean, happen? Nothing."

Janey said, "We have to take her with us."

"Listen, Janey, we can't carry Linda all the way to the Costa farm."

But Janey just set her mouth in a stubborn line and reached for Linda's snowsuit.

Sarah had to go back upstairs to look for Jethro's things, which were washed and put away in Brad's room. Sarah packed them and another pair of heavy socks inside a faded flannel shirt. With Roger's shower going full force, she had to yell to Mom that she was taking the little ones outdoors for a while.

They started with Linda on the sled. But the snow was too

soft, so Sarah got the toy wagon instead. They set off once more with Linda riding on the clothes and Janey pushing at the rear. Only one car came their way, the driver swerving when he saw the small procession on the otherwise empty road. Sarah, who had yanked the wagon onto the rutted shoulder, had to lift Linda out to get the wheels back on the flat surface. Linda didn't want to get into the wagon again. Janey got in to lure her back. Sarah had to lean hard to pull that load. The wheels squealed horribly.

By the time she made it to Mrs. Costa's driveway, she was hot and out of breath. When Mrs. Costa came to the door, Sarah held out the clothes and tried to explain about their being washed. But Mrs. Costa was way ahead of her. Mom had already been in touch. "The boy's all cleaned up," Mrs. Costa assured Sarah. "I told your mother we expect this sort of thing, having transits here every summer like we do."

"So Jethro's all right? You'll let him stay?"

"Of course, I will, poor kid. People do such awful things these days. Probably they wanted him while he was earning. See, these transits mostly go south in the winter, but there's not that much work for them. Who knows where they dumped the boy? It's a wonder he made it back here. And he's such a willing kid, too. Right now he's down back cleaning out the chicken coop. You know much about him?"

Sarah, halfway down the porch steps, paused. "Not really. Why?"

Mrs. Costa's face was blurred behind the glass of the door she held ajar. "I'm worried he might be illegal," she said.

Janey, sitting with Linda on the wagon, said, "He's an alien."

"That's what I mean." Mrs. Costa pushed the door wide. "Sonny says we can't keep any illegal alien."

"Well, you don't have to worry about Jethro," Sarah assured

her. "I know for a fact he's . . ." She faltered. "He's very honest," she went on. "That's why he worked for you before you knew he was here. He wouldn't take anything."

"Still, he talks funny. I mean he's real polite, but you can tell he's . . . what your sister said."

Sarah shook her head. "That alien stuff is just a game with him. It isn't real." She hurried on down to the wagon. She had to get Janey out of there before she said anything more to cast doubt on Jethro.

Jethro, wheeling a load of manure out of the long shed, didn't see the girls until they came as close as they could stand.

"You'll need another shower," Sarah said to him.

He nodded. "She washed my hair at the kitchen sink, and then she made me wait with it all soaped, and after that she sent me into the shower. It was my second time in one."

"How did you get clean before?" Janey asked him. "In a bathtub?"

"It depended on the season. The pond or the pump. I never used Mrs. Lockwood's washtub. Mercy did, though. First time I saw her, when she came half-drowned. Mrs. Lockwood sent Mr. Lockwood and me out of the kitchen while she bathed her. Likely Mercy brought bugs with her, too. And poor Mrs. Lockwood constantly battling them. She had no special soap like Mrs. Costa's."

Janey asked why Mercy came half-drowned, but Sarah told her to take Linda inside to look at the chickens.

"I want to stay," Janey protested. "I want Jethro to talk to me."

"Just for a little while. Then you can come back."

As soon as Janey led Linda inside the shed, Sarah turned on Jethro. "My mother knows you're here now. So will everyone else soon. So you have to tell me what I need to know about you, and I'm not kidding."

Jethro looked down his arm and began to pick off a feather here, a feather there. He didn't speak.

"Jethro," Sarah burst out, "if you don't trust me by now, who can you trust?"

But still he held back. Was he reluctant to talk with her because she questioned what he told her? That would account for the ready sympathy that seemed to flow between Janey and him. Janey never doubted anything he said.

"Sooner or later," Sarah informed him, "someone's going to ask you about your family. If you don't have any, they may take you away."

"They won't," he retorted. "I'll hide."

"Not here," Sarah pointed out. "Not anymore. How can I help you if you won't tell me what's really going on? Do you think I'd go against you after all this time?"

When he finally answered her, his voice had grown harsh and taut. "When I was growing up," he said, "I knew my place. I behaved as though the young master was my playmate. At the same time I had to be prepared, always, for the turnabout that proved he was not. Do you hear what I am saying? I had to let him knock me flat or kick me downstairs, not for any reason connected with me, but just because he might happen to be disappointed or aggrieved. If his pony went lame and he could not ride that day, or if he left his book outdoors and it was rained on, he would spend his anger on me. I was expected to be cheerful and obliging through it all. And all the while I had to be watchful of his parents. I learned that to please his father was to displease his mother. I took nothing and no one for granted."

"All right." She had to go along with him for now. "But that was a long time ago. What about the people who helped you?"

Jethro nodded. "It took me awhile to learn . . . to believe. Only with Mercy was it different. Right from the start, you see, we were equals. In ages and in other ways. I could almost see myself in her. And just as soon as I was able to help her, I began to help myself, too. If I were to abandon her now," he concluded, his voice dropping, "I would be abandoning myself." He was looking at Sarah, reflecting on something he saw in her. Not himself, she supposed. Nothing like that.

Janey and Linda emerged from the shed. Quickly, before they could interrupt, Sarah made one final attempt. "I still don't understand why you think Mercy may be here or may come."

His hands, clenched, fell to his sides. "All right. I'll walk you home. You should not be out in the woods anyway. It isn't safe."

"Of course it is. But we did come on the road."

"Still, I will go with you. In case of the catamount."

She couldn't let that go unchallenged. "Show me its footprints first."

"They were in the cornfield farther along. I myself never saw them. The snowfall covered them."

Just as I thought, Sarah wanted to retort. She had to force herself to keep still.

They set off for home the way they had come, only this time with Jethro pulling the little ones in the wagon and Sarah walking beside him. When a car came speeding from behind, Jethro snatched up both girls and swept them off the road.

Janey kicked and laughed. She didn't see the alarm in his face. Sarah waited with the wagon. "If Mrs. Costa catches you acting like that," she warned, "she won't believe you about being here before."

"There were no such things before."

"Jethro, Mrs. Costa thinks *before* means last summer. If you want her to go on thinking that, you'd better get used to cars and stuff."

Jethro set Linda in the wagon. "I try. But when they come fast and close . . ." His voice fell away.

"I bet I know," Janey declared. "You get carsick. I used to throw up all the time." She skipped along beside Jethro.

Sarah almost told Janey that Jethro had never been in a car.

"Down," Linda demanded as soon as they were homeward bound again. But well before they turned the last corner where the road rose to cross Singing Fish Brook, she began to lag behind. Sarah had to wait for her while Jethro and Janey walked on. Eventually both little ones were willing to ride the rest of the way in the wagon. That meant that at long last Sarah could rejoin Jethro, who said to her, "Something bad happened to Janey."

"No," Sarah said. "What do you mean?"

"She is afraid to go home. She said they might hurt her and Linda."

Sarah gasped. "She's making that up. No one's ever hurt her. They love her."

Jethro just looked at Sarah.

"Well," she added, "they had a fight before we left the house. It scared Janey, that's all. They mostly never fight, so it upset her."

Jethro mulled this over. When he finally spoke, his voice was so low Sarah had to move closer to catch his words. "I know how it goes on and on, even though it is over. Maybe that is what is happening to her."

What was he talking about? If only he would speak up instead of mumbling. And make sense.

Halfway up the driveway Jethro stopped. Climbing out of the wagon, Janey came to stand beside him. The front door opened, and Roger stepped outside. Seeing the children, he raised his hand like a traffic cop. Everyone stood still, except Linda, who waddled to meet him. He scooped her up and carried her to the others.

"Is this the guy who loused us up?" he asked, extending his hand toward Jethro.

"I am sorry, sir," Jethro mumbled.

"I take it you're clean now?"

Jethro nodded.

"Well . . ." Roger beamed at them all.

Sarah stole a glance at Janey, who gazed up at Roger open-mouthed.

"Since I had to come home early," he declared pointedly, "I thought we might take advantage of what's left of the snow. Who wants to go coasting? Janey?"

Looking puzzled, Janey whispered, "Yes."

"Come on, then. You get the flying saucer from the shed, and we'll go up Anursnack Hill." He turned to Sarah. "You were good to get them out of the house before. Out from under. And, Sarah, would you mind seeing to them later if your mother and I go out for dinner? We could use a little time to ourselves."

Sarah nodded.

"Thanks," he said to her with a big, delighted grin.

Janey came dragging the flying saucer. "You're not mad anymore?" she asked him.

"No, honey. I guess I just went off the deep end. It was stupid of me. I'm sorry."

"He seems kind," Jethro remarked as Roger and the two little ones headed for the hill that rose between the shop site and the highway.

Sarah shrugged.

"Did he mean that he fell in the millpond off the deep end of the dam?"

"No. It was just his way of saying he lost it. Lost his temper," she added. "Did you have trouble understanding Mercy?"

Jethro grinned. "At first I thought she was a foreigner."

"You mean," asked Sarah, "she had a different way of speaking or a different language?"

"Mostly a different way. But I could understand her more

than Mr. and Mrs. Lockwood. Perhaps because I came from another place. My mother had a special way of speaking. I have a bit of that way still."

"What was the first thing Mercy said?"

"First she jumped back, afrighted. Then she called me by a name and said she knew me. I thought she had lost her senses. She insisted I was the son of the dreaded King Philip. When I said I had no knowledge of such a king, she pleaded with me to recall that we had met before. Even though years had passed and we were both older now and changed, I must recognize her."

Squeals and shouts reached them from the sliding hill, and great gusts of Roger's laughter.

Jethro said, "I never imagined that one day we should go sledding together on this very hill. It seemed much higher then, farther to climb and longer to slide down. We could have gone from the top all the way onto the frozen pond, but Mercy always tumbled off before we hit the ice. She would not risk the pond, she said, never again the pond."

"When did she think you two had met?"

"Oh, she changed her mind about that. After days and days of talking and listening. She had to be made to see that we were in my time, not hers, before she could give up believing that we had faced one another when she was five or six and I about nine years old. That was hard for her to do. And then she decided I must be descended from the son of that king, my looks bespeaking my relation to the boy she saw in prison in the year of our Lord 1676."

He turned from Sarah, drawn by the sounds of hilarity on the hill. And by memories? Stories of his own making? Sarah turned, too, looking where he looked, squinting against the low sun in the western sky, wondering how it looked to him who believed that Mercy was true.

CHAPTER 17

For Mercy's Sake

The weekend began uneventfully. When Sarah made no attempt to seek Jethro out, Janey pressed her about him. Mom, overhearing, asked Janey whom she wanted to see.

"The alien," Janey promptly replied. "Jethro."

Mom asked her why she called him an alien.

"Because he is," Janey told her. "He's from outer space."

Mom laughed. "I see. Well, why don't you girls take Barker outside? He's getting restless in the cellar. Maybe he's almost ready to go free."

"What if he can't find food?" Janey protested.

"Then he'll come back. Or we'll feed him outdoors."

It was a mild afternoon, clear and springlike. Sarah pulled the caged crow on the wagon all the way to the edge of the woods. Janey trudged alongside, her knapsack crammed with the crow's favorite tidbits. He turned first one way and then another, shaking out his feathers and muttering as if talking to himself. When they released him, he stepped along the wagon rim and stretched out his neck toward Janey. As soon as she moved within range, he lunged at her cupped hands and gulped down Cheerios and raisins.

"He doesn't want to be free," Janey said. "Let's take him home."

But Sarah thought he needed a little more time to realize that he could fly off at will. She leaned back against the boulder where she had first left food and clothing for Jethro. Suddenly there was a clamor overhead. Crows landed in the treetops. Barker stretched his wings and added his rasping croak to their raucous gabble. Flapping his wings, slowly gaining height, he headed for those other crows.

The treetops seemed to explode with hurtling black bodies. A few feathers, sun-struck to purple iridescence, wafted downward.

Janey screamed, "Barker! Barker!"

Sarah, trying not to let her own alarm show, pointed out that sooner or later Barker would have to get used to being with other wild crows.

"But he's a pet," Janey shot back. "Jethro says so. I'm going to look for him. Barker!" she started calling again as she stomped off.

Sarah shouted after her, "You can't look for a bird that flies."

"I can so," she retorted, her shoulders slightly hunched as if she expected a blow from behind.

"Fine, fine," Sarah grumbled. "I'll come with you."

Every few steps Janey lifted her face to the bare treetops and called to Barker. Sarah suggested looking where the pine trees were. Barker seemed to like the pine needles. Janey surged ahead and then stopped beneath a huge white pine. Sarah, who had lost sight of her for a moment, found her again, somehow diminished, a small figure with long braids like black ropes draped over her flappy pink jacket. The forlorn voice that issued from her scarcely rose to the dense green branches above.

> *The crow can always provoke the child into giving chase. It flaps along the ground and scuttles just out of reach, trailing her precious moppet made from corn husks or her cloth cap. The crow's coarse laughter taunts the child and puts her in a rage. She lunges for it, sometimes even striking out at it. Feathers float up in her face. But the crow always returns the treasure before sundown, and sometimes with an extra gift from the treetops or the earth.*

"Barker!" Sarah roared. "Barker, come!"

And then they both saw him, his wings outstretched but unmoving. He seemed to glide toward them like a statue borne on an invisible shaft, a thing of mystery that silenced Sarah and stopped her in her tracks. There was only a split second like this, after which Jethro's head emerged—hair, face, neck—and then more of him as he crested the rise on the far side of the brook. If Jethro made a sound, the rushing water blotted it out. He approached in eerie silence, his face drawn, as if he, too, were unnerved.

When he finally halted across from them, he reached up to dislodge the crow balanced on his head. Then he called over the splashing water, "I thought she had brought him, sent him to me. Mercy."

No more Mercy, Sarah resolved. Not for me. Not anymore.

Jethro tucked the crow inside his jacket. "There's a tree down away upstream. I'll cross there."

But they came along with him, the girls on one side of the brook, the boy with the crow on the other. They didn't try to speak again until they reached the blowdown. Jethro stepped nimbly along the trunk of the chestnut oak that made a bridge across the brook. Then he released the crow into Janey's eager hands.

"Don't squish him," Sarah warned.

Jethro grinned. "That crow has been through worse than being hugged by a little girl."

"Through what?" Janey wanted to know. "What do you mean?"

"Oh, for goodness' sake," Sarah began to object. Now that the crow was back safe, she wasn't about to put up with any of Jethro's craziness.

But Jethro was already informing Janey that Mercy's crow stuck by Mercy through every ordeal.

"Does she want him back?" Janey asked. "Is Mercy going to take him?"

"She would if she could," he answered.

> *The crow would entice the child from the prison if it could. It tries to tease her into giving chase as she used to. Baffled, it sulks. Then it flaps off alone to seek morsels from the street, from a cart or barn. It never fails to return with some meager offering.*

Turning from Janey, Jethro faced Sarah. "If Mercy remained, she should be safe. Only I cannot think what happened to *him.*"

"I don't know what *him* you're talking about," Sarah replied stiffly.

"You do. I told you about Zerobabel Quelch. It was he who brought Mercy out of prison and then years later had her bound hand and foot to be swum in the millpond. With all the settlers to witness. If she floated, it would prove she was a witch like her mother, and the crow her familiar."

Janey clutched the crow. "What did he do to Barker?" she asked.

"Tucked him in Mercy's apron. She was bent over him with her arms crossed, thumbs tied to toes."

"You shut up," Sarah ordered. "You're frightening Janey."

But Janey said, "I want to know. I don't understand."

"Of course, you don't," Sarah agreed. "It doesn't make sense. None of it does." She glared at Jethro.

"Well, what happened to Barker?" Janey persisted.

"The storm saved them. A hailstorm. It was early summer, not the season for hail. The settlers were terrified. They had come uneasy, unaccustomed to this witch test, which was more used in Connecticut Colony, where Zerobabel came from. So when the storm shot little balls of ice upon them, they took it as a sign against the swimming. But even as they cowered, Zerobabel Quelch stood tall on the millrace, bearing the full brunt of wind and ice. And there he cried out upon Mercy and her dead mother. He would not release the goodmen and goodwives from their duty. He ordered Mercy cast into the water."

Janey gasped. She pressed her face against the crow.

"It's a story," Sarah shouted at her. "It's like a scary television movie."

"It is what Mercy herself told me," Jethro rejoined.

Furious that she couldn't cut him off, Sarah was forced to challenge him. "Did Mercy happen to say why those settlers went along with her uncle? If he was a madman, what were they?"

"When the settlers rebuilt their homes and began to farm the land again, they had need of Mercy, who grew up with her mother's way with animals. But the more they came to rely on her to help with a sick sheep or an injured pig, the more they feared her healing power and the crow that was always with her. No matter how often Mercy's uncle shot at him, he would not be killed. Remember, in Mercy's time it was ungodly to make pets of wild creatures. Then, too, Mercy refused to bind and cover her hair, as was the custom. To be different was to be suspect. To be stubborn was to be witchy. So she grew up shunned, with no one to speak for her, no one to save her."

"What happened to her in the pond?" Janey demanded. "What happened to Barker?"

"For a while Mercy's skirt billowed and held her. Then the wind whipped the water to a froth, and the stuff of her petticoat and skirt was soaked and drew her down, the crow with her. But the ropes came loose. So Mercy, holding the crow, swam underwater until her breath gave out. Just in time she fetched up at the spillway."

"What's a spillway?" Janey asked him.

"You have one here. It's in the dam. To let the water out when the pond is high. In the dry seasons it can be closed to save the water for driving the wheel. On that day, the day of the hailstorm, the water gushed out of the spillway and tumbled in a great fall to the brook. Mercy was sucked right through; she dropped beneath the waterfall and huddled there against the dam. But she could breathe again. No one saw her. She pressed the crow's beak shut for fear he would give them away. She has no idea how long she stayed that way. She could hear nothing but the crashing water, not the storm, not Zerobabel, nothing. She considered trying to run along the brook, but did not dare. So in time she struggled back through the spillway against the full force of the water."

"Back into the pond where she couldn't breathe?" Janey exclaimed.

"She had no choice. She could not remain beneath the falls. She hoped the people had fled the storm. But the struggle through cost her her strength. She lost her way underwater, and when she finally surfaced, she could barely drag herself out. It was dark then, the storm still raging. She was too spent to notice that the pond was changed, the dam was changed, the mill itself was changed."

"Why?" Janey asked him. "Why was everything changed?"

"Because she was no longer in her own time. She was in mine. Mr. Lockwood found her wandering, dazed. She let him lead her into the house, to Mrs. Lockwood. And that is where I first set eyes on her."

"What about Barker?" Janey pressed. "Where was he?"

"He was found that very day, soaked and battered but full of life. You never saw such a greeting as the one between them."

Janey scowled in puzzlement. "If Mercy is somewhere else now, won't she be worried about her crow?"

"It's not somewhere else," Sarah put in; "it's some*time* else." She turned to Jethro. "Janey doesn't understand all that stuff about different times. You're just confusing her."

"Yes." Jethro nodded agreeably. "And it must be hard for you who doubt everything I say."

"What do you expect?" Sarah flashed. "I've tried. You know I have. And I'd still like to help you. But why should I change what I believe just because you say so? It's one thing to read about, and another to think it's true. If I thought you could really go through time, I'd make you teach me how. I'd be glad to take my chances on another time."

"You cannot mean that."

"I do. I know something about running away because I've tried it. Well, not exactly running. I stayed with my best friend where we used to live, and when it was time to meet Roger at the store to come back here, I didn't. I stayed away. I called Mom so she would know I was all right."

"Were you?" Jethro asked.

Sarah had no intention of admitting how miserable and scared she'd been. "Sort of. But it didn't work out, so I quit. But if I could go into another time, that would be something else, going away from here, away from Roger."

Jethro threw up his hands. "It isn't like that. You can't just depart at will and go home when you choose. Mercy thought she knew how to make it happen, but she could not tell what future time it would be. It isn't a—a pleasure trip."

"Then what is it?"

"I do not know. Maybe it's like this brook. It's always here, isn't it? This same brook, in Mercy's time and mine and yours. The same, only not the same. Not these drops splashed on the tree trunk. You won't see them again. Never those very same drops of water. And those pebbles swirling, they'll be pushed under the bank or carried along, getting stuck and moving again. Water, pebbles, mud, leaves—all traveling in the same direction. They won't go back. Nor can we to what we were." His voice shook. "Nor can we. And if that is so, how can I find out what happened to her? How can I be certain she is safe from him?"

Sarah had to answer Jethro on his own terms. "But Zerobabel didn't come with Mercy into your time, did he?"

"We couldn't be sure. While she was with us, Mercy began to feel safe. Until the day the stone-picker came to the mill seeking work. Usually Mr. Lockwood dressed the millstones himself, but he welcomed this man who called himself Bezaliel Mason and declared himself practiced in stone dressing. Mercy never set eyes on him. But the moment she heard his voice she took fright. She could not be calmed. She implored me to help her escape him. I must wear her cloak, she insisted, the cloak she had from Mrs. Lockwood. I must put it on to trick that man, the stone-picker."

"I still don't get it," Sarah put in. "Why was she afraid of him?"

"Because she could tell he was not what he said he was. You must understand that by this time we were used to Mercy's frights about people. She had grown happy in our company, working, evenings at the fireside, even during jaunts away from the mill at sugaring time, when it was she who led

us to the likeliest trees. But no matter how hard Mrs. Lockwood tried to persuade her, Mercy never joined in when others were concerned, not even for the husking bees at the
harvest. Yet this time we could all three tell that her fear was
different, more serious."

"So he was her uncle Zerobabel?"

"How could I know? Mercy was in a frenzy then. All I can
be sure of is that if she is here now, all that has seemed so
strange to me will be unfathomable to her. She will be dumb-
founded. In my time she was even amazed at simple things
like our windows and Mrs. Lockwood's clock and the glass
lamps and the crockery. In Mercy's time the plates and bowls
were made of wood until Mercy's uncle brought two pewter
trenchers and a salt with him. You might think Mercy would
find the new things splendid and wonderful, but she was only
made uneasy by them."

Sarah tried to imagine herself in a world transformed, but
all she could picture were gadgets from sci-fi movies.

"Mercy held fast to her own notions," Jethro continued.
"She called our kitchen the hall. She baked pumpkin stuffed
with beans and savory and fresh milk. Mrs. Lockwood kindly
learned her ways. But not Mercy. She was ever reluctant to
change her own. She even brought young plants to the herb
garden, mullein and nettles that Mrs. Lockwood pulled for
weeds. But Mercy dug them in beside the pennyroyal and yar-
row and rosemary as healing plants they would need by and
by. Mrs. Lockwood let them stay."

Sarah couldn't help thinking of how her mother would re-
act. She said, "Well, if Mercy still shows up, she can help
Mom plant her herbs."

"You think your mother would have her?"

"I keep telling you, Jethro, my mother and Roger take in
foster kids. But," Sarah added, "I don't think Mom is like
Mrs. Lockwood. She has her own ideas about how things
should be."

Jethro mulled that for a moment. "So does Mercy," he concluded in a worried tone. "Mrs. Lockwood used to say that Mercy had a will to be reckoned with."

Sarah couldn't help relishing the prospect. "I can't wait for her to show up."

"If she does," Jethro put in.

Janey rubbed her cheek against the top of the crow's head. "If she doesn't, she won't have her crow and she won't have you, either."

"If she stayed in my time, then it is long over for her." Jethro sounded like a grown-up coaxing a child to reason. "If she grieved for the crow, that is over, too." He seemed to be groping for plain words Janey would understand. "If she stayed with Mrs. Lockwood, she might have managed. She might grow and be—" His voice broke. "And grow old," he finished, "perhaps with a family of her own. And die."

"Die," murmured Janey, for whom Mercy was only here and now.

They stood in the mottled sunlight, the brook trundling over rocks and branches. A blue jay dropped down to the water. Somewhere in the woods a woodpecker drummed, while out on Mill Road a car swooshed by, its fleeting presence muffled by the trees and brook.

Sarah understood that either she had to meet Jethro on some common ground, or else she had to break away from him entirely. She gazed at the water rushing on and on to the pond, where it would be held for a while, lie still, and then move on. Here was Jethro, facing his loss of Mercy as time ran on, too.

"But she isn't lost," Sarah tried to tell him. "She's past." It seemed to Sarah that she was caught in a struggle for Jethro, with Mercy pulling him down into that past. Sarah had to find a way to keep him from slipping out of reach.

"I only know," he said, "that what was in Mercy's past

didn't stay there for her. She dreamed the same dreams. Those dreams come into your life whether you want them to or not, whether they began this year or last year or long ago. They are what you never forget, and they are always with you."

Sarah stood her ground. "All right. Part of you may always be in your past, but mostly you're here now in the present. Your life is still happening. It's ahead of you, too."

He nodded slowly. "Even so, there are things I have to do, to know, before I can look forward. Mercy hunted for a certain millstone to prove that what she told me about herself was true. Even after I showed that I believed her, she craved that proof. Now I understand how she felt. And I have been thinking that if she stayed behind in my time, there might be another kind of stone, one with her name on it. If there is a burial ground hereabouts, maybe you could help me look for it."

"Of course, we'll help you," Janey told him. "Whatever it is." She turned to Sarah. "Say you'll help."

Sarah wished she could believe that easily. And yet, in spite of all her natural resistance, it was happening. Everything Jethro said about Mercy kept tilting Sarah toward acceptance. If Jethro could pin his hopes on finding a gravestone for Mercy, who might have married and changed her name or else moved away, then she still had a mighty firm grip on him.

"Tell him," Janey insisted.

"Yes. All right," Sarah agreed.

So, she thought. She had made her choice. But was the common ground she moved toward Jethro's? Or was it Mercy's?

CHAPTER 18

On the Brink

When Sarah and Janey got back to the house, Brad was home. He had caught a last-minute ride with someone. He had phone calls to make and things to do. But for a little while he was just there.

Janey basked in his attention. "Do you want to see Barker? We nearly lost him, but Jethro brought him back."

"Who's Jethro?"

"He's our new friend. We're allowed to talk about him now," she added in the face of Sarah's silence.

Brad turned to Sarah. "A boyfriend?"

"No," she answered curtly. But she couldn't duck the subject now. "He's living with Mrs. Costa." Sarah lowered her voice. "He's kind of weird."

"How weird? You know, Sarah, if he's doing drugs—"

"Not like that." How much could she tell Brad? "He's just sort of foreign."

"Foreign isn't weird," Brad told her.

"I know," she said. "Come upstairs. I need to talk to you alone."

Brad followed Sarah to her room. "What's going on?" he asked. But before she could get a word out, he went on to say that he'd already heard that things had been a bit rough at home lately. Mom had just told him she was going to start back at work in the store two days a week; Roger would manage things at home.

Sarah hardly heard what he was telling her. "It's this boy, Jethro. He keeps saying things like they're true, only they can't be."

"Like what?"

She was stumped. Finally she thought of an example. "He's afraid of cars and trucks. He says he's never been in one."

"Maybe," Brad suggested, "he was in a terrible accident like Dad. Maybe if Dad had lived, he'd be the same way. He might've gotten amnesia from the accident."

Amnesia. That had never occurred to Sarah. Then she rejected the idea. "Jethro's just the opposite," she said. "He has too much memory. It's full of . . ." She wanted to say it was full of people with names like Mercy and Zerobabel. "It's full of things no one's ever heard of," she finished guardedly. "Like a king in Massachusetts."

"It sounds like he's got more imagination than memory." Brad glanced at his watch.

To hold him a moment longer, Sarah asked him what a transit was.

"A transit?" Brad frowned.

Recalling what Mrs. Costa had said, Sarah added, "Transit worker."

"Oh," said Brad. "That would be someone who works for a bus company or a subway system."

As he headed for his own room, Sarah suddenly thought to tell him about the things she had borrowed for Jethro. "I know I should ask first."

"That's all right." Brad seemed distracted. "Listen, Sarah,

I haven't mentioned this to Mom yet, but I have a chance to go kayaking over spring vacation, which means I might not be home until after finals. I'll need my sleeping bag, but that's about all from here. Take anything else you think the kid can use. I'll leave some stuff out for you."

"Jethro did use your sleeping bag for a while," Sarah told Brad. "It might be sort of cruddy. Maybe," she put in anxiously, "you should take Roger's." She didn't dare mention the lice. What if there were bugs rolled up inside?

Brad didn't object to the idea. She heaved a sigh of relief.

That night after Brad went off in the car to be with friends in Brookline, the house seemed unusually quiet. Scraps of Mom's and Roger's conversation about the new shop drifted up to Sarah.

"If Ken's right and it's part of the old bulwark," Roger was saying, "the backhoe could undermine the dam."

"Still," Mom answered, "we can't decide by ourselves."

Sarah went downstairs and into the kitchen.

"Those slabs are just too neatly laid out," Roger went on.

Sarah took an apple, forgot to wash it, and wandered into the dining room, where she asked Mom what was going on.

"You know, we just got the backhoe digging again," Mom said. "It's reached some kind of stone paving."

Sarah peered over at the plans spread out and weighted at the corners by a stapler, a book, and two pieces of kindling. There was a diagram of the shop—or what it would eventually look like. There was no picture of the hole in the ground and the stones. "So what do you suppose it is?" she asked.

Mom pushed back her hair. "It could be part of a burial ground. That would be exciting. Or it might just be part of the bulwark for the previous dam."

"We're pretty sure it's connected with that heap of stones we uncovered last fall," Roger added.

"I just hope we don't get held up too long if we have to

bring the engineer in on this again." Mom tapped her pencil on the diagram. Sarah, leaning forward, dislodged the stapler; the paper snapped itself up and rolled loosely over to Roger's side.

"Sorry," Sarah mumbled.

"Doesn't matter." Roger rolled the paper more tightly and shoved it into a tube. "It won't do us any good to look at it until we're ready to move ahead."

Sarah bit into the apple.

"That sounds good," Roger remarked. "You want one, Molly?" He was already on his way to the kitchen. Sarah heard the water run. Roger wouldn't forget to wash his apple.

Mom said she would like a cup of tea instead. Roger filled the kettle and set it on the stove. It seemed to Sarah as though Roger were performing, like one of those fathers on a TV sitcom that make you feel good about the American family. Suddenly what Brad had mentioned about Mom and Roger's taking turns being home came back to Sarah. But she didn't want to think about it, so she asked her mother what was happening with the old cloak. Mom told her that an expert in early American textiles hadn't been able to date it exactly, but that since it was ample enough to cover a very full skirt, it was probably pre-Civil War.

Sarah tried to picture Mercy as Jethro had described her. Long black hair. What else? But nothing more came to mind. Only a feeling about her, angry and determined. Around this faceless image Sarah flung the gray cloak, ample, although too tight for Jethro at the shoulders. Sarah tried to infuse the picture with more features, but they wouldn't appear.

Sunday morning, just before Brad's ride picked him up, everyone went out to the shop site to look at the problem Mom and Roger had been discussing. Roger held Linda, but Janey crept to the edge of the excavated area and peered down. Brad jumped inside. "If it's a grave, maybe it'll turn out to be an unsolved murder." He grinned up at them.

"I'm not sure that's funny," Mom remarked.

"Well, it does look like something belongs here. I bet it's haunted."

"Right," Roger responded. "Haunted by whatever was stored here—turnips or a cow."

"Frenchy thinks it's an old cellar hole, but Ken's afraid it's connected with the dam bulkhead."

"Couldn't you tell when you built the dam?"

Roger shook his head. "We found so much of the old stonework still intact, especially toward those piled-up stones, we just left it. Our engineer felt that much of what remained of the last dam was perfectly sound. He could even tell what its dimensions were, about twelve feet thick and fourteen feet high. So we kept a lot of the original substructure."

"Well," Brad declared as he hauled himself up out of the hole, "let me know what you dig up here. I've got to get ready to go."

"Will you be back for my birthday party?" Janey asked him. "It's— When is it, Mom?"

"Next weekend," Mom told her. "Saturday."

Brad shook his head. "But I promise to call you."

Mom said to Janey, "You can invite some friends from Sunday school."

They were walking back to the house together. Linda, set down, splashed through every mud puddle she could reach.

Janey stuck with Mom. "Can I have anyone else?"

"Anyone you like," Mom promised rashly.

Sarah knew whom Janey had in mind. Janey was showing signs of becoming more than Mom and Roger had bargained for. They might regret keeping her out of kindergarten this year.

That afternoon Sarah went back by herself to the problem hole. She knew that Brad had been kidding about a grave, but

Jethro's plea nagged at her. Staring down, she felt reassured. Anyone could see that the paved area was the size of a small room.

> *Again and again the child is drawn to the place where Papa last worked before the fever took him. She fears that he may be changed by heaven and that she will nevermore see him as he was. Here at the base of the hill she seeks him grimy from digging, with flour dust in his hair and in the creases around his eyes. She creeps up on the place, as if to surprise him. There is nothing. Already a fine new grass has sprouted where he dug. She kicks at one pale green clump. It tumbles down the slope and lands at her feet. She tramples it, grinding it into the dirt.*

Sarah slid inside, debris pelting her as she dropped. Standing with her head below ground level, she turned to the wall of earth and stone that might or might not be connected with the previous bulwark. All she could recall from when the brook was diverted was how the remnants of the old dam had seemed to disappear beneath that small mountain of stones.

She tried to visualize the reconstructed dam the way it looked when it first spanned the distance between the wheel pit and mill at the far end from here and the place where it merged with the stones at this end. She had only a vague memory of a massive sloping structure with some kind of framing over it that had to be removed before the water was let through. She had no trouble recalling the squared opening in the dam, the tumbling vent with its steel pipes for raising or lowering the water level once the pond filled. Only now did it come to her that she had been even more stupid than she had realized on the day of the freak storm. She had grabbed one of those metal pipes. It was a wonder she hadn't gotten herself electrocuted.

What exactly had happened when the lightning struck? Was she holding on right in front of the tumbling vent, what Jethro called a spillway? Had something really grabbed her ankle, or had she only imagined it in her panic? She tried to recover that moment underwater when she felt herself held down. She experimented, closing her eyes and holding her breath as long as she could. She could feel her heart hammering. She could feel something close around her ankle, fingers like metal cutting into her. And then? Then nothing. Her breath giving out, darkness pulsing with that harsh, unnatural light. Acid yellow.

"What are you doing down there?" came a voice from above.

Sarah yelped with surprise and with something else, something akin to terror. Panting, she had to wait a moment before she could rail at Jethro, who crouched above her.

"Don't you ever sneak up on me like that again!"

"I wasn't. I was looking for you. What is happening here?"

"It's where they're going to build the new shop. Where they'll sell the flour and herbs and antiques and stuff. Roger's furniture repair shop will be in back."

"But here? I have seen the huge machine from a distance. I did not realize—" Jethro broke off. Then he asked, "Is the digging finished?"

Sarah shrugged. "It depends on what they find, I guess. Why?"

But he only shook his head. That usually meant that he was grappling with something important. She guessed that he was torn between what he considered must be a secret and his longing to share it with her. She knew better now than to let her own frustration show. Concentrating on getting out, she looked for a toehold in the naked earth so that she could haul herself up the way Brad had. In the end she had to accept Jethro's hand as she accepted his silence.

But it was predictably easy to get a response out of him by informing him that he was about to be invited to her house.

"I am?" His look of delight mingled with anxiety.

"I think so, yes. To Janey's birthday party."

"The young master had birthdays," Jethro said. "What must I do?"

"You won't have to do anything. Well, maybe play a game."

"At the Lockwoods' we sometimes played at word games. Those evenings were . . ." He faltered. "When Mercy came, she sat quietly at first. Then one night she laughed at a word that was strange to her, and we laughed with her. After that she joined in. And before we banked the fire and retired to our beds, we would each read a passage from the Bible. Mercy always chose the same scripture, the psalm that ends, 'Yea, the darkness hideth not from thee; but the night shineth as the day: the darkness and the light are both alike to thee.' And Mr. Lockwood commended her every time for committing us to our sleep with her reading. And the dark house would smell of the apples we had roasted. And the night seemed to hold us safe."

Sarah couldn't speak. She was still so new at listening like this, at letting his memories resolve into images of her own. And it was happening with a force that seemed almost to threaten her. She could feel more words welling up in him, longing to be spoken, to be heard. She had no flashboards to raise against such a torrent. All she could do was hold still and hope that he would receive her silence as she had his. Otherwise, if he released the flood, she would be swept right along with him into the unknown.

CHAPTER 19

A Gift

Mom's first day in Brookline working in the store coincided with the beginning of the February school vacation. Faced with a whole week with nothing to do and nowhere to go, Sarah decided to make herself useful to Frenchy and Ken in the mill. They gave her a sash brush and let her put primer on all the windows leaning up against the inside walls. She got herself so covered with paint that there was little danger of her being asked to deal with the little ones.

It was only later on, when she stood facing Liz Ackerman in the driveway, that Sarah felt a little awkward. Even on a blustery afternoon like this Liz always managed to stay neat-looking, all of a piece.

"Any idea what's eating Janey?" Liz asked. "Something happen between you two?"

Sarah thought for a moment, then shook her head. But she felt she had to explain that she was busy this week doing things that Janey was too young for.

"No," said Liz. "It's something . . . more than that. I asked Roger, but as you know, it's sometimes as hard for him to talk as it is for Janey."

Jethro's comment about Janey came back to Sarah from the day he walked them home. He had noticed that Janey was afraid to go back to the house. "Mom and Roger had a fight," Sarah said. "The shouting upset Janey, but it was no big deal, and it was days ago. She's fine now."

"She wants me to come to her birthday party next Saturday. Maybe I can get a few minutes with your mother then." Liz opened the car door. "Anything on your mind?" she asked, almost as an afterthought.

For one crazy moment Sarah thought of blurting out everything Jethro had told her, contradictions and all. But she knew exactly what would happen if she did. Liz would go charging over to Mrs. Costa's, and then Jethro would be stuck somewhere else where he could play basketball with boys his own age, whatever that was, and get a halfway decent education. Still, Sarah longed to let it all go. Liz let the moment stretch out a little longer. Sarah finally spoke up. "Janey's problem might have to do with Roger being here instead of Mom."

"Possibly." Liz nodded thoughtfully. "Though usually he's so good with her."

Sarah responded with a noncommittal shrug.

When she got to the house, Roger was sanding something out in back. Janey and Linda played nearby. Sarah considered going over to Costa's to see Jethro. She went into Brad's room to see what he had left out and found a scribbled note telling her to help herself to any of the old notebooks and school things on top of his desk and also his Swiss army knife, since he had a better one with him. She slipped the knife into her pocket. Then she went into the bathroom to clean up. But by the time she was ready to go, Roger and the little ones were inside, and Sarah was stuck with them after all.

The window painting was endless and boring, but she kept going to the mill each day, listening to Ken and Frenchy talk about the job and their kids and politics, and hearing in their talk a liking for Roger as well as Mom that surprised her. On Thursday, when Roger was in charge at home again, she quit work early and took off down the road, first jogging, then slowing as she ran short of breath. As she neared the Costa house, she could hear a machine roaring somewhere behind the house.

Sandy, stretched out on the porch, drew himself up and uttered one deep-throated bark before collapsing again with a lazy thump of his tail. Mrs. Costa opened the door and shouted above the din that Sonny was trying to teach Jethro a thing or two about the tractor. Sarah felt in her pocket for the knife, then decided to hold on to it until she could give it to him herself.

As she turned to leave, Mrs. Costa said, "He tells me he's invited to your house on Saturday. That true?"

Sarah nodded. "I think so. Or anyhow he will be. It's my foster sister's birthday."

"Seems peculiar," Mrs. Costa observed. "Him being so much bigger."

It was all Sarah could do to keep from pointing out that it was one of the less peculiar things about Jethro.

On her way home a passing car slowed and then stopped just ahead of her. Sarah's instinct told her to get off the road. But the driver leaned across the car and rolled down his window to ask directions to her own house. She told him it was the last house before the highway.

"You going there?" he inquired. "Can I give you a lift?"

He sounded perfectly nice, and he seemed to know Mom and Roger. But his smooth voice made her skin prickle, her shoulders tighten. "I'm meeting someone," she told him. She jumped down into the spongy wetland where she had to fight her way through the dense undergrowth. She couldn't keep from plunging wildly from one hummock to the next until at last she caught sight of the osiers that bordered the brook. They were just turning red and stood out like welcome signposts. Now she was able to gain her bearings and seek the fallen oak, which she crossed on her hands and knees. The brook churned with debris from its flooded banks. Even when she made it to the other side, she could barely find any solid footing.

As she stood there waiting for her heart to stop pounding, Jethro showed up. He had tried to catch up with her on the road and then had cut straight through to the blowdown.

She had to draw a deep breath before she could ask him in an ordinary tone how the tractor lesson had gone.

"I am too dull," he answered. "There is so much I don't understand. Spark plugs, for instance. And oil is not what I thought. Yet some parts are not unlike the mill—gears and cogs and the like. Do you think your family might put me to work when the mill starts up?"

"You can ask. Only don't tell them all that stuff about a hundred and fifty years ago. They won't buy that. They'll just think you're . . ." She shut her mouth on the word *weird* and chose instead Mrs. Costa's: "Peculiar."

Frowning, he straddled a bough of the chestnut oak. When she pulled out the knife and gave it to him, he rolled it from one hand to the other.

"Is it yours?"

"It's for you. An unbirthday present."

"Unbirthday?" He laughed. Carefully he opened the big blade, then the smaller one. He said, "I have always wanted a jackknife."

"There's lots more things in it. Let me show you." Grabbing it back, she pulled open the screwdriver. He fingered the notched part and asked what it was for. "Opening bottles and cans. And the squiggly thing is a corkscrew. Do you know how to play mumbly-peg?"

"Mumble-the-peg, yes. The young master and I played at it. I bettered him almost every time, although I tried not to. He did not like to lose. He would kick or thrash me."

"I can't believe no one ever stopped him."

Jethro swung his leg over the bough and moved up the bank. Then he squatted, flipped the knife, and sent the blade neatly into a mound of moss. "I have told you. It was what I was for." He drew the knife out, wiped the blade with his fingers, and handed it to Sarah. "It was all I knew before they fetched me away. When I was in Philadelphia, the people I stayed with brought me to hear a woman speak from a platform. She was like me. She was a woman of color. But she was a lady, not a slave. She said it was a crime to make a slave of another human being and a sin to accept it, to allow it. She worked to end slavery."

"Abraham Lincoln ended slavery," Sarah informed Jethro. "You must have heard of him."

Jethro shook his head. "Did you ever hear of Miz Mary Ann Shadd?"

"No," Sarah answered.

"Well, she is the lady who lectured in Philadelphia. I expect she had something to do with ending slavery, too." He nodded at the knife in Sarah's hands. "Your turn."

She flipped the knife, but it landed flat.

"Like this," he said, showing her again. The blade struck in.

"I wish you could slow it down. It's so quick it's like magic."

He nodded, smiling. "Like the tractor for me. Magic."

She tried once more. This time the blade dug in, but at such a slant that it slowly sank.

"You practice," he told her. "Keep the knife for now. Then we'll be matched. We'll play territory."

"Is territory a kind of mumbly-peg?" she asked.

"It is. I will teach you it as soon as you are ready."

She pocketed the knife, and they parted. She was in a hurry now to get home before Roger began to wonder where she was.

He was already starting supper when she came pounding through the mudroom. He told her he expected her to have the table set before Mom got home.

"Who was the guy," she thought to ask, "the guy who was just here?"

"What guy?" he said, handing Janey a raw carrot.

"The one looking for you or Mom. I thought he might be the engineer."

Roger shrugged. "He didn't show up here. He must have gotten lost."

But how could he get lost? Sarah wondered. This wasn't just the last house; it was the only house until the highway.

Her silence caught Roger's attention. "Sarah?" His voice was low. "When was this? What did he look like?"

She didn't like Roger's face so close to hers. She tried to pull back. "I don't know. Maybe a half hour ago. He was in a car. I couldn't see him that well." Was that true? She believed so. But it occurred to her that she would recognize his voice if she heard it again.

Roger said, "Well, whoever it was, I expect he'll find us if he wants us." He spoke in an offhand way, but the words seemed to come from the back of his throat as if he were choking on them.

CHAPTER 20

The Cellar

S arah was more nervous about Janey's birthday party than
Jethro seemed to be. Roger had prompted Janey on the
telephone and then had taken the phone from her to confirm
that the invitation was real. Sarah tried to imagine Jethro on
the other end. His first experience with a telephone?

"How did he sound?" she couldn't help asking Roger.

"Taciturn."

"What?"

"Not much of a conversationalist."

Sarah hoped Jethro stayed that way. Each day after school
she spent a lot of time over at the shop site, where the men
were digging by hand, scraping the earth down to the level of
the slabs and hauling up crumbly subsoil in a clamshell post-
hole digger.

"We ought to use some kind of suction device," Ken grumbled. "I'm a builder, not a stone-picker."

Stone-picker. The word hovered over Sarah's thoughts. But

it wasn't until she was in bed that night that the connection came to her. In Jethro's story the stone-picker had frightened Mercy.

Once during the night Sarah started awake at a sound like a cry. Lying rigid, listening hard, she was able to identify other night sounds: the rumble and swish of cars and trucks on the highway, infrequent at this hour, but never absent. In between, though, were swaths of silence pricked with small, wild voices: the soft cascading notes of an owl, muted but insistent; the chittering of raccoons quarreling over a road kill; the crow, his strident complaint muffled by walls and floors.

What had stirred him up? He was beginning to stay outside now, but this evening he had come begging to be let in. Something out there had frightened him. Something made him restless, even though he was safe in the cellar. Something or someone. Better keep him in tomorrow, Sarah thought; he ought to be on hand for Janey's birthday.

> *The child kicks with all her might and does not move.*
> *A leg cramp cuts all the way to her chest, to her*
> *throat. She cannot swallow. The crow perches on her*
> *bound wrists. It probes her face before dropping to*
> *retrieve the strip of pork rind it has brought. I was*
> *kicking, she whispers. I dreamed I was kicking. She*
> *has wet herself again. She is cold. She is ashamed.*
> *Stay, she pleads. But the crow flaps away to fetch*
> *more scraps of pork. The child chews the salty meat.*
> *She cannot swallow.*

Roger made a carrot cake with cream cheese frosting, which Janey wanted to put on. He let her smear it all over the cake, all over the counter, and all over her own face and Linda's. She even fed some of it to the crow.

She was barely cleaned up and in her party dress by the

time Mom got Linda up from her nap. Then Liz and Jethro arrived at the front door together. Liz had a small package in hand. So, to Sarah's astonishment, did Jethro. And it was gift-wrapped.

He stared in wonder at Janey. "You look—look like a real girl," he blurted. Everyone laughed too loud and didn't seem to know how to stop. Liz Ackerman's present was a Peter Rabbit mug. Jethro's was a set of soaps in animal shapes and packets of bubble bath, over which Janey squealed with delight. Mom and Roger made polite comments. Sarah was speechless.

Next Janey ripped apart the paper covering the big present. It was a toy theater with puppets. Linda grabbed at the props as they tumbled to the floor. Fending her off, Janey insisted on having the theater set up in her room. Within minutes the two younger girls were upstairs engrossed in the new present.

Liz suggested taking advantage of the quiet moment. She needed to talk to Molly and Roger.

Jethro stooped down to pick up the box of soaps. He touched a blue sea horse, sniffed his fingers, and wrinkled his nose.

"Did Mrs. Costa get it?" Sarah asked him.

Jethro nodded. "She said it would make Janey happy." He was gazing at the bookshelves. Then he walked to the fireplace, spread his hands on the brick facing, and leaned down to the worn hearthstone. He groped like a blind person, seeing with his fingers. After a moment he knelt. His arms, slightly raised, appeared to encircle something. "Maid," he murmured.

"Made what?" asked Sarah.

"Maid, the dog. She would lie here with her chin on her paw. When I set a log on the fire, she would flop right over on her back. She was huge, about to whelp. I was to have one of her pups for my own."

Sarah was keenly aware that Liz and Mom and Roger were talking in the very next room. Upstairs the girls' babble erupted from Janey's room and fell like a curtain, leaving Sarah and Jethro alone.

He turned slowly. "It is bigger. The windows are different. What happened to the wall?"

"Jethro, be careful," Sarah started to say to him.

But he had already dropped to his knees again and rolled back the rug. "There!" he declared, triumphant. He described an invisible line. It was only when Sarah stood with her back to the windows that she saw a difference. Between Jethro and the outside wall the floorboards were perfectly matched, the nails neatly covered with wooden plugs. Going the other way, toward the fireplace, the boards were more like waves, some of the cracks between them filled, some not.

Jethro sat back on his heels and let the rug unroll into place. He nodded toward the kitchen and dining room. "That is all new, too. When I first walked in here, I thought my memory had tricked me." He rose. "If I close my eyes, I can see it right."

"But you mentioned a kitchen," Sarah reminded him. "Where you first saw Mercy."

He spread his arms. "The parlor here. And this is the kitchen." He turned to the hearth. "Here was Mercy. And see," he added, peering into the fireplace, "here is the cooking crane and the very pots. The house in Philadelphia had a cookstove that stood on its own legs." He faced Sarah. "Do you believe this? Do you believe me?"

Caught up in his urgency, she could only nod. At this moment she did believe him.

Slowly he turned all around. He gazed at the ceiling, at the light fixture with bulbs shaped like candle flames. He shook his head, and in a brusque, diminished voice he said, "Will I never see them again?"

"Jethro!" Sarah had to break his mood. Any moment now Mom and Roger and Liz would return and they would all have ice cream and cake together. She probed as gently as she could. "Jethro, why did you believe Mercy when she said you were King Philip's son?"

Gradually he focused on Sarah, on the room as it now was. "But I didn't. Didn't I tell you that? I heard her out, but I knew it was impossible. King Philip lived a long time ago. Of course, it took awhile before I found out who he was. He wasn't a real king. By the time I learned that he was an Indian chief who called on all the tribes to help him drive the American colonists out of Indian lands, by the time I realized that he really had existed and was famed, by then Mercy had told me much more about herself. She even showed me where she had been kept in the cellar."

"In the cellar here?" Sarah exclaimed.

"In the root cellar, yes. It was all she could recognize, all that was left of the house she knew. That was where she and her mother were kept until they were moved to a real prison in Boston and were held in irons, hands and feet, with only watered cornmeal once a day, and whatever scraps the crow could bring them. I know what it is to shuffle along in chains because you cannot take a step. The irons binding Mercy weighed many pounds. She could not even shuffle. She could only lie in filth beside her mother, waiting for the birth, the death."

Sarah whispered, "You can't make up something like this."

"No," he agreed, "you can't. That is what I finally concluded, too. It wasn't until after Mercy spoke of all this that I found out about King Philip. He was killed in 1676. His wife and son were captured. The colonists debated how to deal with them. They were dealt the severest punishment of all: separated and sent as slaves to the Spanish Indies, perhaps to the very island where I was born. So it is possible, what Mercy thinks. Thought. That I so resemble King Philip's son that I must be his descendant." There was a note of challenge in his tone. "And who can say," he finished, "that I might not be descended from an African chieftain as well?"

The grown-ups emerged from the dining room subdued. They stood around and didn't even call the little ones downstairs. Something was going on. It looked to Sarah as though it was more serious than Mom and Roger yelling at each other.

Liz finally spoke up. "Listen to them upstairs," she remarked. "That toy theater's a big hit."

Sarah's mother said almost listlessly, "What? Oh, yes."

Roger tried to rally them. "Let's keep this birthday going."

"Is something wrong?" Sarah asked them.

"No," Mother and Roger retorted at the same time.

"Later," Liz told her.

Sarah took that to mean: Not in front of strangers, or aliens. Suddenly protective of Jethro, she blurted, "Mom, Jethro found where the house was added onto. Where the floor changes."

Sarah's mother made an effort to respond. "Where did you learn to tell these things?"

"He's had a lot of experience with old houses," Sarah answered for him. Already she regretted raising the subject.

Roger remarked dryly that it was something of an accomplishment to gain a lot of experience by the age of . . . How old was Jethro anyway?

Quick as a wink, Sarah picked up from what Jethro had said about Mercy's being nearly his age. "Past fourteen," Sarah pronounced, averting her eyes from Jethro.

"Why don't you let him speak for himself?" Liz inquired.

"Because it's hard being the only stranger. When are we going to have ice cream and cake?"

Everyone dutifully assembled the birthday feast. Then the

little ones came back downstairs, and everyone told Janey what a gorgeous cake she had decorated, and then she blew out six candles.

"You get your wish," Sarah exclaimed.

"Good," Janey told her. "It was my best wish, and—"

"Don't tell. Remember about secrets? It won't work if you tell."

"Can I just whisper it?"

"You can to me," Mom said to her. She bent down, then started to laugh. "You're tickling my ear." In an instant her face went from laughing to something quite different. Her eyes filled with tears. Catching Janey up in a tight hug, she managed to shake back her great cloud of hair, and the tears did not fall.

Roger cleared his throat. "How about some cake for those of us who don't get wishes?"

Janey cut such huge slices that they had to be divided into portions. Jethro said he had never tasted anything like it. Roger looked pleased. He said it was comforting to learn that all teenagers didn't prefer junk food. Jethro looked baffled. Before he could ask what a teenager or junk food was, Sarah offered to take him down to the cellar to see the crow. She all but dragged him toward the door to the cellar stairs.

He tried to hold back. "The way down is there," he declared, pointing into the living room.

"No," Sarah corrected. "It's right here in the kitchen."

"Let me show you," he insisted.

Because the others were all staring at him, Sarah had to give in and follow him into the living room. He stared at the half wall between the living room and the kitchen. "That's where the stairway used to be."

"Whisper," she ordered, her own voice low, but Mom was already joining them and asking Jethro how he had guessed about that.

"It's where it was," he responded doggedly.

Roger and Liz came in, too. "He's probably been here before," Roger suggested. "Is that right, Jethro?"

"Yes, sir."

"You lived here?" Mom pressed. "When?"

"Some time ago," Sarah put in. "Just for a while."

Mom pursed her lips. "Funny," she mused, "I thought the kitchen-dining room wing, including the cellar stairs, was done around the turn of the century."

"I don't know when it was done," Jethro managed to inform her before Sarah got him out of the living room.

Once they were back in the kitchen, she opened the door to the cellar and practically pushed him onto the stairs. "Can't you shut up in front of them?" she snapped. "Mom'll keep pestering you about this house now." Sarah switched on the light, transforming the dark space below into a dim, cluttered room.

"Why will she pester me?" Jethro asked.

"You know too much." Sarah was fuming. "And wait till they find out you're not in school. You'll be on that bus to the regional high school so fast you won't know what hit you."

"But why? Why should she care whether I'm in school? And why does she care where the stairs used to be, or when they got moved?"

"Because," Sarah informed him as they tramped down into the cellar and looked around for the crow. "Because those are her things. Antiques, including this house, are her almost favorite subject. And kids who aren't getting proper care are the other most important thing. It's why she takes in foster kids. That's how she and Roger met. He was doing it, too. Sooner or later she's going to decide you need a home and a future. Only sooner or later you'll get careless and tell her you're from before the Civil War and that you knew someone named Mercy from colonial times. And then it won't be the school bus you're on. Jethro, are you listening to me?"

Sarah picked up the crow and held his wings close to his body so that he wouldn't flail. Jethro, who seemed to have ignored her tirade, looked as though he were swimming through the gloom, his hands before him shoving at unseen objects. He came to a full stop midway between the furnace and the door to the root cellar. There he pressed a nonexistent wall or door, his hands bending back at the wrists. He toed the floor, scuffing the cement along an invisible line.

Sarah deposited the crow in the cage and walked past Jethro. Then she turned to face him. He wasn't fooling. He looked stricken. He swallowed hard before whispering, "Let's go back to the others."

Stepping to meet him, Sarah reached for his upraised hands until her palms opposed his, not quite touching. "See?" she said to him, showing him that there was no barrier between them. "You can just keep coming." But he didn't seem to hear her anymore. Unnerved, she snapped, "Jethro, stop it!" And something in him responded, although he still appeared to be in two places at once. No, she realized: not places. Times. Moving slowly backward, she felt herself drawing him past a barrier that only he could see. He stumbled once. Then he seemed to relax. His hands dropped to his sides.

She felt wrung out, but she kept on moving away from him until she backed into the door to the root cellar. She reached behind her for the latch.

"No," he whispered hoarsely.

"There's nothing in here. Nothing much." She waved around in the darkness until her hands found the string for the light bulb that hung from the ceiling. But the string pulled right off in her hands.

Jethro stood in the doorway, not speaking.

"Is this the place?" she asked him. "Is this where slaves hid?"

"One place," he answered.

"The place where Mercy and her mother were kept?"

There was a slight inclination of his head.

"But there's no window. You can see that. Was it there before?"

Jethro nodded. "Mercy told me her mother scratched their names along the inside edge, and also a few words. Mercy thinks they were from that psalm. Her mother scratched them with an arrowhead she wore around her neck for strength, a gift from an Indian, more proof that she was a witch. Mercy looked for their names, for the writing. She said that when she and her mother were taken away, bound and tied to a wagon, Zerobabel caught sight of the arrowhead and wrenched it off. Mercy has a clear memory of that, because it happened after they were brought out into the daylight. She remembers how her mother's head snapped back and then forward because the thong around her neck was so tough. And Zerobabel Quelch told her mother it was a taste of what would come when she was turned off the ladder with a noose around her neck." Jethro's voice was so low and intense Sarah could almost hear Mercy speaking through him.

The crow uttered a two-note croak and fell silent.

Jethro hunched his shoulders. With the dim light from behind, he resembled the crow drawing up his wings and sinking his head between them. "Was the crow here, too?" she asked.

"Here and on the journey to Boston. Zerobabel tried to shoot him when he caught sight of him in a tree, but the soldiers stopped him lest the warring Indians hear the shots and become alarmed and ambush the settlers. Mercy recalls that journey, how long it was and how dreary. She did not understand that it was the last time she would breathe fresh air and see the sky for a long, long time."

"So she and her mother went straight to prison?"

"That time is not so clear to her. Only when her mother was taken away for the trial. Mercy was left with prisoners she did not know, one of them babbling and howling, quite out of her wits, and another covered with horrible sores that gave off a sickening stench. Then Mercy's mother was brought back, and a man came to fit leg irons on them with locks, and for the hands as well so that they could not perform their evil mischief. You see, witches are supposed to change their shapes and other people's and get small enough to escape. Like that book about Wonderland. I suppose Alice was some kind of witch."

"She wasn't a witch. She was just a little girl having an adventure. Actually it was a dream."

"Well, Mercy was just a little girl, too. But it wasn't a dream. It was true, a true nightmare. And afterward it kept on happening through her dreams. She could never escape it."

Sarah asked, "Did you get to see the writing on the windowsill?"

He shook his head. "The window was boarded up during cold weather, but the board and batten plug could be lifted out. I meant to look at it another time. Do you think it's still there?"

Sarah felt along the wall, but she couldn't reach all the way to the top. Everywhere she touched she felt the bulging unfaced stones and granular runnels where mortar filled the pockets between them. "I don't think there's any wood here," she told him.

Jethro stepped beside her and stretched tall. She couldn't see his hand, but she guessed it was feeling around a square-shaped area close to the ceiling. "No," he agreed. "No wood." Then he added, "But the names must still be there. Underneath the stones and plaster."

He groped his way out of the root cellar. His face was drained, bleached like ash. Sarah led the way upstairs and opened the door into the bright kitchen. She felt as if she were emerging from a grave.

All about them were the shambles of the birthday party. Liz had gone, but Mom and Roger sat at the kitchen table, speaking in guarded tones. As soon as Sarah and Jethro appeared, their conversation came to an abrupt halt.

"Ready for more cake?" Roger asked expansively.

Jethro blinked.

"Come on," Roger urged him, reaching for a clean plate. "I'll join you. We both will."

They sat amid balloons and party napkins and ate carrot cake again. Sarah was famished. There was a gaping hole inside her, full of sadness and misery and hunger.

CHAPTER 21

Crimes and Punishments

Sunday dawned gloomy and wet. Intermittent rain turned everything muddy and sodden. Mom and Roger were inclined to stay home again, but when Janey begged to go to Sunday school, Sarah volunteered to baby-sit. It seemed to her like a good time to check out Mom's books on antiques and history.

Linda wandered into the living room, dragging her blanket and sucking her thumb. Seeing the books strewn about, she plopped herself down in their midst. "Read," she commanded.

"Bring me something," Sarah told her.

But instead of going upstairs for one of her own books, Linda picked up one that Sarah had pulled from the shelf.

"That's a grown-up book. You wouldn't like it."

"Yes, I do. Read."

"It's too long. It doesn't have pictures," Sarah explained.

Linda dragged the book onto her lap and opened it. "Picture," she declared, pointing to a full-page portrait of a child. "Doll."

Sarah glanced down at the picture of a young girl that had

been painted, the book said, in 1670. "It's not a doll," Sarah said. "It's a real girl a long time ago." The child portrayed wore a head scarf knotted under her chin. Her plain dark frock had only one adornment, a lace collar. The child's stern expression did give her a doll-like look. What made her human was the way she clutched something—a ball or maybe an apple—against her tummy.

Could Mercy have looked like that when she was little? Imagine Margaret Bredcake sweeping the child into her arms and kissing her on a day like this, the Sabbath. How could that be considered wrong?

> *Running. The stinging wind, the warm breath of the sun like Mamma bending to enfold her. The goodwives shake their heads and whisper among themselves that Goody Bredcake and her child are disregardful, brazen. Wicked.*

Linda leaned against Sarah. "Read," she murmured.

Sarah flipped through some pages. Linda snuggled close. A chapter heading caught Sarah's attention: "Crimes and Punishments." She began to make up a story she pretended was in the book.

"Once upon a time there was—a name on the page supplied her with the heroine—"a girl named Lydia. . . ." Sarah scanned a long list of crimes. "Lydia was naughty."

"What?" mumbled Linda. "What naughty?"

One of the crimes punishable by death was disobedience to parents. Sarah skipped that page and the next until she came to Sabbath laws. "No one shall run on the Sabbath day, or walk in his garden, or elsewhere," she read, "except reverently to and from meeting." This was followed by yet another list that concluded, "No woman shall kiss her child on the Sabbath or fasting day." So there it was. That much was true.

"Read," Linda said.

"The naughty girl, Mercy—I mean, Lydia—decided she'd better be good. So her mother kissed her, but not on Sunday, and they lived happily ever after."

Linda sucked noisily. Then she withdrew her thumb. "More."

"No more now," Sarah replied, reading to herself about whippings and brandings and death penalties for pirates and Quakers alike. So much for the good old days, she thought. What was so great about times like those?

At lunchtime she said something about it to Mom, who rubbed her eyes a lot and seemed distracted.

Roger said, "Those Puritan settlers had strong religious beliefs. Life was hard."

"So Quakers had to be banished or killed?" Sarah demanded. "And how about stubborn and rebellious children?"

"Aha!" he exclaimed. "Now we get serious." He grinned. "Makes Mom and me seem like old softies, doesn't it? In the seventeenth century it would be...," Drawing his fingers across his neck, he left the sentence unfinished.

Sarah turned to her mother. "How can you like that crummy period?"

Mom pulled herself out of her private musings. She said, "I thought you were into the abolitionist movement."

Sarah shrugged. That reminded her that she hadn't done a thing on her report yet. "I don't know," she answered. "It's hard to keep track of all the different times. They're all old."

"Look at it this way," Roger suggested. "Those strict laws were made long before the Revolution. It took a couple of centuries for people to get to the point where they defied laws they thought were wrong. That's what the Underground Railroad was all about. Then there's nearly the same span of time between then and now. Things change slowly. But they do change."

"Always for the better?"

He and Mom exchanged a long, bleak look. Then he said, "In some ways. But there are still—" He broke off, his eyes on Mom.

"There are still atrocities," Mom finished. "The civilized world expects better, but every age has had them."

Sarah pushed away from the table. "They really hanged people for witches?"

Mom nodded.

"And put kids in prison because their mothers were there?"

"We'll talk about it later," Mom said, nodding toward Janey.

"If you're going to read about those laws," Roger said, "you'd better have a look at what people thought and felt, too." He got up and walked into the living room. By the time Sarah joined him, he was glancing through one of his books. "Okay," he told her. "This is the other side of the law you were asking about. It was written by the father of a young child who was imprisoned for months with her mother."

"When?" Sarah wanted to know. "Where?"

"Right here in Massachusetts. The father petitioned the court for the sake of the child, who, 'being chained in the dungeon was so hardly used and terrified that she hath ever since been very chargeable, having little or no reason to govern herself. And I leave it to the honorable Court to judge what damage I have sustained by such a destruction of my poor family.'"

"What was her name?" Sarah whispered.

"Dorcas," he said. "Dorcas Good."

Mom carried Linda through to the stairs. Linda waved toward the book Roger was handing to Sarah and said, "Sarah read book again."

Roger nearly choked. "You read that stuff aloud? To our baby?"

"About a doll," Linda reported.

Roger subsided. Mom promised Linda a very short story before her nap. And Sarah settled down with the book Roger had just read from.

But she had had enough history for a while. The rain drummed steadily and darkened the house. Sarah glanced at one page and then another. She was barely attending when she came to a diary entry in which a man from colonial times wrote down his wife's dream: "She thought she saw a scroll in the sky in the form of a light cloud with writing on it. . . . The writing she could not read but there was a woman before her that told her there would be a great dearth because of want of rain and after that a pestilence for that the seasons were changed and time inverted." *The seasons changed and time inverted.*

> *It is hard to awaken into the nightmare. Dreaming brings daylight and running and the wheel turning and the water sending forth splashes of summertime colors. It brings Mamma laughing and Papa striding from the mill and the crow playing games with its touch of meanness.*

The rain bore down for another hour or so, and then suddenly stopped. A hint of sunlight edged the low clouds. Rain-blackened branches cast dull shadows beyond the house. Everything inside was quiet, Roger working, Mom reading, Janey playing in her room.

Sarah took a flashlight and headed for the cellar. She shut the door from the kitchen firmly behind her.

The crow sputtered in his cage. Sarah decided to let him loose in the cellar for a while. Freed, he stepped cautiously onto her shoulder. Then, his claws digging in for an instant, he flapped clumsily off to perch on top of the freezer.

Sarah dragged a crate into the root cellar. She turned the

flashlight on the end wall that sort of leaned against the sloping bank on which the house was built. Then she played the light along the adjoining wall, tilting the beam to the uppermost section, which might barely reach above ground level. Had there really been a window there in Jethro's time? He had been right about the living room and the stairs.

Sarah beamed the light over the rounded stones. When she stood on the crate, she could almost see a squared demarcation in the stones. But as soon as she backed off, the pattern, if it was a pattern, vanished.

She turned the flashlight at an angle until she again detected a kind of outline. She moved gradually until all at once what had seemed there was not. Just as she stooped for the crate, there came a rush above her, a sudden frenzy. Her hands flew to the top of her head; the flashlight dropped.

Falling to her knees, she groped in the dark for the flashlight, which had gone out. When she switched it on again, the beam was faint. Quickly, before it died, she tipped it up. Even in the dimness she could see the crow slamming against the place she had been examining. Each time he bashed the stone, he flapped and clawed at what would have been the window, except that it wasn't there.

Sarah shoved the crate against the wall, climbed on it, and held the nearly useless flashlight as high as she could. But the crow was so wild she couldn't grab him with only one hand.

"Mom!" she called. "Mom, come down here!"

The crow was making such a racket she couldn't hear anyone upstairs. The flashlight flickered and died. Now when she could use both hands, she could only flail blindly, striking her knuckles against the stones. "Mom!" she yelled. "Help!"

"Sarah? Where are you?" Roger's voice came close. "What are you doing in the dark?"

"Here," she sobbed. "Up at the window. Hurry!"

He was groping for the light string that wasn't there. "What do you mean? There isn't any window."

"The crow thinks there is," she countered. "He keeps hitting it, trying to get out. Stop him."

Roger brushed past her. She heard him gasp and then grunt and then mutter, "Idiot bird." Then he caught the crow. "All right," he said, though whether to the crow or Sarah, she couldn't tell. He carried the crow into the main cellar and stuck him in the cage. "How did he get out?"

"I let him out. For exercise. Then I left the door to the root cellar open for light, because the string's off."

"I guess it's not a good idea," Roger remarked mildly. "He really went berserk."

"I know." She waited for the expected lecture on being responsible, but he must have had something else on his mind because he forgot to deliver it. "Thanks," she managed to get out as they started up the stairs.

"It's getting time for him to go free," Roger observed.

"Janey's afraid something will happen to him," Sarah answered.

"I know," he replied. "No need to push it right now. But the crow was telling us something in there. Don't you think so?"

Sarah nodded. If she said what was on her mind now, Roger would think she was as crazy as the crow. But even ending in silence, this was the closest she and Roger had ever come to a real exchange.

CHAPTER 22

Territory

The following Monday afternoon when Sarah got off the school bus, Liz had already left. Sarah felt let down.

She found Roger on the phone arguing with someone about the problem hole and objecting to any further delay.

Janey asked Sarah to come upstairs and watch a play in her theater. Linda said, "Read. Read book."

It was easy to tell that Roger had been attending more to the shop site than to the kids.

"Later," Sarah told them, getting out before Roger could stop her. She went to the mill and climbed the stairs to see what Frenchy and Ken were up to.

"Finishing," Ken said. Turning on his ladder, he waved her over to a milk carton that was sliced open at the top and full of nuts and bolts. Handing the carton up to him, she asked how long before the mill would actually start working.

"Soon as the shop's ready," Ken told her. "There's inspectors going over it now, engineers and archaeologists from the state. All sorts."

"What are they looking for?"

Ken shrugged, but Frenchy said that they'd discovered that the land around it had been scraped. "Probably happened years ago," he added, "when the highway was under construction. Someone selling topsoil and making a bundle on the side."

Sarah climbed down to the ground floor. There was a sleeve around the shaft; it blocked her view to the lower level where the power train connected with the great wooden waterwheel. She walked outside and around to the wheel pit. That January day when she had slithered and climbed on the icy wall that joined the dam seemed now to have happened in another age, another lifetime. Today the sky was a milky blue with cloud wisps distant and pale. The brook rushed madly beneath the road and vanished. Birds darted and dipped to the fall of water and flew up, a trail of drops in their wake like tiny sparks from the sun. The air smelled of mud and skunk cabbage. Sarah could hardly recall that strange warm wind, the yellow and black sky, the icy grip of the water tightening around her chest, the jagged lightning.

She was still standing there when Ken and Frenchy came out of the mill. She heard the trucks back out to the road. She waited until they were gone before working her way down and approaching the problem hole. She knew from the architect's drawings how the path would curve away from the mill before turning toward the shop, but she couldn't actually place the path to be.

It seemed to her amazing that someone could lay out the path and design the structure out of nothing and draw a picture of them before they ever existed. She knew that she had no control over the vision that had come to her on that January Sunday when she glimpsed the mill in ruins. She could neither summon it nor banish it any more than she could call up Mercy from the past. Did that mean Mercy wasn't there? Did that mean that all traces of those other lives were erased from this place? What made them seem at times so present? Sarah couldn't tell. But she had a feeling that she was on the verge of finding something she didn't yet know was missing.

The child recalls dreaming about this place. Or was it somewhere else? It is hard to recognize now, for where she thought Papa had uncovered the Indian bones and covered them again there now stands a small sumac tree, taller and redder than any of the weeds that surround it. She snaps a milkweed pod from its brittle stem. Downy seeds float on the air and land weightless on her shoulders and arms. Brushing the fluff from her black hair, she catches one white seed in her fingers. For just an instant she is surprised to find that it is not blue and that the hand it alights on is not Papa's.

Jethro materialized beside the shop site. Already the light had drained from the sky. The wispy clouds had a fuller look about them, a heaviness, as if they were sinking to earth.

"Want to play that mumbly-peg game?" Sarah asked him. "What do you call it?"

"Territory."

"How does it go?"

Jethro knelt on the ground near the problem hole and drew a circle in the dirt with a stick. Then he drew a line through the middle of it. "We try to take over each other's half," he explained. "If it's my turn and the blade strikes on your territory, we change the dividing line. Then on your turn you try to gain it back and get more of mine."

Sarah tossed the knife. It landed outside the circle. Jethro said she could try again, but she refused. She watched him send the knife right onto the dividing line. It didn't gain him new territory, but it was neat and sure. She hoped she could make one toss that good before it got too dark to play.

"You know," she said to Jethro as she wiped off the blade, "if you really know what all that stonework was for and I can tell everyone like I'm guessing it, then the shop can be built and the mill will start and you might get a job in it."

"The people coming to look at it," said Jethro, "will soon find out. But you may as well know," he went on. "This is where Mr. and Mrs. Lockwood hid slaves escaping to Canada. When there was serious danger, we went underground here. If it was just a busybody about the place, the cellar was used." He gazed down into the hole. "There doesn't seem much of it left. Something must have happened besides the fire. I wish I knew what it was."

"And I wish I knew what you were talking about," Sarah broke in. "You never mentioned a fire before."

He stood up. Sarah rose, too. She couldn't see the territory outline anymore, only the knife lying open on the ground. "Here is the calf shed." Jethro indicated the front of it or the doorway. "That is all you see from the house and the mill. But down below, concealed, is a stone door that pivots on an iron bar. It leads to another chamber and out again through a kind of tunnel. It is all inside the dam."

"You mean, was," Sarah insisted.

Jethro seemed unfazed by her correction. "I don't know how much of it was destroyed the night of the fire."

"How did the fire happen? Why haven't you told me about it?"

"It is a constant danger in mills. The grooves in the mill-stones must mesh just right, or the oats and corn will not come fine. But if you run the stones too thin, you ruin the grinding surfaces, and the stones give off a horrid burning smell and sometimes sparks. With flour dust everywhere, it can happen just like that. But this time it may not have been that simple."

"Why not?"

"Here is all I know," Jethro told her. "The stone-picker

came to the house for his dinner. As soon as Mercy, who was in the woodshed, heard him speak, she became so agitated that Mrs. Lockwood had me take her to the secret place in the dam. You must understand that Mr. and Mrs. Lockwood already thought Mercy sometimes lost her reason."

"You mean, thought she was insane?"

He nodded. "Later Mr. Lockwood gave me candles and matches and bread and sweet cider and sent me to stay with Mercy until the stone-picker was on his way. By then someone had come to warn Mr. Lockwood against Bezaliel Mason, the stone-picker. It seemed that not long since he had seized free men in another town and then declared them to be runaway slaves. That was his real calling, the way he made his living."

"So that meant you were in danger?"

"More than that. The hiding place was, the station on the Underground Railroad, and all the people connected with it. So while Mr. Lockwood hid me, he had to act as though he still believed nothing was amiss. When he paid the stone-picker and saw him leave, Mr. Lockwood assumed he had given up his search. But later Mr. Mason's horse came wandering in from the meadow where he must have been tied and broken loose. So then Mr. Lockwood supposed that Bezaliel Mason had not given up but was biding his time."

"Were you still in the secret place?"

"Yes. Mr. Lockwood feared for me. But he made Mercy go to Mrs. Lockwood." Jethro fell silent.

Sarah waited. She knew that all in good time the story would come out. "It's getting really dark," she said. "Do you want one more turn?"

He dropped to his knees and flipped the knife. She had to crouch down to see where it landed. It slid on its side. He picked it up and handed it to her. "Just before dark," he resumed softly, "the fire broke out. All the neighbors rallied with bucket lines from the pond. Mercy told me that Mr. Lockwood was sorely burned. Mrs. Lockwood feared that if the heavy timbers fell on the dam, it would cave in, so she sent Mercy to fetch me out." Again he broke off.

This time Sarah remained still, the knife flat on her open palm.

Jethro raised his hands to his face and then let them drop. "When Mercy came to me, she was raving. At one moment she called the stone-picker Bezaliel Mason and the next moment Uncle Zerobabel. She begged me to help her escape. She urged me to put on her cloak to get him off her track, in case we failed to get away together."

"Get away where?" Sarah interrupted. "Where did she want to go?"

"She had a notion," Jethro went on. "She was desperate. She thought we might go through the dam as she did before. Both of us. And if he followed, she meant to double back. She meant for him to be caught in another time."

"With you?"

"Well, yes. Thinking me Mercy. When he discovered otherwise, it would be too late."

"But how could you do . . . what she said?"

"Go through?"

Sarah nodded. That was partly what she was asking.

"I knew there was an escape door. I had to tell her about it. But I had never seen it used. Still, it was there, leading into the dam and out of it beneath the falls. Under the spillway. I did not know what to believe about going through time. What I feared was that the slave hunter would get me. So when she insisted, when she implored me, I could not refuse her."

"Then you must have believed you'd come through in another time."

"Yes. No. Well, by then I did believe it about Mercy. I did not see how it could happen to me. Yet I must have believed . . . something. If she was right about the way through and if she was right about the stone-picker, and if he tried to follow us and then found only me, she would be free of him. In a way I must have believed that was possible. There was so little time. Not enough time to think. It took all my strength to raise the iron lever that released the pins. I had to push the stone wide enough to bring us through."

"Us? So she did go with you."

"She was just behind me. Out under the falls we could see through the water that the mill was ablaze at the top. I climbed stones like steps to the spillway. It was not like . . . The water sizzled from burning timbers. I reached back to pull Mercy through with me into the pond. She handed the crow to me. I reached again. I thought I had her, and then I did not. I struggled through the spillway against that wall of water. It was hot . . . hot. The pond refused me, forced me back. I had to pull myself with both hands, but I don't remember letting go of the crow. I grabbed something that was burning, then grabbed something else. That is all I remember."

Fingering the knife blade, Sarah puzzled about the crow. She peered at Jethro through the dusk. "Do you understand how it happened?"

Even in the gathering darkness she could see that he was just as baffled as she was.

"Did Mercy understand?" Sarah pressed.

Jethro shook his head. "She knew her mother was no witch, but she did wonder whether witchcraft helped her escape into my time. She thought that her uncle might have been partly right, that maybe the pond held some kind of spell. She knew the Indians believed that the hill belonged to their ancestors, and the brook that bounded it."

"The Place of the Departed," Sarah murmured.

"She cast about for explanations: a tempest, the crow, the dammed water, and the turning wheel. Or else the driving fever that afflicted him with cruelty. And her with hate."

"That doesn't explain how," Sarah objected. "In books time can be folded and skipped through, or ghosts appear because of unfinished business. But you're not a ghost." Sarah stopped short of asserting that neither was Mercy. "Anyway," she finished, "I don't believe in ghosts. I don't believe in witchcraft, either. Do you?"

He pondered her question before answering. "I do not believe that Margaret Bredcake was a witch. I think she was clever and generous and—"

"And what?"

"It is hard for me to say this." He drew a breath and plunged on. "And beautiful. In a way she did cast a spell over Zerobabel Quelch. He was bewitched. To free himself, he looked for other witch signs."

"You've told me all that." Just thinking about it made Sarah's skin crawl.

"Mercy's aunt often told her she had her mother's wildness along with her beauty."

The first time her uncle touches her, she is startled. He has chanced upon her gazing into the hill, into the past she cannot be certain she fully remembers. He grasps at the mist of milkweed seeds wafting between them. His fingers disentangle the white fluff from her long, loose hair. With sudden violence he grips her head and thrusts her off, berating her. Where is her cap? Why does she not cover herself as modesty dictates?

Sarah waited for Jethro to go on. She flipped the knife, and they both bent over, foreheads nearly touching, to see where it landed.

"It is too dark to play," he said. But he picked up the knife and sent it down. "Not as good as yours," he commented.

She couldn't even see where he had drawn the last dividing line. She rose to her knees, poised for one last toss. Jethro's voice came to her through the darkness, so soft it was like an echo.

"Mercy guessed what it must have been like for her mother. Then, later, when he would not let Mercy be, when he bothered her and punished her in turn, she had no doubt."

Sarah sat back as his meaning sank in.

"If you fail to play your turn," Jethro resumed in his usual tone, "we will lose all the territory to the dark."

She raised the knife. In the instant before she flipped it, something hurtled from above. Her breath caught. Then she saw what had split the darkness and struck the ground between Jethro and her. It was another knife, larger and easier to see, even though its blade was impaled in the dirt.

She looked at Jethro. From the way his head tipped back she could tell that someone stood just behind her. Someone so sure of his aim that he had swiped Sarah's turn. Afraid of brushing against the knife hurler, she froze.

Jethro stood up, his gaze still fastened somewhere above Sarah's head. Then the man spoke. Guided by his voice, she was able to swivel on her heels and move out of his range.

"I just had to show you two how it's done while I could still see." He leaned over to extract the knife. There was a click. The blade snapped and vanished. He stepped back. But not far enough.

His easy, confident manner was so insulting that Sarah blurted, "That was dangerous. And—and rude."

The man laughed. "Wrong about dangerous. Right about rude. I didn't think I'd scare you."

That was close enough to an apology, so she made an effort to be polite in case he was the engineer or something. "Are you here to look at the site?"

"The sight. You might say so. But it's like night already."

Then he was gone. Where? Which way? After a moment she heard a car door slam, a car take off down the road.

Jethro scuffed out the scored circle, then, as she stood up, yanked her away from the edge of the hole. His hands felt icy. For a moment she gripped them as if it were she who had pulled him to safety.

"Can you see your way home?" he asked.

"Of course, I can," she retorted. "I already am home. I'm fine," she added, because she wasn't. It had just come to her that she recognized the man's voice. "Did you see him?" she asked Jethro.

"No. But I think . . . It sounds like . . ."

"Like what? Like who?"

He kicked loose stones into the hole. "Nothing. Talking about all this gives me notions, that's all."

"Me, too," she admitted, fending off creepy thoughts about the man. "We've probably heard him talking out here. Ken said the place was crawling with inspectors today."

"I suppose so," Jethro agreed. "That must be it."

On that note they parted, Jethro swallowed up by the night, Sarah running toward her lighted house.

CHAPTER 23

Uncertainty

Things were happening all around, and they were not happening. The historian and the engineer were making progress, but not the shop itself. Beneath all of that, which Mom and Roger talked about all through supper, were the secret things Sarah could tell they were thinking about. And darting around and about everything else were Sarah's own secrets. They burst beyond her grasp and sprang back again to tease away her thoughts. It amazed her that they escaped her mother's notice, but then they were most present in her silences, not her words.

"Could you take me and Jethro to the library tomorrow?" Sarah asked her mother.

"Jethro and me," Mom and Roger corrected in unison. Then Mom added that she would have to think about it.

"In other words, no?"

"I didn't say that, Sarah." Mom sounded tense and tired. She said she would do her best, but there were a good many unpredictable things cropping up just now. When Sarah said, with feeling, that she could see that, Mom and Roger exchanged one of their looks.

"When you say something like that," Mom told her afterward, "it makes me realize that you're coming through."

Sarah nearly dropped the stack of plates in her hands. "What did you say? Coming through what?"

"Through . . . you know, out of your difficulties. You seem so much happier. And that," Mom added, rescuing the plates, "makes me happy."

Sarah said bluntly, "You don't look happy."

"I'm worried, that's all. But not about you."

That evening Janey came into Sarah's room while she was doing her math homework and stood waiting for Sarah to notice her. Of course, Sarah knew she was there. Breathing.

"What's up?" Sarah said to Janey.

"Dad says we have to let Barker go."

"We've let him out before. He comes back."

"But Dad says we have to keep him out. For his own sake."

"That's because he had a bad time in the cellar awhile back."

Janey's voice fell to a whisper. "He'll die if we let him go."

Sarah said, "We can still feed him."

"Do you think Dad's doing it because of that time the crow pushed him?"

"The crow didn't push him," Sarah started to explain. "Dad thought I did, and I said it was the crow, but I didn't mean push, only that . . ." If it was too complicated for Sarah, how could she make Janey understand? "Listen, Janey, I have homework. We can talk about it tomorrow. Okay?"

"Okay," Janey agreed.

The truth was that Sarah was no longer sure what exactly had happened that day. She couldn't separate Roger's anger and suspicion from Zerobabel Quelch's accusing Margaret Bredcake and later Mercy herself of possessing a familiar in the form of a black crow. Sarah needed to learn more about witches in colonial times. She hoped the library had some books about them.

It suddenly occurred to her that she ought to let Jethro know if they were definitely going to the library tomorrow. She found her mother sitting on her bed, talking with Roger. Sarah wasn't surprised when they broke off.

"I have to call Jethro if we're going tomorrow."

"How about Wednesday instead?" Mom suggested. "Since it's half day. That way I can leave you two there while I do some errands."

Sarah nodded. Then she blurted, "Something's going on. Why won't you tell me?"

"Some things are private," Mom answered.

Roger said, "There is one thing we can tell you, though. We've decided to get the mill going without waiting for the shop to be built. We'll have a grand opening and have people in to help launch it. A little favorable publicity may help move those state officials along."

"You mean you'll grind stuff and everything?"

Mom nodded. "And give everyone samples."

Sarah went downstairs to use the kitchen telephone. It felt funny calling Mrs. Costa and asking to speak to Jethro. The television was loud in the background. What were they watching? What did Jethro make of sitcoms and car chases and sex?

"Sarah?" He sounded perfectly normal, as though he were used to talking like this.

"Be here Wednesday a little after noon and we'll go to the library." She spit the words out so fast and hung up so abruptly she astonished herself. Something like terror had seized her at the sound of Jethro's voice on the phone. All her doubts about him came rushing back. He was not an escaped slave from before the Civil War. He did not travel through time to the twentieth century. He was just fooling around, playing some kind of sick game. Probably he even went to high school. Probably he thought she was the stupidest girl in the world.

She sat down, swinging her knees away from the table, leaning over them, and covering her burning face with her hands. Stupid, stupid, stupid. Probably he was still laughing over there at Costa's farm.

When she went to bed, she lay stiff and hot with shame, not wanting to think about Jethro on the telephone, not able to stop thinking about him. She thought she would never get to sleep, but all of a sudden she snapped awake and realized she had drifted off.

For a second she held still, in case there was something outside that had waked her. But all she heard were the spring peepers and wild ducks squabbling on the pond. She told herself that if she saw something now like a vision of a child in a dungeon, it would be a sign that Jethro had not been stringing her along. But she saw nothing. She slept without dreaming until Mom called her out of bed the next morning.

On Tuesday after school she tried to get started on her report, but her mind kept wandering. She could hear Mom on the phone telling Roger that the archaeologist or historian or someone had dug up some early eighteenth-century document in which Singing Fish Brook was listed as Sin and Flesh Brook. Also a newspaper article about the fire that gutted the nineteenth-century mill.

That night at supper they talked some more about it. "Lord knows what Puritan drama produced Sin and Flesh Brook," Roger remarked. "What kind of details did you get on the fire?"

"Not much," Mom said. "Apparently there was a violent storm, with lightning. But it was also thought that it could have been caused by poorly picked millstones. Someone charged that it was started deliberately, but there's always some crackpot after a disaster like that trying to stir up trouble."

Sarah seized on this. "Did they say who did it?"

Mom said, "I don't think anyone took it seriously."

"Anyone hurt?" Roger pursued.

"The miller was injured. Someone disappeared, probably the only fire victim."

Sarah thought: Bezaliel Mason. Then she thought: Jethro. But where did that leave Mercy? "Did the article mention anyone else?"

"I don't think so," Mom answered. "When the mill toppled, it smashed the midsection of the dam. The miller said . . ." She paused. "He said he was sick at heart. He doubted he would rebuild."

"Could I see the article?" Sarah asked her. "Would it be in the library?"

Mom shook her head. "You'd have to go to the state archives or the historical society. I don't think they allow children access."

"I'm not a baby," Sarah retorted. "I don't break or tear things."

"I know. But they make these rules to protect the records so qualified people can find out the sort of things we've just been learning."

"Well, can you get one of those qualified people to find out whether anything more came out about the fire afterward?"

"All I can do is suggest . . . ask."

Sarah sat back and let the conversation go on without her. Even if she was blocked by those rules, there ought to be some way to find the root cellar windowsill where Mercy's mother supposedly scratched her name and Mercy's and that bit about the darkness.

"When was this house built?" Sarah blurted.

"You're interrupting," Mom said.

Sarah waited. Finally Mom told her that some of the house was built in the eighteenth and early nineteenth centuries, but that it had been added to off and on, as Jethro had pointed out, and there was reason to believe there was a dwelling on this site before all that. Sarah struggled with the centuries. If Mom said the nineteenth, that meant the 1800s. That would do for Jethro's time, but not for Mercy's. "How can you tell there was a house here even earlier?" she asked.

But the phone was ringing. Mom got up to answer it.

"Experts look at the way beams are joined," Roger told Sarah. "Even the way the wood is cut can tell us about its age."

"So what does the wood show you here?"

"Nothing, really. I thought you were asking in a general sort of way. Actually it's the deed that goes farther back. Also some of the stonework in the cellar looks a lot older than the rest of the foundation."

Mom returned. "Liz," she said cryptically to Roger. But they both glanced over at Janey, who was fidgeting at her place. A passing thought that Janey might be in some kind of trouble glanced off Sarah's mind. But what kind of serious trouble could Janey get into? Sarah went back to considering the walled-up cellar window. She glanced at Mom, and then at Roger. Neither of them looked especially receptive to a suggestion that would involve wrecking part of the foundation. Sarah tracked a silent conversation between them. When her mother clamped her mouth shut, Sarah spoke up.

"When you die," Sarah said to her, "who will get this house?"

Mom's mouth opened, but nothing came out.

Roger began to laugh. "You have designs on it?"

Sarah flushed. She wanted Mom to answer. She wanted to

know that in the future she would be able to look for the names on a walled-up seventeenth-century window ledge.

"Tell us what's on your mind," Mom suggested. "Why all the questions?"

Sarah drew a breath. "I might want to, you know, find out more about it. The way that historian is doing with the mill and the hole where the shop goes."

"Is there dessert?" Janey asked.

"Cookie," Linda demanded.

Mom said, "Just a minute," to them, and to Sarah she said, "All of you children will share in whatever property Roger and I have when we die."

"But what if the others don't care about the house?"

"Are you going to die?" asked Janey.

"No, darling, of course not. Sarah's asking about a long, long time from now, when you're all grown up. By then we might not even have this house anymore."

"Then what's the point?" Sarah exploded. "What's the point of doing all this work?"

"Sarah," Roger responded, "your mother's just saying that we can't predict the future. Can we end this discussion now? Before we upset younger members of the family," he added meaningfully.

Sarah knew he was speaking of Janey. Anyway, what did Mom mean about a long time from now when Janey was all grown up? Mom sounded as though she had forgotten that Janey was a foster child. There was no telling how long a foster kid would stay. Some left after a few weeks or even a few days. Only one boy had been with them for months. And Janey? It had been more than two years now since she'd come. That was very long for a foster child. Who knew where Janey would be when she grew up?

Before bedtime Janey sidled past Sarah's door. This time she spoke up right away. "Can I sleep with you tonight?"

"No," Sarah told her. "It's a school night. A busy day to-morrow."

Janey looked impressed. "How come?"

"Jethro and I are going to work in the library."

"Can I come, too?"

"No, it's work. You'd be bored."

"I could look at books," Janey pressed. "Sarah, would Mom tell us if she's sick and going to die?"

"Oh, for goodness' sake," Sarah retorted. "You've been watching too many junky TV shows."

Janey raised a finger to her mouth and began to tear at her nail.

Sarah knew that her question about inheriting the house had really gotten to Janey. "Okay," she declared, "I'll let you come with us tomorrow if you promise not to bother us."

"Okay," Janey agreed. She sounded infuriatingly humble and grateful.

"Can we end this discussion now?" Sarah demanded. What made her fall back on the very words Roger had used? She supposed she sounded just as stuffy and at least as mean. Well, she would make it up to Janey tomorrow. She would make time for her and take her to the children's room to check out some books. Everything would be different tomorrow.

If Jethro actually showed up.

CHAPTER 24

Finding

J ethro did show up on Wednesday, but he seemed more interested in the finishing work at the mill than in going to the library. When Sarah told him about Sin and Flesh Brook, he took it in stride. After all, he wasn't the doubter; Sarah was.

Helping to get Linda ready, Sarah told Mom that she had promised to let Janey tag along with her.

"That's nice," Mom said. "Keep her right with you."

"I thought we'd leave her in the children's room. She loves it there."

"Sarah," Mom told her in a voice constricted with something Sarah didn't understand, "you have to keep her with you. All the time."

Sarah was about to reply that no child was ever alone in the library when she caught a glimpse of Mom's mouth, set in grimness. It scared her a little. Finishing the double knot on Linda's sneaker, Sarah dropped her head and nodded.

In the car Jethro sat in back on the edge of the seat. His eyes flicked from one passing vehicle to the next. When an eighteen-wheeler roared across the intersection and headed west on the highway, his whole body recoiled. The moment Mom pulled up at the library, Jethro let out a long, soft sigh. Fumbling, he had to use two hands to open the door.

"Wait for me," Janey reminded him.

"Remember what I said," Mom reminded Sarah.

And there they were, Sarah and Jethro and Janey, walking into the Ashbury Library on a Wednesday afternoon when the place was swarming with kids of all ages.

Sarah saw and was seen by two girls from her homeroom. They stared at Jethro. Sarah surged ahead of him, anxious to get away from prying glances. She hurried to the children's room, where Jethro, enthralled, kept stopping and exclaiming. To Sarah's embarrassment grown-ups turned to smile at him. She supposed they guessed he was a foreigner.

When eventually she was able to drag him away, they went to the main desk to ask where books on the Massachusetts Bay Colony could be found. The librarian asked what specific subject they were interested in.

"King Philip's War," Jethro answered.

"Witchcraft," Sarah declared.

The librarian sent them downstairs to the nonfiction room. She told them the numbers they needed to look for there. Janey dropped her books. As they knelt to retrieve them, the two girls from Sarah's class swung by. "Hi," one of them said to Sarah.

"Hi," Sarah mumbled from the floor.

"Hi, Grissom," the other called back over her shoulder. Grissom. Not Gruesome.

Downstairs Jethro was bowled over by the number of big volumes. "How can you ever read them all?" he asked Sarah.

"You can't. No one does. Unless," she added, "you're an historian."

"If I stay here," Jethro told her, "I'll read every one." He took a book at random and opened it. Then he exclaimed, "Oh, look!"

Sarah stepped close enough to see pictures of an old-fashioned locomotive, an oxcart, and a stagecoach. She reminded him that he had come to find out about King Philip, not to read about transportation.

"But I know these things," he blurted. "It's good to see them." Then, a little regretfully, he shelved the book and moved on with her. "Some mornings," he said, "I wake up wondering . . . hoping it was a dream. You can't imagine what it's like to be a stranger."

"Yes, I can," Sarah told him. But could she compare moving to Ashbury with being thrust through time into another century? "I told you," she said, "I ran away. Just for a few days."

"But it makes no sense. You have a family."

Sarah nodded. And then she found herself telling Jethro that her father had been killed, his car rammed by a drunken driver.

"What was he like?" Jethro asked.

But Sarah had only Brad's recollections. And Mom's.

"So we have something in common," Jethro declared. "I did not know my father, either. Or," he added, "if I did, I didn't know that he was my father. But my mother is as real to me now as on the night I was taken from her."

"Why didn't she try to escape with you?"

"There was another child. A smaller boy. He was not allowed in the house, but she could see him from time to time. She would never leave him." Jethro paused. "If I had known then how soon all the slaves would go free, I might not . . ." He shook his head. After a moment he finished his statement another way. "I wonder what it would be like to know what will happen a few years ahead."

Sarah almost told him then and there about the woman's dream she had read about, the foretelling. What stopped her were the final words about the seasons being changed and time inverted. He might take them as a clue to the way through time, not some ordinary superstition.

She found the other history section the librarian had mentioned and picked out a book on witches. She looked in the index under "crows." Nothing. Then she tried "familiars." That was better. She saw something about toads and a great deal about cats, especially black ones. Then, finally, she came to one short paragraph about birds. Crows were traditional familiars because they were black and clever and associated with death. She read on. Some people believed that animals were put under spells by witches; others, that they were demons in the shape of animals to do the devil's work. Still others thought witches could themselves become animals.

Janey shoved a book at her. "Will you read this to me?"

"Tonight," Sarah promised. "Right now I have to work." She opened another book. It had disgusting pictures in it, torture things and gallows. She exchanged it for a more modern-looking book.

Jethro came toward her with a book open before him. "How will I find out about King Philip's son?" he asked her.

"Look in the back." She showed him the index, but there was no reference to King Philip's son.

"King Philip was a great chief," Jethro told her. "His Indian name was Metacom. He waged a hard campaign against the white settlers. When they killed him, they stuck his head on a pole. People came to look at it."

Sarah gulped. "Civilized people did that?"

Jethro nodded. "I wish I could find a picture of him."

Sarah helped him look, but none was to be found, at least nothing that could be called a reliable portrait. Sarah told Jethro he could borrow the book and finish reading all about the war.

"Will they let me?"

"You'll have to get a card at the desk."

He scowled. "How is that done?"

"Just tell them where you live. They'll give you one. You have to be sure to get the book back on time, or you'll be fined."

"I have to go to the bathroom," Janey said. She was getting tired of looking at books that no one would read to her. Sarah glanced at the clock. Telling Jethro she'd be right back, she took Janey to the women's room, where she again ran into the girls from her class.

"Who's the cute guy?" one of them asked Sarah.

Cute guy. For a split second Sarah was struck dumb. "Jethro Philips," she said. "He's a neighbor." She yanked Janey out and along to the stairs as fast as she could. "Don't tell Jethro," she warned Janey. "Don't tell him what those girls said." Cute. And there was Jethro hoping he would come across a picture of himself in the person of the great rebel chief Metacom, who called himself King Philip and had a war named after him.

Jethro was sitting on the floor, the book about Massachusetts Indians off to the side, another, smaller book clutched so tightly in his hands that his knuckles had gone white. He seemed to be in a trance. When Janey went running over to him, he held the book up. It was one of those Sarah had rejected because it was old and had funny print.

"It's the same book!" he exclaimed.

"The same as what?"

"One I already read. Before. At the millhouse."

"That just means it must have been written a long time ago. There are probably newer, better ones."

"But this is it!" he nearly shouted at her. "The very one."

"Listen, Jethro." She lowered her voice, hoping to tone him down. All she needed was to have those girls hear him ranting like this. "There are lots of copies of every book that gets published. Even this library has more than one of some books that are very popular."

He opened the book to the flyleaf. "Look," he directed.

She saw a very long title and no author's name. The paper was thick and yellowed, but not brittle. Opposite the title page was the flowing script he pointed to: "Given to the people of Ashbury in memory of my husband John Lockwood who abhorred slavery and labored for the freedom and dignity of all human beings. Nancy Green Lockwood, July 9, 1864." Sarah took the book from Jethro. It seemed to be all about laws against the Quakers and other dissidents in colonial New England. Sarah found a publishing date: 1837.

"We'll borrow it," she said. "For both of us."

Jethro nodded. "You will read it in the house where I first read it."

At the circulation desk he seemed surprisingly poised and not the least bit nervous about answering questions. Yes, he lived in town. With Mrs. Costa on Mill Road. No, he could not say how long. Yes, an indefinite period of time. The librarian sensed that he was unaccustomed to the procedure and perhaps to the language as well. She watched him sign his name with small, deliberate sweeps. She was extremely polite, and he responded with the distant civility of a king or the descendant of a king.

Fortunately he spoke little, only inclining his head as he thanked the librarian and gathered up his books. Sarah, conscious that his quiet dignity could be interpreted as craziness if he disclosed the reason for his noble manner, prayed that no one from school showed up. In a minute or so they would be out of the library and, if she was lucky, running to Mom's car waiting for them on the road.

CHAPTER 25

From the Shadows

On Thursday afternoon Roger stopped outside Sarah's door, which she had left ajar, and remarked, "Your friend Jethro has quite a mechanical knack."

Sarah, lying on her stomach, pulled the pillow over the book Jethro had found at the library. "Why? What did he do?"

"Tricks, like how to keep the flow steady. We're running water through the race now. Did you know he's asked for a job at the mill?"

Sarah mumbled into her pillow that she guessed so. If she kept quiet, maybe Roger would go away before he began wondering about Jethro's schooling.

"What I can't figure out," Roger continued, "is where he picked it up. You don't learn about nineteenth-century milling practices at the vo-tech high school."

"Daddy," Linda wailed from somewhere downstairs.

"Dad!" Janey called up to him. "Can Linda put something on her face?"

Groaning, Roger departed. Sarah heaved a sigh of relief and shoved the pillow aside. The book was frustrating. So much of it was about colonial laws, and the strange spelling slowed Sarah down. Then all at once she would come across something out of a court record that she almost recognized. One man, about to be hanged for a witch, hurled a last defiant warning: His accusers, who thought they would be rid of him, would see "strange things."

Sarah thought of the day Margaret Bredcake died. If Zerobabel really believed that the black catamount on the milldam was her spirit and that it remained in the water, Sarah could see how he might regard the pond as cursed. First the catamount, then Mercy, the witch's child. Would he have wrecked the dam to cleanse the place of its curse? Would he have had the water run unchecked to keep it from gathering its evil power once more? If only all the answers to these questions could be found in a book.

At least Sarah was beginning to understand how believable it all was. Prisoners who were ordered released but who couldn't pay for their keep remained captives till they died. One woman sold herself as an indentured servant to get out. Mercy would have remained in prison indefinitely if her uncle Zerobabel had not paid the prison lodging cost for mother and child and the price of the leg irons and handcuffs. That was how he could lay claim to the mill and bind Mercy in servitude. Believable, all believable.

But no book could tell Sarah what those months in prison were like. What did Mercy see and hear? And smell? What did she feel? And what were those dreams that Jethro spoke of that sustained her and later haunted her?

Sarah kept trying to figure it out. If Mercy spent months in leg irons and handcuffs lying in unimaginable filth, she must have been skin and bones and probably covered with sores. And she would be unaccustomed to strong light, to any light. Maybe her aunt cleaned her up before Zerobabel set eyes on her. Then when did Mercy see King Philip's son? Before or after she was made presentable?

Sarah stood up. Staring down at the books strewn on her bed, she was amazed that they had brought her this far, that they could help her rearrange pieces of the scrambled puzzle Jethro had presented to her.

"You've spent the whole afternoon up here," Roger said in passing. "Is anything wrong?"

She shook her head. She couldn't tell him that she was searching for a person she sort of knew but had never seen. Now that she could feel herself drawn into Mercy's life, it almost seemed as though she and Jethro were changing places. But Sarah couldn't let him stray too far. He was still the only one who could supply more of the missing pieces of the puzzle. Tomorrow after school she'd get him alone.

But it was a struggle to divert his attention from the mill-works, especially since Sarah couldn't mention Mercy in front of the grown-ups.

Mom noticed. "Did you and Jethro have some kind of quarrel?"

"No. Why?"

"You seemed so easy with each other on Wednesday. Then Roger says you spent all yesterday afternoon in your room."

They watched Jethro lean into the wheel pit to help Frenchy with some adjustment. Jethro's oak-leaf skin shone in the late, low sun. Here he was, absorbed in the present, which was just what Sarah had urged on him, and here was Sarah pursuing lives that had no more substance than the presences that might or might not haunt the millpond.

She couldn't help herself. She had to know more about Mercy and her mother. Not as actors in an old blurred movie, nor as characters in a rambling, disconnected story. Sarah needed to penetrate the blur and raise them from the shadows, if only to have their story finished, to lay Mercy to rest.

"You've been reading a lot," Mom continued. "Is it for your report?"

Sarah nodded. She had forgotten about it again, and it was due at the end of next week.

On the bus on Monday, rehearsing excuses, she decided to switch her report to the mill, since it was occupying her family's every waking moment. By the time she got to school, she had convinced herself that she would have no trouble convincing Mrs. Segal.

"It's not ready," she said lamely when she failed to produce an outline. If she spouted the mill-as-history excuse, all the kids would take it as showing off. "I changed what I'm doing," she added.

"You need permission to change your subject. Don't you think it's a little late in the day to start something new?"

Sarah had no answer. No one had called her Gruesome lately. A couple of kids had even spoken to her across the lunch table. She wasn't about to spoil all that now.

It wasn't until she was home again that it hit her that she really was committed to starting a new project. She had no idea how to begin. Besides, she couldn't keep her mind on anything but Mercy.

"Dad says, can you watch Linda and me?" Janey stood at Sarah's door.

"Since she's in the house anyway," Roger prompted from downstairs.

"Since you're in the house anyway," Janey dutifully repeated.

Sarah yelled to Roger that she had to work on her overdue report.

"They can watch the tube. Please, Sarah. Liz couldn't come today, but I waited around. Please. I've got to get to the mill."

"Okay, okay," Sarah replied. He had to be desperate to allow daytime television.

"Will you play with us?" Janey asked.

"I have to work. Go feed the crow."

"I did. He won't eat."

Sarah swiveled around in the chair. "How come? Is he sick again?"

"I don't know," Janey answered. "No one has time to take him to the doctor."

"Let me work for a while," Sarah said. "Then I'll come look at him."

Satisfied, Janey went downstairs to Linda. She asked only twice whether the hour was over. Finally Sarah gave up and joined the little ones.

The crow did look unwell. Some of his feathers stuck up at odd angles. The purple gloss around his neck was gone. It gave Sarah a queasy feeling to see him so wasted and dull. If he died, would she be losing another clue in her search for Mercy?

Sarah took a pail, a spoon for Linda, a ladle for Janey, and a shovel for herself and led them out to dig for worms. On the sheltered side of the retaining wall where Mom and Roger had planted bulbs last fall and where jonquil and daffodil buds nodded on bendy stalks, Sarah dislodged the spongy leaf mold. Janey collected the insects they uncovered, but Linda refused to share her worms. Still, there was no shortage.

Sarah was gathering up utensils when she became aware of a man standing near the mudroom door. He seemed to be waiting for them, expecting them.

"Hi," Sarah said as they approached. She guessed he was one of the people examining the shop site. "Are you looking for Roger? He's in the mill."

The man shook his head. "Just taking a break."

Sarah wondered whether she should invite him in. It was the sort of thing Mom and Roger always did. She tried to calculate how long Roger was likely to be gone.

"Hi, Jane," the man said as Janey stood to one side of him, stock-still.

Then again, thought Sarah, there was that rule about strangers. Or was he a stranger if he already knew Janey? Come to think of it, his voice did have a familiar ring.

All at once the queasiness hit Sarah again. The voice she almost recognized insinuated itself into her head. She had to shake it, to shake off the notion that this was the man who had invaded the game of territory.

"Come on," she said to the girls. "We should get these things to Barker before they crawl away." She had to prod Janey to get her moving again.

Inside, she asked Janey who the man was.

"What man?" Janey said. She handed a worm to the crow. He blinked and cocked his head but wouldn't take it from her.

The child hopes she is not dreaming. The crow seems to be bringing her an apple with a speckled green skin. A whole little apple. Her mouth waters. But just as the apple descends, the coiled peel stretches and sags. An empty apple after all. Still, it is moist, and it bears a cidery tang. The child bites off a full circle of peel and nods toward Mamma. The crow hops from one to the other. It dangles the remaining peel over the woman's face. The child can almost see Mamma as she once leaned over the scrawny nestling that was all mouth and eyes, Mamma guiding a worm down its gaping craw. This is not a dream; it is a memory from before the darkness. Now it is Mamma and Mercy who must be fed. They turn their eyes to the tiny square of light through which another peel may be delivered. They are the nestlings now, without arms or legs, grotesque and helpless.

Sarah tried everything they had dug up and a variety of leftovers from the refrigerator. The only thing the crow would eat was the special cheese Mom bought direct from a goat farm. After downing most of it, the crow drank some water.

"Progress!" Sarah exclaimed. But Janey still looked worried.

Supper that night ended up being cold cereal and milk because all the leftovers had been messed with and picked over. Mom and Roger were so wound up about the mill and shop that they barely complained. They had just learned that the archaeologists were almost done at the site.

"What exactly are they looking for?" Sarah asked.

"I guess they're hoping to come across a date or a name. The engineer won't let them move those stones that lead to the bulwark."

"You mean there might be a name on one of them?"

"In the early days," Mom told her, "people put names and dates on things they made—doorframes, spinning wheels, whatever. Sometimes they'd add a line from the Bible or a dedication."

"Would they maybe leave a message?"

"Who knows?" Roger answered. "It would be great to find anything at all, but I'll be glad when this delay is over. By the way," he added, "do you know why Jethro's been out of school this week?"

Sarah shrugged. Jethro needed another warning.

That night Sarah awoke with a start, certain that the crow had let out one of its piercing squawks. "No, no," she heard. The cry came from across the hall. Sarah sprang out of bed and flung open her door. Mom and Roger were ahead of her, the light already on in Janey's room.

"It's all right, sweetie," Roger was saying. "You were having a bad dream."

Janey wrenched herself from side to side, her braids flapping, her dark eyes looking somehow bruised in her swollen face. Mom had to fight to quiet her.

"Get away," Janey screamed, "get away."

Mom, looking stricken, glanced up, but when she started to pull back, Janey clutched at her.

"Hold on, Molly," Roger said to Mom. "It could be a flashback. She doesn't know what she's saying."

Standing in the doorway, Sarah couldn't help wondering whether Janey did know. What had brought on this nightmare? Sarah had a feeling that if only she could think back clearly, she would find the answer. She stayed there until Janey began to calm down. Mom was rocking her now.

Sarah turned and went back to bed.

CHAPTER 26

Stranded

S aturday morning Sarah was out of the house before anyone else was up. The woods were awash with early light.
Tree swallows swooped before her, some of them carrying tiny
green shoots in their beaks. Jethro was surprised to find her
out already. He greeted her cheerfully and seemed unaware
that he had been ignoring her.

"You'd better be ready for some questions," she told him.
"Roger wants to know why you haven't been in school this
week."

"We're so busy just now," Jethro replied, "I don't think
he'll bother about it until after we have the mill running."

We. Already Jethro regarded himself as part of the team.
He sounded as though he didn't need Sarah anymore.

"I've been reading those books," she began tentatively.
"What about you? Did you find anything?"

He nodded. "But nothing especially useful."

It occurred to her that she and Mercy were more or less on
the same side now. "I've been wondering about her," Sarah
said.

"About Mercy?"

"Who else do you know?" Sarah snapped.

"You are cross with me?"

"Jethro," she said, trying to put a lid on her temper, trying to bring him back to what they shared, "I keep telling you. You're too smart about mills, and you're there too much. And you can't level with them the way you did me."

"I have been watching people come and go," he told her. "Where the shop is to be. I have been there, too," he added, "in the early morning. Looking. I am very careful." He brushed his hand across his eyes. It was the first time she had seen this gesture in weeks, as though he were trying to sweep confusion aside.

Suppressing a twinge of guilt, Sarah pressed her advantage, asking him what the Lockwoods had thought when Mercy first showed up.

"They were used to people who were frightened or hurt," he replied. "And angry. Mercy seemed a bit like one of those fugitive slaves they hid. They could tell that she was desperate and—and other things."

"And you could see that, too?"

Again his fingers swept his face, clearing memory. "Yes." Then he said, "You know, since first coming into your time, I have not seen so well as before. I am more used to it now, though. I'm seeing better."

It crossed her mind that what clouded his vision might simply be pollution, but she knew he was speaking of his own bewilderment, too. Even though he noticed that his vision was adjusting, he didn't seem to realize how much he had already changed. Would his recollections fade as he lived more and more in the present?

"Tell me what Mercy was really like again. When she came."

Jethro seemed to be sorting out a few clear images from a

jumble of memories. "In the kitchen," he began. "At first I thought she was teasing me. Then her face went dark, and I thought how like a witch she looked with her long black hair and wild eyes. Those eyes—"

"What?" Sarah pleaded. "Say it."

"Something about them was terribly old. She looked like one who has walked through fire and bears its scars." His voice dropped. "Yet something else in her eyes was childlike. That was what helped me to believe her. And even so it took time. And she was the most impatient person I have ever known. There was an old millstone here that Mercy said was from a pair used in her time. She tried so hard to find the other one that matched it. She said it was proof, it would make me believe."

"Did she tell you everything? Did she tell you what it was like after prison?"

Jethro eyed Sarah. "I have told you. You know that at first Mercy's aunt tried to ease things for her. That Mercy was wayward, stubborn."

"And all through those years? Jethro, there must be so much more."

"Haven't I told enough? It is all said. How when she revived a downed ox or a half-frozen lamb her uncle called it sorcery. How he charged that only a witch would have a crow for a pet. And the rest, all the rest, I do not want to talk about. All you need to know is that it got worse, until she taunted him. Until she challenged him to try her."

"And that's when he had her thrown in the millpond?"

Jethro nodded.

"And there was a hailstorm?"

"Sudden, yes, like the tempest that came with Margaret Bredcake's death. Zerobabel declared that only a witch could raise such a storm. She does not think he meant to drown her. He believed she would float, proving that she possessed unnatural powers."

"Well, she did," Sarah pointed out. "She escaped him. She came through time."

> *She grows crafty. She averts her eyes and practices the art of escape. Once, when he comes upon her by herself and pulls her inside the mill, she sees again with the eyes of her child self how he yanked her mother out of the cellar and kicked the door shut after him. How later Mamma returned but was not there. Then, when he falls to his knees and cries out against bedevilment, she laughs with a voice as harsh as the crow's. And the dreams come again, the old dreams of running and running.*

"Then what unnatural power did Zerobabel possess that he could seek her out in a later time in the person of the stone-picker?"

"Maybe," Sarah suggested haltingly, "he didn't. Maybe it was the stone-picker's cruelty that made her think of her uncle."

"Yes," Jethro said, "I did consider that. But he was the same, don't you see?"

Sarah didn't see, but she kept her reservations to herself. "Was she thin?" she went on.

"What?"

"Was Mercy very thin? One book on witchcraft said that in the water tests the thin ones usually sank and the fat ones floated."

"She was about my height," Jethro said. "Her bones showed. Her ankles and wrists had a knobby look. I think it was from the irons."

"Do you think she could have lived a long life? In your time."

"I don't know. Yes, maybe so, if she could feel safe." Jethro sounded drained. "I did not want her to pass me by. She was just beginning to trust . . . to be happy. We believed we would be lifelong friends." He glanced toward the mill.

Sarah wished she could offer him some kind of assurance, some comfort. "Maybe something will turn up," she suggested. "So that you'll know for sure." But he already knew that Mercy was out of her own time, like him. Stranded.

He refused to meet Sarah's eyes. He only said as he walked past her to the mill, "Mercy never found the second millstone."

Later, when Roger brought him back from the mill for lunch, Sarah hoped to get some time alone with him. But Janey made him come to her room to see a puppet show. Sarah went along, asking in an undertone about Mercy's meeting with King Philip's son.

"No fair talking," Janey pronounced from the back of the theater.

"People always talk during intermissions," Sarah told her.

"Intermissions are rude," Janey flatly stated.

"You mean interruptions," Sarah informed her.

"Oh. Anyway, I'm nearly ready."

"When you start, we'll be quiet," Sarah promised. She turned to Jethro. "I can't picture her actually meeting him."

"When Mercy's mother died," Jethro told Sarah, "Mercy was left in the dungeon awhile. Mercy has no idea how long. Afterward she learned from her aunt that Zerobabel was at the mill then, overseeing the man who ran it for him. Then there was the tempest and the great black cat. He believed Margaret Bredcake's spirit refused to depart the mill."

"If he really believed that," Sarah remarked, "I should think he would have stayed as far away from the mill as he could."

"He had already moved his household from Connecticut to Plymouth and was making arrangements to move once again to Ashbury. Don't forget he was a man with a mission. He was raised to believe that he was born to lead the war against the devil. Anyway, Mercy's aunt told her that he had her moved to Plymouth jail. She remained there until he gained title to the mill and millhouse."

"And that's where she saw the chief's son? In Plymouth?"

"I think so. He was nine or ten years old. No one would have anything to do with her then. After all those months confined, she must have looked like a half-dead animal, something you might turn over with your foot. Only the Indian boy seemed to regard her as human. They met child to child."

"How come they were allowed to be together?"

Jethro shook his head. "I only know that he tried to help her and that he let her see his own terror. She tried to give him hope. It was much later that she learned that he was separated from his mother and sold into slavery."

"Stop telling that story," Janey said. "It's too sad."

"It is," Jethro agreed. "Will you show us a happy one?"

"I don't know how," she told him. But soon, with Sarah and Jethro egging her on, she began to play out a silly slapstick scene that made them laugh and laugh.

"What's so funny?" she asked in the midst of it.

Sarah and Jethro shrieked and howled. Amid the uproar they were called to lunch. The three of them trooped down to the kitchen still shaking and a little shaken.

It was clear that Mom and Roger were ready to accept Jethro on his own terms. Only they needed to know what those terms were. Jethro managed to dodge most of their questions by keeping his mouth full of sandwiches and beans and answering with grunts and nods. But when Roger said that he would need Jethro's Social Security number if he was going to work weekends at the mill and Jethro responded with a blank look, Sarah decided it was time to break up the party.

She pushed back her chair with much noise. "Not everyone knows things like that," she asserted.

"True," Roger said, "but we'll still need it, especially if the weekend thing turns into a real summer job."

"Summer," Sarah rejoined, "is a long way off."

And somehow, with Jethro eager to get back to the mill and Sarah already at the door, Mom and Roger let the matter drop.

CHAPTER 27

Telling

On Tuesday Sarah asked Liz point-blank what a Social Security number was and what would happen if you didn't have one.

"Everyone has one." Then Liz amended that statement. "Every citizen."

"What happens to someone who isn't?"

"You're talking about Jethro, aren't you?"

Sarah was taken aback. "How did you know?"

"It wasn't hard to guess. Am I right?"

Sarah didn't know how to respond, so she just asked Liz if she could help him.

"I can try," Liz answered. "If he wants to be helped."

Neither of them spoke for a while. Sarah felt torn. She knew she ought to consult Jethro, but she also knew that he was heading for trouble. Sarah drew a deep breath and took the plunge. "He's an escaped slave," she blurted.

"Jethro? What on earth do you mean?"

There was no stopping now. "He told me," Sarah said. "This place, the house and the mill, all of this was a station on the Underground Railroad."

Liz clapped her hands to her mouth. "Oh, Sarah." The words came out muffled. "And you believed him?"

"But that's not all. I haven't told you about the Lockwoods. You can check up on them. You probably can't with Jethro, because he was a slave, and he was born in the West Indies. But there was this girl. Her name's Mercy Bredcake. And she recognized him—"

"Hold on. Mercy *what*? Sarah, maybe you'd better begin at the beginning."

Sarah nodded. But how could she dump everything on Liz all at once? It would be hard enough to convince her about Jethro. Mercy's story would have to be set aside. "It's just that she knew someone who was related to Jethro. There was a family resemblance. That gave Jethro some idea of who he was. The thing is," Sarah rushed on, "what I'm trying to tell you is that Mercy was running away, too. Sort of like Jethro. The man that was after him was kind of like the man that was after her."

Frowning, Liz leaned forward. "Go on."

Sarah faltered. "Mercy was like Jethro in another way, too." But Sarah stopped short of declaring that Mercy and Jethro had come through time.

"All right, Sarah. Let me say something now." Liz smiled at her. "Abused kids very often do have a lot in common. One of those things is a need to escape into other lives."

"What do you mean? How do they do that?"

"By inventing other selves," Liz told her gently. "Other lives."

"You're saying Jethro invented Mercy?"

"I'm saying it can happen."

"Then," Sarah burst out, "who invented Jethro?"

"Try me again. I don't know what you're asking."

"Jethro is real."

"Oh, I see. Yes, of course, he is." Liz was nodding. "To some extent Jethro may have invented Jethro. Some kids, who can't bear what they've lived through, develop alternative personalities, alternative histories."

For a few seconds they sat in deep silence. What Liz said had thrown Sarah. It sounded so reasonable. Sarah groped around for all the bits of evidence she had collected: Jethro's knowledge of the mill; the Lockwoods' book; the cloak. "He can tell you so many things that are true," Sarah insisted.

"I don't doubt it. He seems extremely bright. And imaginative."

"He knows things that are in old books, in history."

"Exactly. He's probably read a great deal."

It hardly made sense to try to go on. But there was one more point that Sarah had to make, because now that she had opened up this far she needed someone older to know about it. "There's also this man. Anyway, we think—that is, Jethro thinks, and I did, too . . . Well, it might be the man that was after him. Or Mercy," Sarah couldn't help adding. She wasn't getting it right. All she could think to add was: "We don't know who this man is. Jethro can't be sure. But we've both seen him. He's . . . sort of weird." Her words trailed off.

"Did you tell your parents about this man?"

"You mean, my mother?"

"You know what I mean."

"I didn't, because I couldn't tell on Jethro."

"What about Mrs. What's-her-name down the road, where Jethro's staying? What does she know about him?"

Thinking Liz meant Jethro, Sarah said, "Mrs. Costa thinks Jethro was there last summer picking vegetables. She told me he's a transit."

Liz nodded. "I think she meant those farm workers are transients, migrants."

"Oh," said Sarah. That made more sense than his being a bus driver or something. "I'm afraid if she finds out what I told you, she'll send him away."

"Sarah, listen to me. There are ways to help a boy like Jethro, even if he's an illegal alien. But your mother and Roger have to know about him, and they have to know about the man you mentioned. And right now you need to be informed about something else they're concerned about. I wouldn't be surprised if some of it's already filtered through into . . . all this you're telling me."

"What do you mean? I haven't been eavesdropping."

"No, Sarah, but things go on in a family that aren't in the open. Let's get your mother in here. You've got to level with each other."

"No!" Sarah shouted. "I already broke my promise telling you."

"More is at stake than you realize." Liz's even tone let Sarah know she was in deadly earnest. "It's not up to me to explain. I'm calling Molly."

After Liz went downstairs, Sarah could hear muted voices. Then Mom and the little ones came clattering up to Mom's room. The television was turned on loud.

Liz came in and sat down on Sarah's bed. Then Mom walked in, shut the door, and leaned against it. "This will have to be quick," she said. "Linda's on a rampage. I had to give her a bureau drawer to unload."

"As I said downstairs," Liz began quietly, "there're developments you need to know about, Molly. They involve bringing Sarah up-to-date about Janey. That's long overdue."

Mom straightened. She glanced from Liz to Sarah and then back to Liz. "We agreed."

"We did. Now she needs to know."

Mom walked over to the window and half sat on the sill. Facing Sarah, she said, "When Janey came to us, there were things about her that were so . . . disturbing we decided not to tell you until you were older. We would have told you this year. Only you started acting . . . acting out. After what happened in December, we put it off."

"So what is it?" Sarah asked shortly.

"Janey was . . . When she came to us, she had been . . . injured. She was abused. Severely abused."

Sarah had to force the words up from her clenched throat. "How could you not tell me?"

"We were trying to do what was best for Janey. Everyone on the case thought she had a better chance if you kids saw her on more or less equal terms."

"You mean, Brad didn't know either?"

"No one knew."

"Not even Janey," Liz put in.

"What does that mean?" Sarah demanded.

"She doesn't seem to remember. Not yet. She isn't ready to deal with any of it."

"Mom! Mommy!" Janey was calling from Mom's room. "Can Linda get in your bed?"

"Yes, all right, honey."

Sarah turned to Liz. "What happened to her?"

"A lot. She was either kept in a closet or tied to her baby brother's crib. All the time. They were malnourished, filthy, and physically abused. I think you did know that Janey's mother's in prison."

Sarah nodded. She had never even bothered to ask about her.

"Her boyfriend is serving an even longer sentence. But not Janey's father. When the children were picked up, he was away. There was no evidence to convict him, only Janey's mother's claim that he was the primary abuser. A few weeks ago he petitioned for custody of Janey."

Sarah tried furiously to fight back tears, but they came dribbling down her face anyway. "I knew it." She felt as though she were choking. "I knew something was wrong."

Mom held out her arms to Sarah, who pulled back and shook her head. "No. I want to understand." But the truth was that she would have given anything to be ignorant again.

Mom said, "Janey's father wanted to come here, to see her. We had to get a restraining order to keep him away. The Department of Social Services backed us up."

"She was afraid," Sarah said. "That time Roger yelled at you, she was afraid he'd hurt Linda."

Liz stood up. "She could fear for Linda, but not for herself. Not directly."

"Maybe," Mom suggested, "she remembers about her little brother."

"What happened to him?" Sarah asked. "Why doesn't she ever see him?"

"He died," Liz told her. "Both children were in terrible shape. He was just a baby. He was too far gone."

Wolves surround a deer caught in the deep snow.
Howling. The child invokes that scene to keep her
from the waking dark, where there is also howling.
She knows she is being punished for some
unspeakable wrong. That is why Mamma howls like
the wolves and never, ever holds Mercy in her arms.
When the howling ceases at last, there is a blessed
silence. Soon, thinks Mercy, Mamma will croon to her,
Poor dear. Then the dream will come again on wings
as black as night. Mamma is only a breath away.

"Mommy!" Janey yelled again.

"I'll be there in a minute," Mom called out to her. And to

Sarah she added, "There's something else. I hate telling you without Roger being here, but I think you ought to know that we've filed for adoption."

Sarah was stunned. "To keep her father away?"

"Not just that. We can't imagine losing her now. I wish you didn't have to learn about it this way."

They could hear Linda beginning to protest and then wail.

Mom said, "I have to see to those girls." As she headed for the door, she suddenly remembered that Sarah had something to tell her. She asked Sarah to save it for later. "Or else tell Roger. I think that's his car coming now." She was out of the room. Sarah heard her exclaim as she entered her own, and then there were peals of laughter from one or both of the little ones.

"How can people do things like that?" Sarah whispered.

"One reason," Liz answered, "is that the abused often grow into abusers."

"Then how can it ever be stopped?" Sarah cried.

"People can change and be changed," Liz answered. "I wouldn't be here if I didn't believe that. Someone caring can help the change to happen. You can help. You've been doing that already. With Janey. With Jethro."

"Hey," Roger called from below, "where is everyone? Molly? Liz? Kids?"

Sarah tried to answer him, but her voice failed. "No," she muttered, shaking her head in misery. "I had it all wrong." But did she have Jethro wrong, too? "So who do you think Jethro really is?" she asked Liz.

Liz smoothed her skirt and walked to the door. "I think he probably is Janey's alien. Only not from outer space. I also think he's been badly treated. I can imagine a situation that was for Jethro like slavery. People are capable of terrible things. But they're also capable of great good. Like those who helped slaves to freedom. And look at your mother and Roger. Unless you recognize the good as well as the bad, you aren't facing the reality about people."

Sarah nodded. It was beginning to dawn on her that every single person possessed a hidden history. Here was calm, levelheaded Liz whose weekly visits for the sake of one foster child had become a kind of lifeline for Sarah as well. Yet Sarah knew nothing at all about Liz. She couldn't begin to picture her at five or twelve. How then could Liz know so much about other people? Even when she was just guessing and might be wrong, she understood far more than Sarah could extract from those books about people in the past, more than she could ever hope to learn about a seventeenth-century child named Mercy Bredcake.

"Jethro needs—" Sarah had to start over. "He needs me to believe him."

"To believe him or to understand him?"

Sarah was stumped. After a moment she said, "I'm not good at understanding. I didn't guess about Janey. I didn't guess anything."

"It's especially hard with people who bury part of themselves or who put on disguises, wear masks."

"You mean Jethro?"

"Janey, too. But the day will come when she doesn't feel she has to be the good little girl anymore. It won't be easy, or pleasant. Anger never is. She'll put you all to the test."

"What do you mean?" Sarah felt herself bristling. "What test?"

"She could go to the opposite extreme and make it hard for you to love her."

Sarah thought of Mercy raging against her uncle. "But what about Jethro?" she heard herself wondering out loud. Now that he was growing used to this time, he was becoming so cool. Was that a cover, too? Is that what Liz meant about understanding him? How could Sarah look beneath the surface if Jethro wouldn't let her?

Liz said, "If I'm going to help him, he'll have to provide some information about himself."

Sarah didn't reply. What was the use? The information Jethro could supply was unacceptable.

"Don't worry," Liz went on. "Many of the kids I work with can't tell me much. Molly and Roger will help. Only right now they have to concentrate on Janey."

Sarah nodded. "And the mill starting."

Liz smiled. "That, too. But it's not the same kind of concentration."

Sarah could tell that Liz needed to wrap things up. "But if you're right about Jethro," she asked, "if he's making all this up because he's had such a bad time, then what will happen if he grows up believing his . . ." She almost said "memory," but to avoid argument, she finished with "story?"

"I doubt that will happen," Liz told her. "But even if it does, his story probably incorporates exploitation, abuse, so in a way he is already dealing with it." Liz fished her car keys out of her purse.

"Wait," Sarah begged. "One more thing." She could feel Liz poised to leave. "What's to keep him from growing up like Janey's parents?"

"I told you before. You and I. Jethro himself. Ask Roger," Liz suggested. "He's a perfect example of the cycle interrupted."

Sarah stared at her. What did Roger have to do with any of this?

But Liz was on her way now. So Sarah was left with another puzzle. Roger an example. Of what?

CHAPTER 28

In the Dark

Liz must have had a word with Roger on her way out because he confronted Sarah on the stairs, forcing her to tell him about the strange man. Standing above Roger, Sarah stared at his shiny head while she tried to think of the wheres and whens he demanded to know.

"But we can't tell for sure that he's Janey's father," Sarah said.

Roger muttered something. Then he asked, "What did Jethro think?"

"We both guessed he must be one of the inspectors. But he reminded Jethro of someone—someone else he didn't want to think about."

"Right. Jethro could tell."

"What do you mean? How do you know what Jethro could tell?"

Roger's head tilted back. The light glanced off his glasses. "I mean, I'm beginning to get a feeling about him, that's all."

Sarah wheeled and stumbled back up the stairs and into her room.

Later she tried to get a moment with her mother, but a hundred things prevented her. They began with Linda and Janey and multiplied at the mill with all its last-minute preparations. It didn't matter whether Sarah pushed forward or hung back. She couldn't understand a word of the strange language that included words like *flutter wheels* and *trundles* and *wallowers*. It didn't help that Jethro was at the center of the talk, resetting the shaker spout, whatever that was, and warning Roger and Ken not to run the grinding surfaces too open, or they would jam and tear off the drive belt.

Wednesday afternoon Sarah had been on the sidelines watching for some time when her mother suddenly latched on to her and drew her aside. "I need to count on you Saturday. It's going to be crazy around here."

Sarah said yes without bothering to ask what she was being counted on for.

Her mother checked something off on her list. "That reminds me," she added. "I asked Marty, the local historian, about the mill fire, and she actually came across a follow-up article. There may have been foul play after all. If her hunch is right, it all fits into your report."

"How? What do you mean? Why didn't you tell me?"

"It slipped my mind. I'm telling you now. The day of the fire there was a man here who people suspected. But the miller was reluctant to help the authorities. Marty came up with the idea that the miller had something to hide. Marty was here when Frenchy pried open the stone door thing. One peek into that little chamber was all it took to find a reason for the miller's caution. He didn't want to blow his cover, if that's where fugitive slaves were hidden. His connection with the Underground Railroad would've been more important than the mill."

"So what happened to the man?" Sarah exclaimed.

"The *man*? I thought you'd be ecstatic about this theory of Marty's."

"I am, yes." Sarah could hardly summon the expected enthusiasm when she was so close to finding out what she and Jethro needed to know.

"Marty said to be sure you understood it's just an educated guess. You can ask her about it on Saturday. All of the people who have been involved in this project will be here then, even though no one wants to risk probing any deeper inside that chamber, which is full of rubble. And don't forget I'm counting on you to keep a close eye on Janey. And not just Saturday. Until we close the Brookline store for good and we're both here full-time, we have to be really careful about strangers."

"When the new shop's open," Sarah pointed out, "there will be strangers all the time."

"I know. But we'll have this thing settled by then. Just stay alert."

Sarah wished she could recall exactly how Janey had reacted when the man spoke to her. She hadn't, though. "What man?" she had replied. Only that wasn't all, either. There had been the nightmare that same night. It all came together now.

Wednesday noon Janey met Sarah at the door with the news that Barker wouldn't open his eyes.

"Mom will take him to the bird doctor," Sarah told her.

Janey shook her head. "She hasn't time."

Sarah found Mom in the bathroom with Linda on the potty. Sarah summoned an indignant tone. Why wouldn't Mom try to save the crow?

Mom sat on the edge of the bathtub. "I can't," she said. "I can't do everything. I can't keep a bird alive if it's dying of old age."

"Maybe he needs some medicine," Sarah suggested.

Linda said, "All done."

Mom looked and said, "No, you're not. Don't you want to?"

"Water," Linda demanded.

Sarah felt like shouting at her mother. If she couldn't cope with all these things, she shouldn't have babies and foster kids. But Mom looked so close to tears that Sarah couldn't say a word. So she left Mom where she had found her, trapped in the bathroom with a not quite two-year-old who had figured out how to get Mom all to herself for a good long while.

"Ask Jethro to fix Barker," Janey said to Sarah when she came down.

"Jethro won't know how."

"Maybe Mercy told him. She fixed sick animals," Janey reminded her.

"All right," Sarah agreed. "I'll ask him. But you stay here."

"I'm coming, too."

"No!" Sarah didn't want to have to worry about her. She didn't want to be in charge. Quickly she left the house and set off for the mill.

Before she reached the road, she heard Janey pounding after her. Sarah spun around. "Go right back," she commanded. "Mom doesn't know you're out."

Janey halted beside the forsythia, her knapsack hanging from her arm. "I told her I was going with you." She backed under the looping sprays of yellow blossoms and planted herself in their midst, her black eyebrows beetling defiantly. Yellow and gray warblers flitted nervously among the flowering branches. In that seething, noisy brightness, only Janey was still as though rooted. For a split second Sarah thought: Mercy.

Flinging back her hair, she casts off a shower of milkweed seeds. She also casts off the thought of her uncle's hand. Then she runs. She does not think where, until she recalls that long-ago dream from when she was so small. In this direction Papa drops

to his heels to catch her up. Here he is, with flour
dusting his eyebrows and blotching his face. He
straightens her blue garland and sweeps her off to the
pond. And she is safe, safe. She trusts the water with
the sky in it and the forget-me-nots whose tiny eyes
are made from the sun.

Sarah reached out. Janey ran to her and slipped her hand
in Sarah's.

Frenchy and Ken were lolling in the sun, still on their lunch
break. Jethro had borrowed their flashlight to have a look inside the shop's cellar hole. Sarah and Janey went off to find
him.

But the excavated hole was empty, except for a ladder tilted
up to them. Sarah looked doubtfully at Janey.

"I can do it," Janey declared. "I already went with
Mommy."

Once down there, Sarah could clearly see the upright stones
that looked like doorjambs and the massive capstone, the outer
edge of which rested on the uprights, the rest of it deeply
embedded in subsoil.

The door slab scraped over loose pebbles. Sarah yanked
Janey back, but this was no quake or avalanche, just Jethro
squirming through the narrow opening like an earthworm. He
brushed the dirt from his hair, his dark eyes suffused with
excitement. "It's there!" he rasped. "The millstone! In that
same room with the shelf. It must have been nearby all the
time. Maybe Mr. Lockwood used it as a building stone. It's
broken. It must have tumbled loose when the dam caved in."

"Can I see it?" Sarah asked him.

"What about Barker?" Janey reminded her.

"In a minute," Sarah told her. To Jethro she said, "Show
me."

Sarah led the way, with Janey following and Jethro behind

to light the passage. Sarah was fine until she felt herself blocked by the unyielding edge of stone. Puffing and grunting, she clawed at raw dirt that crumbled in her hands. "Can't it open wider?" she gasped.

Reaching past Janey, Jethro shoved Sarah's rear end, making her lose her grip on another jutting slab.

"No!" she bellowed, her protest muffled as she tumbled down. She hadn't expected the floor on the other side to be lower. But she turned in time to catch Janey, who was just wriggling through, the knapsack nearly snagged behind her. Jethro, who had worked out a system for himself, slipped through with his body angled.

The sound of the falls came to them as a hushed rumble. No other sound penetrated. Sarah could taste the stale, motionless air.

Jethro played the beam of light over the jumbled rocks they faced. All at once it illumined a man-made curve, the round edge of a millstone.

"How can you be sure it's the right one?" Sarah asked him.

He knelt to pull some smaller stones aside. "If it's the bed stone, it will match the runner." Tugging and clawing, he heaved back a stone.

Janey said, "Can we go home now? Will you look at Barker?"

"Soon," Sarah promised. Then, thinking of what Liz had told her, Sarah went behind Janey and pulled her as close as the knapsack allowed. "I don't like the dark either," she whispered in Janey's ear. "We'll hold on to each other." She could feel Janey press against her.

Jethro dislodged a larger slab, but he couldn't tip it over because of one just below it. Sarah released Janey and dropped to her knees to steady the slab while Jethro lugged the blocking stone free. Several others shifted. Grabbing Janey, Jethro motioned Sarah back with the flashlight. When the rocks stopped sliding, he returned to the partially buried millstone.

"See the furrows?" With the flashlight playing on the grinding face, he traced the curving grooves. "Ours and yours are straight like spokes. Not these. They are shaped like a sickle."

"I don't want to stay here anymore," Janey said.

"We have to get Janey out of here," Sarah told him. "Bad things—"

"I know." He handed Janey the flashlight. "You light this for me."

"You can't know," Sarah insisted. Then she added, "How do you?"

Jethro grunted as he stretched, trying to dig down to the center of the stone. "She is like us," he said to Sarah.

"But she's not," Sarah argued. "Mercy was . . . fierce. Janey's good."

"I'm good mostly," Janey agreed, "but I'm not staying here."

"Of course not," Sarah agreed. "No one is."

Jethro twisted around; his arm plunged to the shoulder. "I'm at the center. There! It is the bed stone. It has no eye."

"Of course not," Janey said to him. "What's the good of an eye in the dark?"

Sarah laughed with Jethro, even though she didn't know any better than Janey what he meant by an eye. What mattered was finding this stone for Mercy's sake. Or Jethro's.

"If it's Mercy's millstone," Janey said, "then is our mill Mercy's mill?"

"In a way, yes," Jethro told her.

"But it's a secret," Sarah hastily added. "No one else knows."

Guiding Janey's hands, Jethro played the light over the rubble. What else was he looking for? Sarah wondered. Wasn't this enough? He had found what Mercy had wanted to show him, even though they could never share this discovery.

"I have to be instead of Mercy," Sarah murmured.

"What?" Jethro tumbled back another rock.

"Nothing," Sarah said to him. "Don't do that anymore. We're not supposed to move any of this stuff around."

"I'll come back later," Jethro replied. "To see if there's a way through."

"Will you think of something to make Barker better?" Janey asked.

"What?" Jethro turned from that bank of stone. "I will try."

But Sarah could tell that his mind wasn't on the crow. It was on the passageway he knew must have been blocked when the mill toppled on the dam in his own time. He hadn't seen the dam being built as Sarah had. He couldn't believe it was utterly closed. He was looking at the piled stones with the eyes of a fugitive slave. He would not give up the idea that an escape route could still be cleared.

CHAPTER 29

Holding On

When Sarah came home from school on Thursday, everyone was cleaning up around the mill. As if on cue, the daffodils began to raise their trumpet heads to the sun.

"We've closed the store till Monday," Mom told her, beaming. "There's a surprise for you. Go look on your bureau."

Sarah ran inside and stopped when she saw the crow hunched and motionless. Jethro hadn't had the slightest idea how to help him, but he'd suggested getting him out in the sun. Yet here he still was, drooping and looking half-dead.

Before she took him outside, she ran upstairs to see her surprise. It was a check, made out to the store, payment for the cloak. Even after she paid Mom back for the cleaning, Sarah would have more money than she had ever had before. Not for long, of course. Frenchy deserved something of it, but mostly it belonged to Jethro.

Back downstairs, she picked up the crow. She could feel how wasted he was, the frail bones just beneath his feathers. Every once in a while a shudder passed through him; his eyes remained shut.

"Did you find it?" Mom called as Sarah emerged from the house.

"Yes. Who bought it? Where's it going?"

"A dealer," Mom told her. "She got it for someone in Connecticut."

"Oh." That meant Sarah wasn't likely to get another look at it.

"Next week, when all this excitement is over, I'll take you to open a bank account." Mom paused. "What are you doing with the crow?"

"Putting him in the sun." Sarah set him on a stump, willing him to revive but not expecting him to. Janey came over to study him. She was dragging a sack with bits of trash in it. The sun made her squint so that she looked as though she were scowling.

At quitting time, when Ken and Frenchy were tossing stuff into the pickup, Jethro came over to tell Sarah that he had been back in the underground chamber this morning and had cleared away more rubble. Sarah reminded him that the engineer had told them to leave the stones as they were. Anyhow, first thing next week the footings would be poured for the shop, and then the foundation.

Jethro said, "I still have three more days."

What for? she felt like asking, but she didn't try to argue with him.

"When is the song?" Janey asked Jethro as she hauled her sack over to Ken and watched him pretend to struggle as he hoisted it over the side.

"What song?" Sarah said. She couldn't help smiling at Ken's antics, but Janey scarcely noticed. She still wore that worried look. Sarah glanced back at the crow on the stump. It hadn't budged, but the sun had, and now a shadow overspread it, turning the bird into a shapeless black lump.

"When the mill starts, I promised Janey she would hear the song of the damsel," Jethro told her.

Sarah, about to rescue the crow from the shade, said, "I don't get it." All she knew was that *damsel* was an old-fashioned word for maiden or girl.

"The damsel song tells you how the stones are running," Jethro explained. At her blank look he tried to show her with his hands how the damsel shakes from side to side as it feeds grain into the millstones.

"You mean, it's a part of the mill?"

"Of course," he said. "I just told you."

They confronted each other, unable to go beyond her refusal to learn about the mill and Jethro's absorption in every detail of the works.

"Then it's not a real song," Sarah concluded.

"But it is," Jethro persisted. "Janey will hear it the day after tomorrow. So," he added stiffly, "will you. If you bother to listen."

Feeling disgruntled and out of step with this Jethro, who bore little resemblance to the tense, uncertain boy she had first known, she left him and went to take the crow indoors.

Roger, on his way out of the mudroom, held the door for her. He paused to touch the crow. "Pretty limp sort of familiar," he remarked with his half smile. "Not much more than a shadow, I'm afraid."

"I wish I really was a witch," Sarah blurted. "Then I could save him."

"I know," Roger answered. "Wouldn't it be wonderful if we could magically help poor creatures like him? And people?"

What Liz had said came back to Sarah: Ask Roger . . . a perfect example . . . Sarah looked at him, just avoiding his eyes, but taking in his expression, a kind of bright energy tinged with sadness. Standing there with the crow in both her hands, she made herself face him squarely. She could see all the things about him she couldn't stand: his baldness and his small face and his funny glasses. She could also see that the sadness in him was for the crow as well as for Janey, and maybe for himself, too. She didn't need to ask him now; she understood that he had been one of those children. She didn't have to know more than that, not now, maybe ever.

Just as she managed to meet his gaze, her eyes filled with tears. One of the crow's wings slipped from her grasp and dangled as though lifeless. With his hand gently cupped, Roger folded the wing back into itself. "It's tough holding on," he said as he lifted Sarah's fingers just enough to tuck the wing back under them. "And just as tough letting go. You do all that's humanly possible, and sometimes that isn't enough. No one can change what's happened. The past is always here. But we can do something about the present and maybe about the future. Sarah?"

She couldn't think of anything to say, so she just nodded dumbly. He slipped past her and went on down the driveway. His voice, his words, stayed with her. She found herself thinking about Mercy again, Mercy holding on. Almost without Sarah's being aware of it, her thoughts switched to herself. Who was holding on now? she wondered. She continued to stand there until Janey came in behind her, buzzing with ideas for different foods to try on Barker.

But the crow wouldn't eat. When Janey gave up, Sarah escaped to her room, where she opened one of the library books, turning the pages and reading bits at random. Without knowing why, she wanted to find that dream again. But this was the wrong book. It didn't matter, though. She remembered the important words: ". . . for that the seasons were changed and time inverted." Lightning in winter, she thought. Hailstones in summer. Could the seasons out of season twist time again?

She rolled onto her back and stared at the ceiling. No cloud, no message. Just cracked plaster and a faint orange stain where the roof had once leaked. For that the seasons were changed and time inverted. She lay there gazing at nothing and seeing more than she could encompass. Roger. Mercy and Janey. She heard no voice, not even a croak from the ailing bird.

CHAPTER 30

The Song of the Damsel

On Saturday a police cruiser came to keep the road open. Two members of the Board of Selectmen were due to arrive, and one of the county commissioners was expected. There would be refreshments, which posed a bigger problem than parking, because the weather was changing, the sky threatening. Everyone said it felt more like December than April.

"The poor daffodils," Mrs. Costa mourned.

"Mulled cider," declared Mom as she hauled out her biggest pots and kettle. "And maybe hot chocolate. Only there isn't enough."

"Jethro says we have to make a dry run," Roger announced on his way upstairs to get his heavy sweater. "Sand, he says."

"Do we have sand?" asked Mom.

"Fortunately, yes."

A small crowd had already gathered at the mill when Roger climbed up onto the wall above the sluice gate to adjust the flow. The wheel turned, lapping the water as it flowed into the wheel buckets. Now for the first time all of the drive train was activated.

Roger led the way inside. On the upper floor he dumped a shovelful of sand into the hopper. "There," he said to Jethro. "Does that do it?"

Jethro shook his head. "More. Much more. It smooths out the surfaces so they will fit exactly. It will make all the difference when you pour in the grain."

"How come that kid's such an expert?" someone asked.

Roger said, "He's got a sixth sense about this. He's just one of the surprises on this side of the highway. You should visit us more often."

A selectman, who was a woman, said that she certainly would and that Singing Fish Mill was a wonderful new lease on life for this cutoff patch of Ashbury. Now the Costas would have a little competition.

Mom spoke up then. She told the selectman, who was a woman, that the mill and antiques shop would not compete with Costa Farm. In fact, the farm stand would be selling stone-ground flour and meal even after the shop was completed.

Everyone looked pleased, even Sonny Costa, who was acting like an official greeter as more people arrived.

Sarah couldn't stand the way everyone sounded like people on the local TV news congratulating one another. But she had promised to stay close to Janey, and Janey wanted to stay close to the hopper so that she wouldn't miss the song of the damsel.

People kept pouring into the mill from both ends of the road, the grounds filling, the mill itself teeming with newcomers stamping and blowing on their hands and exchanging comments about the bitter wind and the wintry sky.

Sarah persuaded Janey that the song wouldn't start for a

while and got her downstairs for a few minutes. Janey clutched her knapsack in front of her, shielding it from the press of people. They worked their way over to the tables borrowed from the church, but there was only a coffee urn, so far no food.

"Here's Marty," Janey said as a stocky gray-haired woman squeezed through the door and was thrust in their direction. Was Janey right? Sarah had seen her around before. But how could this woman in faded jeans and a well-worn jacket be someone qualified to consult restricted archives? She looked sort of like Sarah, only old.

The woman greeted Janey and told Sarah she had been hoping to catch up with her. "I want to thank you for goading me into pursuing the 1851 mill fire here."

Sarah did her best not to look surprised. She asked if there was anything new about it.

"Well," said the local historian, "I do think I'm on to something. There's the miller refusing to cooperate, even after they caught the man who may have set the fire. So he was never prosecuted. Here, that is. He was already facing a stiff sentence in New York. That's where he ended up."

"You mean, in prison? Are you sure? Does Jethro know?"

"Who? Oh, yes, the young mill wizard. Yes, he was here last evening when we were all talking about it. Is he working with you on your report?"

Sarah nodded. "Sort of." So the stone-picker had been caught. A kind of justice, thought Sarah. And for Mercy a chance to live without fear of him. If Jethro never learned another thing about her, this much could sustain him. "Would it be all right if I mentioned this in my report?" Sarah asked.

"Of course. Just bear in mind there's a lot we still don't know. And may never. Some undergrounders believed in publicizing their work, but others maintained the utmost secrecy to protect the fugitive slaves. I think the miller was one of those. I'm not done with him. I'll let you know what I find. I have to brave this mob now and get upstairs."

Janey said she wanted to go back up, too. She wanted to hear the song. So the local historian took her in hand and cleared a way through.

"I'll come find you," Sarah called after them. "Janey, you stay with Marty. She'll take you to Mom."

Other familiar faces swarmed around Sarah. A television camera and sound crew staggered up the steep stairs, the equipment held precariously overhead.

"Hey, Grissom," someone from school shouted to Sarah, "how come you're not up there with all the celebrities?"

"You can't breathe," she answered. "All that hot air."

In a moment three girls had converged around Sarah. They were full of questions and a kind of casual acceptance that was almost friendly. Sarah told them the best thing about the mill was outside. She would show them the waterwheel. They all went out together and pushed their way through the crowd.

The area around the wheel pit was staked off, but Sarah told the man making sure no one came through that she lived here and was allowed to climb up whenever she wanted. So Sarah and her three classmates perched on the wall across from the lever that controlled the sluice gate. It was a wonderful vantage for watching the great wheel lumbering and creaking as water poured into the buckets and splashed noisily out again.

"Awesome," one girl pronounced. Sarah nodded. It did seem to her that there was something magnificent in that turning, the power through water, wheel, and grinding stones. The mill was like some old beast called back to life from extinction.

Sarah's classmates thought it was cool being the only ones who could get that close and be that high. People were taking pictures of them. That made them giggle and strike silly poses.

Then the man watching the wheel pit told them they had better come down because everyone was going inside now for the ceremony.

The girls scrambled down from the wall and ran to the mill entrance. But there was such a jam of people at the door that they were blocked.

"This is her mill," one of the girls said to the backs of people who couldn't move. "Let her through."

But it was impossible. Soon Sarah was separated from the other girls and nowhere close to getting inside. She went back around to see if any of her classmates had given up and returned to the wheel pit. But none of them was there.

All the same, it seemed to her that the place was not empty. It was full of people whose names she knew and did not know. They were Indians treading their sacred ground, fearful witnesses cowed by sudden storms, neighbors roused from their homes to save what they could of the mill. Sarah could feel their presence, even though she would never see them. Or Mercy. But if Mercy was here, so must be Zerobabel Quelch. Still here. Sarah thought of him facing the tempest that raged around him, and inside him, too. She imagined him standing where Roger had stood just a short while ago.

Sarah looked up there on the dam and saw someone else, a man in a silver bowling jacket. He was doing something with the lever for the sluice gate. She glanced around to find someone who could speak to the man in a voice of authority. But there was no one else within sight, no one within earshot. She cupped her hands to her mouth and called up to him, "Hey, don't touch that. It shuts down the water." The man turned and looked at her. She couldn't make out his features because of the pond glinting behind him and the shimmery light beneath the cloud bank. "You're not supposed to be there," she shouted. "If you don't come down, I'll get the police."

To her astonishment he seemed to shrug his shoulders.

"No problem," he said mildly. "No one told me it was out of bounds." He started across the dam. He was sauntering away from her when something struck her hard. He was that man with the knife. Maybe he was the man who called to her from his car and then never showed up. Most certainly he was the man who called Janey by name. Janey!

Sarah turned on her heel and pelted back to the mill door. This time the throng had either filtered through or dispersed outside. Sarah managed to squeeze all the way to the stairway, where she grabbed the rail, ducked under it, and climbed onto the third step. After that she had to haul herself up as much by her hands as with her feet. She could hear someone, maybe the local historian, speaking about grain entering the eye of the runner stone and being worked along the slant of the furrows to the outside edge, where it would be thrown clear as flour.

"Sarah!" The voice breaking into the lecture on milling was Janey's.

It took Sarah a moment to locate her way up on Jethro's shoulders. Sarah pushed through to them and whispered to Jethro about the man on the dam. People close by tried to hush her, but she stretched tall to speak into Jethro's ear. "He's the same man. He could be after Janey."

Jethro scowled. "Where did he go?"

"I don't know. Across the dam. Where's Mom and Roger? Maybe we should get Janey away from here."

Jethro nodded and began to press toward the stairs. Janey protested that she wanted to stay for the song, but Jethro kept doggedly on, Sarah at his heels assuring Janey that she would hear the song later on.

As soon as they were outside, Jethro told Sarah they would take Janey to the underground room. They would be safe there while he went for help. "But if the man comes, if he figures out how the door pivots, I think you can go through the other way."

"Don't be ridiculous," Sarah retorted. Did Jethro mean, go through the escape route or through time? "Just get Janey to the house. I'll stay with her while you get Mom and Roger. And the police."

But he was heading toward the shop site.

Sarah ran to keep up with him. "No. Listen to me, Jethro. Bring her to the house." But for Jethro the hidden chamber was still the only refuge in time of danger. She couldn't stop him.

"Look!" Halting, Jethro spread his hands. Huge snowflakes wafted down on them. "It's one of those times," he said. "And the mill is running."

> *Running. A stinging wind. Warm and cold at once.*
> *Darkness and light. Her long black hair blows across*
> *her eyes and blurs her sight. But Mamma cannot be*
> *far ahead. The goodmen and goodwives frown because*
> *the child running breaks the Sabbath law. She fears*
> *that if she charges into Mamma's open arms, the kiss*
> *bestowed will be noted by all as brazen and*
> *disregardful. It is still not too late to stop. If she can*
> *hold back, everything will be changed. There will be a*
> *different outcome. The night will shine as the day.*

"Snow in April," Jethro said. "You know what can happen. You have to know it in case there's no other way. In case it's all you can do."

"I can't. . . ."

Jethro crouched at the edge of the hole and leaned back, his hands holding Janey's wrists to steady her as she slid to the ground. "Did you never believe me?" he asked Sarah.

"I don't know," she mumbled in a misery of confusion.

"Well, you and Janey hide here. You will know what you have to do."

Sarah started down the ladder, her heart pounding. As Janey followed, her knapsack swung and bounced against Sarah's forehead.

"There isn't any light," Sarah argued.

"There is," Jethro told her. "I left the flashlight on the slate shelf."

"Will you get the police? Will you get Roger or Mom right away?"

He nodded. He was kneeling above her, snowflakes turning his black hair white and feathering his eyebrows.

"Anyway," Sarah thought to add, "it's only worked with the crow."

"Janey has him," Jethro replied. "In her bag."

"Will you just get my mom?" Sarah shot back as Jethro disappeared from the rim of the hole.

"I don't like this place," Janey declared.

"I don't, either," Sarah told her. "We won't be here for long."

"I don't want to go anywhere," Janey said.

"Me neither," Sarah answered. And she meant it. Sometimes people had to run just to survive. But there was a different way for Janey. The way was here.

This time it was easier to get past the stone slab. But as soon as they were inside, Sarah worried about the wider opening. Leaning and shoving hard, she managed to narrow the gap. But how dark it was now. Janey's arms, tightly wound around Sarah's left leg, kept her from laying her hands right on the flashlight. She nearly fell as she fumbled for it. When she finally switched it on, Janey heaved a sigh and released her leg. Sarah beamed the light toward the rock pile. Jethro had actually cleared a kind of pathway to the next great slab. He couldn't know how utterly blocked it was on the other side.

Janey sat on a stone and opened her knapsack. The crow's head emerged. Sarah was surprised to see that his eyes were open. He even let out a laryngitic squawk. Digging into her knapsack, Janey pulled out a bag of raisins, a pad, and another bag with crayons in it. She bit a raisin into tiny pieces and let the crow bite her fingers as she dribbled the raisin bits into him. When he shut his beak, Janey pushed him back inside. In a moment she was drawing a picture.

It amazed Sarah that Janey could settle into this situation so easily. Of course, she had no idea whom they were hiding from. All she knew was that Jethro and Sarah thought she had to be here for a while. Soon she would come out and listen to the song of the damsel and have cider and doughnuts.

There was a tapping on the stone. A whisper came through: "Jane?"

"Daddy?" Janey called out. Leaping up, she knocked over the flashlight, which went out.

"Yes. I've come for you. How do I get in?"

Even though it was just a whisper, Sarah had no doubt. This wasn't Roger. Grabbing Janey, she pulled her close and in a low whisper ordered her to stay absolutely quiet.

"But it's Daddy," Janey argued out loud.

"That's right," came the voice Sarah recognized. "Where's the light?"

Sarah had the flashlight in her left hand, Janey's upper arm in her right. She could feel a change come over Janey. Did Janey actually realize who the speaker was, or was she only aware that he wasn't Roger? Either way, she went very still, so inert that Sarah could let go of her arm. Only now she wanted Janey to go on sounding normal, accepting.

"Let's find that picture you made for Daddy," Sarah prompted. Her voice rang falsely bright. Groping for the pad and crayons, she ripped off a sheet of paper and thrust it into Janey's hands.

"Just hand me the flashlight," urged the soft voice on the other side.

"In a minute," Sarah forced herself to respond. "One minute. Janey has to finish her picture for you. Then we'll pack up and come out."

"Never mind the picture."

"She's finishing it right now. You'll love it."

Janey was doing nothing of the kind. She was as still as the crow.

Sarah snatched up the paper and a crayon. She wanted the man to hear the sound of a child drawing, but as soon as she began to scribble on the uneven floor, the crayon snapped, the paper tore. Grabbing another sheet, Sarah hauled herself up by the slate shelf. She set the paper on the smooth stone and with the flattened crayon stub made sweeping strokes.

"That's better," she babbled. "It's too bad the first picture tore, but this one's even better." She could hear the man on the other side of the door slab speaking in an urgent undertone. She kept on scrawling and praising the picture that Janey was supposedly completing for her daddy, promising that any moment now she would hand it and Janey through.

And all the while Janey sat as though frozen in the utter darkness.

Sarah was still making audible crayon scratchings when shouts erupted outside. She knew inside her head that it meant help had come, but she didn't dare breathe, not until she heard someone she recognized. "First get up here," a strange voice ordered. "Right now." Other voices converged around that one, and then, through the clamor, Sarah heard Roger yelling, "Sarah? Janey? Are you all right?"

Sarah stooped down to Janey. "It's Daddy," she tried to say, but her teeth were clenched, and she couldn't get any words out. She was shaking so violently that she couldn't even put her hands on the flashlight. It seemed in that cold dark place as though time kept on stretching and twisting until at last she heard her own voice calling out to Roger.

Sarah struggled with the slab until someone on the other side dragged it open. Next she boosted Janey out. Janey was already in Roger's arms when Sarah came through. His arms spread out to draw her in close beside Janey. They stood like that, all three hugging, the snow turning thin and dissolving into a fine rain. Anxious and relieved all at once, Jethro and Mom leaned down to them.

Janey pulled back. "Did I miss the song?" she asked.

"It's happening right now," Mom said to her. "Come and hear it."

"Did Jethro tell you?" Sarah asked Roger. "The man was trying to shut down the water."

Roger thrust Janey up to Mom. "I'm not sure what he was up to. The police have him. They'll handle it."

Janey twisted out of Mom's grasp. "My knapsack. Barker. They're still in there."

"I'll get them," Jethro told her, sliding down into the hole.

While Mom and Roger took Janey back to the mill, Sarah waited for Jethro, who seemed to be taking too long. Still on edge, she shouted to him to hurry.

"Coming," he answered, his voice muffled. "I'm just looking . . ." After a moment he shoved the crayoned paper at her. "Come back inside and show me where Janey did this."

"No. I'm never going back in there." But she took the paper. "Janey didn't do it. I did. To stall. I pretended—" She broke off. She was looking at the white pattern that emerged through the blue scribbles. Not a pattern, but writing in the sloping hand of an earlier time. The first letter was an oversize *M* that tailed into a flourish.

Jethro called to her again. "Sarah, are you still there?"

She nodded. Then, realizing he couldn't see her, she answered, "Yes," in a small voice. "Mercy," she read out loud. "Mercy and . . . Trv . . . Trv . . . ?"

"Truth!" he shouted, exultant. "TRUTH!"

As she held the paper up to the dingy gray light, raindrops slid off the crayoned surface but soaked the bare letters. She read: "Mercy and Truth are met together," the paper going limp in her hands.

"Where?" Jethro demanded. "Where is it from?"

"The shelf," she answered, watching the message darken.

When Jethro came out with the knapsack, she was still holding the sagging sheet of paper. Reaching for it, he ripped it in half. For an instant he looked aghast, until she reminded him he could make another.

"The writing is still in the stone," she said.

"I know," he responded. "I could feel it. She must have used something like a sharp nail. She didn't have her mother's arrowhead."

Walking back to the mill, Jethro pondered the message on the slate. "Mercy couldn't have scratched all those words at the time of the fire, not with Mr. Lockwood hurt and every hand needed. She must have returned later to the hiding place, discovered the bed stone from her time, her proof, and then scratched the message for me to find. Hoping I would seek her there. And letting me know she remained in my time." Carefully he folded his half of the paper and held out his hand for Sarah's.

She looked up at the wintry sky. But already it was changed, the clouds on the move and seamed with light. Even the air had lost its bite. "It isn't exactly like those other times," she said. "Anyhow, this time no one came through."

"Something did, though. Mercy's message." He stared at the remaining half of it, which Sarah still held. "I was so afraid," he told her. "I feared that Mercy might have gone into a different future and was lost. She knew I would worry. She knew I would keep searching. That is really why she left this message for me."

Sarah couldn't muster a reply. When would it occur to him that someone other than Mercy could have gouged those words?

"What?" He stopped. "Something is wrong?"

Sarah, just ahead, turned to meet his dark, intense gaze. All this time he had been poised on the discovery that could set him free from Mercy, from the past. And maybe from Sarah, too. If she raised the question Jethro in his need had ignored, the haunting might continue, at least for a while.

"Not something," she answered thickly, handing him the rest of Mercy's message. "Me. I think I had it wrong about Mercy being in the past. I mean, of course, she is. But she's also here, now. In this place. In you." And in Janey, too, Sarah added silently. Even in me. As she groped for the right words, Roger's came to her: "The past is always here."

Behind Jethro a rim of sunlight pressed beneath the lifting cloud bank. Anursnack Hill, diminished by time and human endeavor, seemed to regain a semblance of its former scale. Mist rising from newly budded trees obscured the cut marked by the highway beyond. Sarah had this one brief glimpse of the hill standing in translucent fullness over the brook and pond, over the Place of the Departed. She thought: Did Mercy see it like this? Did Jethro? But he was facing the other way, toward tomorrow, and anyhow, as the light expanded, the hill was restored to its present-day contours.

Jethro said, "Last night I found out that if Mercy stayed in my time, she could have felt safe again. And now I know she did stay, she isn't lost. And Janey will be all right. That's what matters."

"Yes," Sarah agreed. "And also that this time it's not the same in other ways. It doesn't have to be. Besides," she added, "if today had been like those other times, something would have happened to the mill."

"Something nearly did happen," Jethro countered. "You stopped it."

"I did?" Sarah was mystified.

"The man at the sluice gate. You thought he was going to shut down the water. What if he was opening it all the way? That would have sent a torrent through the gate. It would have thrown everything apart, all the works. Think how that would have disrupted everything. Maybe in the confusion he meant to grab Janey and run."

"If I'd guessed that," Sarah murmured, "I'd have been too scared to stop him."

Jethro grinned. "Then I'm glad you were foolish and brave. But I'm also glad you didn't try the escape door. I'm glad you weren't as brave as you once sounded when you said you would take a chance on going through."

"I'm glad I didn't want to," Sarah maintained.

Janey ran to meet them. "Give me my knapsack. I want Barker to hear the song of the damsel." She flung herself at Sarah, who staggered and just caught her.

Trust the water as the fledgling trusts the sky. The child runs on between darkness and light, in and out of time, past the fear, through the dreams.

Somehow they all managed to reach the upper floor, where everyone crowded close to watch the grist milled. When Ken dumped a bushel of whole wheat into the hopper and opened the slide valve under it, all the machinery seemed to spring to life. The grain streamed onto the damsel and into the eye of the millstone. And as it rotated, it gave a kind of growl that merged with the clanking of the conveyor chain and the chattering screens. Yet none of this din could mute the rhythmic clacking of the spout, the damsel, its song accompanying the hum of the revolving runner stone and hailing the flour that poured into the waiting sack.

The song overspread them with the clouds of sweet-smelling flour dust. Everyone's faces turned to masks. Everyone's except Jethro's. Sarah saw him wipe his hand across his face, not at some invisible film, but to brush away the fine powder that would not melt like the snow that had fallen out of its time.

Jethro coming through, thought Sarah. Coming through for good.